RESCUED

A SECOND CHANCE ROMANCE MYSTERY

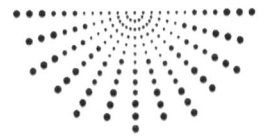

LYZ KELLEY

Belvitri
Services

A SPECIAL GIFT JUST FOR YOU.

I have a present for you…

…your very own ebook exclusive when you sign up for my newsletter.

Newsletter Sign Up:
https://geni.us/LyzKelleyFreeBook

CHAPTER ONE

A chill gripped Karly Krane, even though the mountain air was finally above seventy degrees. Today would be the first time she'd seen Thad since he walked out of her life 3,726 days ago.

Her heart thumped in synch with the car radio's toe-tapping tune, but she wished the usual carefree bliss had followed along. She twisted the radio's knob full volume to distract herself and avoid pondering the one thing she didn't want to think about.

For ten years, she'd struggled to understand why. Why, after she and Thad spent a good chunk of every day together for six plus years, he decided to leave Elkridge. Leave her.

During their final three-minute phone call, she told him to never ever talk to her again. At eighteen, she had no notion of how long never-ever could last, because on that sunny spring morning, he did as she asked and disappeared from her life, only to show up again more than a decade later, wounded and alone.

The soul-slicing pain had created a festering wound, and the hurt still burned deep, buried underneath the rubble of rationalization.

If only she hadn't promised her brother she'd look in on Thad. If only she didn't need his help.

I guess it's time to put the big girl panties on and get this done.

From the back of her mother's hand-me-down red and tan Subaru hatchback, she retrieved the extra-large, folded up dog kennel and began reconstructing the metal frame next to Thad's recently patched plank porch.

A movement spotted out of the corner of her eye hitched her breath. *Thad?* She swallowed her anxiety. No, just an elk passing by.

Get a grip. He doesn't matter anymore, remember?

"Yeah. Like that's the truth," she mumbled, and stood to wipe her hands on the jeans she'd washed so many times the chic, manufactured threadbare was threadbare.

She opened the back passenger car door. The standard poodle mix studied her with his intelligent brown eyes and expressed his opinion of her procrastination with an impatient whine.

"Take it easy, Custer. This is for your own good." She scratched the dog under the chin, then leaned in to kiss his nose and fluff his ears. "This is your last chance. Don't let me down."

Karly's throat burned as she remembered

the urine and feces stench which greeted her when she entered the hoarder's home. She and three other shelters committed to finding homes for the animals, although the local kill shelter had already euthanized eight that couldn't be saved. The thought of others suffering the same fate made her sick.

The large furball shifted nervously in his security halter. "You need to get it together. You hear me?" She rubbed the dog's fuzzy chest, unclasped the buckle, then lifted the dog's muzzle. "You're too smart, and I don't mean that in a good way. A little girl is depending on you. You'd better straighten up. Three weeks. That's all we've got."

The young sixty-pound male, sensing freedom, nudged past her and gave her arm a good yank when she grabbed the end of the leash. She gently snapped the lead back, reminding him of his training, before shutting the door.

"See, Custer? This is what I've been talking about. Stop fooling around. I need the money, and you need a forever home."

"Talking to animals again?" The familiar voice made the goose bumps pop up on her skin and shiver. She sucked in a rush of air.

There he was. Heart-stopping, gorgeous Thad Lopez. "You scared the poop out of me."

"I didn't want to interrupt your lecture."

Like a hunter tracking a deer, he watched her. Methodical. Calculating. Measuring.

He shoved his hands into his pockets, which pushed his jeans low around his thin hips and cleverly displayed his black cotton boxers. A sight she had no right to gawk at, but curiosity made her look anyway.

An army green baseball cap sat low on his forehead, and the long-sleeve performance V-neck tight across his chest made him look downright delectable. If it wasn't for the intensity in his amber eyes, she might have sighed. Damn her breakable heart for the pang of regret.

"Why are you here, Karly?" Thad asked in a low baritone that had once been a tenor.

"You've changed."

Gone were the long hair, baggy clothes, and stand-aside cocky attitude. And looking him directly in the eye wasn't possible anymore. He'd sprung up a couple more inches.

"You haven't." He scratched his shoulder to relieve an itch. "Your hair is a bit longer, and you've grown some curves, but that's about it."

Curves? Figures you'd notice. She gestured to the large, curly mutt looking at her with those please-don't-leave-me eyes. She forced her attention back to Thad. "Rumor has it you've been looking for work."

Thad shifted his weight off his left leg and leaned against the side of the cabin, then crossed his arms. "Are you here to offer me a job?"

His mocking disbelief almost made her get back in the car and leave. She would have if she hadn't promised her brother, Kenny, she'd try to help Thad.

And if she didn't need the income to save her business and her four-legged friends.

And if she didn't believe an injured soldier returning home deserved and needed community support.

And if this wasn't literally Custer's last happily-ever-after chance.

All of which added up to a quadruple load of responsibility, an obligation she couldn't ignore.

Custer circled her legs and sat on her left foot—rather than beside her where he'd been trained to sit—then released an impressive, guttural growl, perfectly expressing her feelings.

"As a matter of fact, I do have a job for you." She raised her chin a couple of centimeters to generate a pump of courage. "I've partnered with several organizations who train service dogs." Karly glanced at Custer, who at the moment was having a good scratch behind the ear, and doing his best to demonstrate that the past several days of training hadn't made one iota of difference.

She fidgeted and cleared her throat. "I

know a hunting dog isn't the same as a service dog, but training is training. Since you were always good at figuring things out, I thought you might like to help. The pay is forty-five hundred dollars if he passes the service tests and the service family adopts him." She rushed on, no longer certain this last-minute training idea was smart. "I keep thirty percent. You get seventy." She swallowed hard to keep the trepidation from choking off her air. "It's real money for a couple of weeks worth of work."

He studied the dog, then her, his eyes narrowing with disbelief. "Double the time, and you'd be lucky to get that dog to sit properly."

She plucked her foot out from underneath the dog's hind leg and moved to the wire kennel to lift up the plastic protector with Custer's fact sheet displayed inside. "A little girl in Arizona has a rare disease and requires oxygen full time. She needs a large-breed dog that can carry the tanks and follow her around, even down park slides and around the yard. The insurance company picks up most of the cost. You would be making a difference."

"That's not why you're here." The humor dancing in his eyes called her bluff. *Damn you, Thad Lopez.*

"Yes, it is. My kennel is overcrowded, and Custer needs a handler." She fussed with the dog's eyes, gently rubbing the crusty goobers out, then dithered over a piece of dried mud on his leg, doing her best to not look at the man who at one time held her whole heart and all her dreams.

Well, the "at one time" bit wasn't quite true.

He still had that giant magnet, the one even now drawing her closer and closer and closer, like a *Star Trek* tractor beam. She didn't want to feel the tug. He'd broken her heart—smashed it into a million tiny pieces —and she wouldn't allow him to do it again.

When the silence got to be too much, she sought his face. He looked tired. No. He looked like life had dragged him out of his bed, beat the crap out of him, and left him by the side of the road.

Don't feel sorry for him. Don't you dare.

He dumped you. Remember?

You're doing this for Kenny and Custer. End of story.

"I'd better go." She pointed a thumb over her shoulder. "It looks like you need to get back to whatever it was you're doing…or something." Thankfully the trembling on her insides didn't cause her voice to jitter. She tugged on the dog's leash. "C'mon, Custer. In you go." The dog entered the kennel, circled and then flopped onto the metal floor before she secured the latch.

"Karly. That dog is not why you're here."

It really sucks letting people into your heart. They get to know every mood, tic, and nuance. There isn't any place to hide or find refuge from the hurt when things sour.

"I'm here to offer you work which will help a little girl who needs a service dog." At least that wasn't a lie, but the excuse didn't answer his question. Guilt nibbled on the edges of her integrity.

Wiping her sweaty palms on her jeans, she retreated to her car's hatchback to grab the donated items. "Here are Custer's supplies."

He didn't move, or offer to help. He just watched her drop the dog's printed ceramic bowls and a twenty-pound bag of dry dog food by the crate.

"You should call Kenny." She made the wide-arc trek back to her car, maintaining her distance. "He's worried about you being alone out here on the ridge."

"I need the quiet."

You need something, all right. She twirled the key ring around her finger, in time with her whirling misgivings. "Kenny's worried. He thinks you should be around people. Not spend so much time by yourself."

The muscles across her shoulders tightened when he shifted to rub his unshaven jaw. The red, puckered skin on his hand disappearing under his shirtsleeve drew her sympathy. He noticed, and his expression hardened. He obviously didn't want her sympathy. In fact, his go-away attitude made it clear he didn't want anything from her.

She clenched her fist and let stubbornness and the keys press into her palm. "Something happened over there—something bad—didn't it?" She had trouble drawing in a complete breath, because she wasn't sure she was ready to hear the truth.

"Tell Kenny I'm all right." Thad brushed off her comment as easily as a mosquito.

"Tell him yourself." She dropped her shoulders to keep the concern from destroying her need to remain indifferent. "You've been in the zone. You know what it's like to get letters and phone calls. Soldiers need to hear from people back home—remind them who they're fighting for."

She closed her eyes and wished she hadn't blurted out that last bit. "Elkridge supports our military veterans." She drew a line in the red soil with her cross trainers, then squinted into the sun. "That's what people in small towns do, right?"

A shadow drifted over his eyes, and he became eerily still, except for his fingers twitching randomly at his side. Nothing in his relaxed stance showed alertness, but still, after all these years, she could sense the underlying emotional turbulence that had always plagued him.

What are you thinking, Lopez?

Thad walked to the dog crate with a slight limp and lifted the eight by eleven plastic envelope holding the training details. He shook his head. "You need to take this dog with you." His whispered statement barely carried on the breeze. His expression escalated to serious. "I can't do this. I can't train him."

"Look, I know this is last minute and all, but—"

"No." His voice was raw in a way she'd never heard from him before. "You don't understand."

Custer's ears drooped, reflecting how she

felt. This wounded soldier was his last hope —her last hope.

The overlarge mutt stood and shifted uneasily in the wire box.

"No, you don't understand." She gestured to Custer. "By law, I can only keep a specific number of animals in my kennel. I'm over the limit now. If you can't train or keep Custer, then someone needs to take him back to the kill shelter, and that won't be me. You hear me? I. Will. Not. Do. It." She opened the driver's side door, slid behind the wheel, and rolled the window down. "If you don't want to train him, *you* take him to the kill shelter. The address is on the paperwork."

He took a step toward her. "Karly, don't you dare put this on me."

"The way I see it, you've been asking for work around town, and I've just given you work. Is it the responsibility you don't want, or is it because of me? If it's just me…that's a pathetic excuse for refusing to help a little girl."

"Our history has nothing to do with this, and you know it."

She studied the former soldier, who looked both comfortably familiar and vastly different. "When it comes to you, I don't know squat. What I do know is I have a business to run. Every day I have to decide which animals to keep and which animals I can't save. I can't keep them all." *Like I couldn't keep you.*

Thad studied the dog for a good long while before his head dropped onto his chest in acceptance. "Give me overnight to think about it."

Cautious. Introspective. Calculating. Things never changed.

At least he'd given an inch. If he'd set his mind against helping, nothing would have changed it, short of the sun falling out of the sky.

"Then think about it—hard. I meant what I said. You're Custer's last chance. I know you can train him. You're the only one I know who's more stubborn than he is."

She rolled up the window, and then shoved the gear into reverse, spinning the car around so fast she lost sight of him in the cloud of dust.

A seething cauldron of emotions boiled her senses to the point of numbness. She shoved the car into drive.

Halfway back to town, she realized the one question she needed to have answered for so long had gone unanswered.

Then again, maybe discovering the *real* reason he left town wouldn't help.

Sometimes knowing the why of things didn't heal a hurt...and this hurt had almost destroyed her.

"DON'T LOOK at me like that." Thad glared at Custer.

The dog gave him a woe-is-me look that just about did Thad in. He'd sworn never to train another dog. Damn mutts could burrow in and tear a man in two when they paid the price for their loyalty.

He fisted his hand, fighting back the memories blowing into his head like a sandstorm—memories of trauma, pain, loss.

With every tick of the second hand, details came trotting back to remind him of his time in the hospital, and worse, reminding him of the brotherhood killed by his carelessness. Loneliness and isolation were his legacy in the aftermath. He'd thought he wanted to get away, disappear, but the past few weeks had proven he didn't know what the hell he wanted.

Custer whined and pushed his nose through the metal grid. "I'm okay. It's okay." Thad poked his fingers through the metal holes to provide comfort and a scratch.

The vibration of his phone brought him back, and he looked at the number. A smile meandered into place. "S'up, Neon?"

"How's that mountain life treating you? See any bears yet?"

The friendly conversation eased his knotted muscles and wrestled down the relentless voice in his head. Day and night, the sound of his father's disgust rattled on and on and on. He couldn't sleep or eat, and sometimes he wondered whether breathing was still the right thing to do.

Thad shifted to look at the mountain ridge behind his cabin. "They're around. Elk. Moose. Mountain Lions. Fox. They're all here. You can look them up on the internet if you don't know what they look like."

"Bugger off."

Thad managed to summon a laugh, something he hadn't been able to accomplish in weeks, and all because of Neil Doucette. "Just because you're a city boy from New Orleans who thrives on spicy food and women, doesn't mean I live in Dulltown, USA. What's up?" Thad asked, trying to keep a gut-wrenching regret from seeping into his voice. "Ready to go back to work?"

"It won't be the same without you, buddy. I always thought you'd be a lifer."

"If it weren't for that IED, I'd still be there." Thad closed his eyes, fighting against the sounds and sights and smells of war.

The first day of basic training, he and Neil were as different as odd and even. Seven months of training and bullet-flying conditions created moments where opposites could become best friends. He counted Neon among the best.

"Nothing will ever be the same." A heated blade of guilt slid into Thad's gut.

"Catch your meaning, Monk. I wish—"

"Don't be getting all pansy on me." Thad dropped his head and closed his eyes to lock down the memories. "No looking back. Remember? You promised."

"You got it."

The silence weighted his shoulders like a sixty-pound rucksack on a ten-mile uphill march. The cool mountain breeze brushed across his skin.

"Hey, have you seen Kenny's sister?" Neon pushed to break through the conversational lull. "From her recent picture, she's a hottie."

"Her name's Karly, and, yeah, I've seen her."

"And?"

"And what?"

"Don't tell me you're still flipping that coin—heads or tails." Neon's chuckle reminded him of prairie dog chatter. "Every girl who ever turned your head looked just like her. You need to pull your head out and decide one way or another. You could have been killed protecting Kenny. And don't give me any of that protect-your-brother bull. You've gotten in more shit shielding his six than at any other time. I don't get you, man."

"No, I suppose you wouldn't. It's history."

"That's crap, Monk, and you know it. You have the hots for this woman, or you wouldn't have dismissed every girl I've ever introduced you to."

"Maybe if you introduced me to women who wanted more than a meal and a roll in the sack with a guy in uniform, then maybe I wouldn't have bailed."

"Dude. Women are all the same."

Not all women. "Neon. You've got a red neon sign with the words 'come to daddy' plastered on your chest. One of these days, you'll want something different. Something steadier."

"I doubt it. If you want to stay a monk the rest of your life, that's your problem." Neon gave another snort and a chuckle. "Hey…I forgot. Did you ask her yet?"

No confessions here. "Didn't get a chance. Besides, she wouldn't apologize." *She didn't before.* "She was too busy dropping off a dog."

"A dog? That's just harsh."

Thad's gut seized and knotted. "She doesn't know. No one stateside does except my mom and sister, and they're in Texas. I'd like to keep it that way."

He'd spoken in such a hushed tone, he wasn't sure if he'd said the words aloud. His brain traffic seemed rather congested these days.

"Hey, Thad? You okay, man? 'Cause if you need me to come up there and kick your butt, I'm still game."

"No. I'm okay. Just need some space to breathe, and a few months to get the dust out of my pores."

His voice remained stable and level, but the tilt-o-whirl of life unbalanced him. No matter what Karly believed, another dog wouldn't help him find his steady.

"Didn't you tell me Colorado was lacking in the air department?"

A laugh managed to leak out as Thad shook his head. "You mean oxygen, not air."

"You know what I meant."

"I swear, sometimes I wonder how you made sergeant."

"I keep telling you. Those Air Force ladies have multiple levels of talent when it comes to tutoring."

"The next time I take some classes, I'll keep that in mind. However, you should stick with the Army women. I wouldn't want that large, protruding object on the front of your face to get busted up again. It would ruin that pretty Hollywood profile of yours."

"I can handle those boys in blue."

"I'm sure you can, but when you get a nasty one, it's somehow always perfectly timed to get the whole platoon involved. Keep in mind, I won't be there to bail your sorry ass out anymore."

"Go to hell."

Already there, dude. Already there. Thad released a self-deprecating snort of humor. At least he could still laugh, even if the cause was a bit off-kilter. The IED hadn't taken that from him, even if it had taken pretty much everything else.

He gave the dog watching him a long study. "Hey, Neon. I'd better run. I've got a dog I'm supposed to teach a thing or two."

"If anyone can train that dog, it's you."

"Thanks for the vote and call. Hey, and watch out for Kenny, would you?" *'Cause*

Karly would lose it if anything happened to her brother.

"Will do, Monk. You have my number. Keep in mind the phone works both ways."

Yeah, but I can't handle hearing about the guys right now. "Catch you later."

Thad shoved his phone back in his pocket and slowly lowered into a squat in front of Custer's cage—searing pain blasting up his leg to the middle of his back. He gritted his teeth and stuck his fingers through the wire to give the dog a good sniff.

"Bet you didn't know George Armstrong Custer was my favorite United States Army commander." *But Karly did.* "He's a screwup...just like me. I joined the military to show my dad I could take a bullet—tried damned hard to make it happen. I should be dead." He snorted in disgust, "I couldn't even manage to do that right. I got my friends killed instead. How pathetic is that?"

He opened the kennel and let the dog smell him some more. Custer turned to look down the road with a sorrowful face.

"You'll see her again. Don't worry. But here's your first lesson." He slid his hand gently over the dog's head. "Women are trouble. Heaps of trouble. They can kick you in the balls and break your heart. Stay away from them." He gave the dog a good scratch behind the ear. "That is, unless the female in question is under the age of four and needs you to carry her oxygen tank."

CHAPTER TWO

Not much had changed in Elkridge, and that's what Thad had counted on. The sleepy little town nestled between two mountain ridges was exactly what he needed. No major shopping malls. No loud construction noises. No fast movements that put his military-honed senses on high alert and reminded him of a place he didn't want to remember.

"Hey, Coach."

The owner of Tool Shed dropped his chin to look over the top of his bifocals. The years had put a little more weight around Bill's middle, and he was a bit more hunched at the shoulders, but his old football coach was still sharp and observant. There were few things in life Thad was grateful for—Bill Mason was one of them.

"Howdy, Thad. My son-in-law said you were in the other day. How are the repairs coming?"

Thad grabbed the brim of his ball cap, lifted, and scratched his head. "That cabin needs a ton of work. I came in for some caulking and weather stripping, and I need to order a window." Thad pulled a crumpled piece of paper out of his pocket. "Got something with those dimensions?"

Bill accepted the scrap and peered through the bottom of his lenses. "I don't have anything in stock, but I can order it for you." He waited for Thad's nod, then walked around the counter and pulled the rest of the items off the shelf. "Anything else you need?"

"That'll do for now. I just need to fix the holes before I freeze to death. Going from the desert heat to the mountain air is a shock to the system."

"Just as bad as coming back from 'Nam and the humidity." Bill rang up the supplies. "That will be five bucks even."

Thad added up the price on the sales stickers. "I might have barely passed algebra, but I can still add, sir." He threw a ten on the counter. "Keep the change."

"Stop with the sir crap. I don't see any officers around here."

"Yes, sir." Thad's mouth twitched, and his chest rumbled with a snicker.

"Still a stubborn shit." Bill snatched the money off the counter and shoved it into the cash register drawer. "It's not much, but I've got a couch you can sleep on till that window comes in. You'd be warm at least."

Not looking for handouts. "Thanks, Coach, but I'm good."

"Figured you'd say that." Bill placed the items in a brown paper bag. "We're having a meeting tonight over at the lodge to discuss our volunteer rescue training calendar. Why don't you stop by, meet some of the guys? We even have a few ladies in the group now."

Matchmaking? Please...not you too. "Thanks for the offer, but I think I'll pass. Besides, I need to find something I can do to put food on the table."

"The Army should have set you up with a pension with ten years in."

"They did, but money doesn't stick around when there's a family to support. My mom lost her job and hasn't been able to find work."

"I'd give you a job, but—"

"I'm not asking for charity, Coach. I've got enough for now." He capped off his irritation by attempting a smile. "I'll find something in time."

"I talked to the town council last month about creating jobs to keep our young folk here. Too many are joining the military and coming back busted up. It's either working the ski resorts or construction, with not much in between. I heard they got some openings at the Elkridge Lodge."

"That snobby place? No, thanks. I'd rather do construction. 'Cause skiing is out." *Never could afford those lift prices.*

The store bell rang just as Bill was winding up for another soapbox rant.

The storeowner shoved his glasses farther up the bridge of his nose. "Hey, Rivers. I was just telling young Thad here about our meeting tonight."

Rivers Black walked toward them with a slow, methodical gait. With each footfall, he measured Thad—the boy then, and the man now.

"Rivers," Thad greeted.

"Lopez." Rivers' eyes squinted to continue the assessment.

Thad recalled the night his racist father tried to teach the "Injun" a lesson. His father misjudged the Native American, just like his dad misjudged most everything else in his pathetic life.

"How was hunting season?" Thad asked to be courteous.

"Freezer's full."

"You still making jewelry, belts, and stuff?"

"Yep."

The grunted responses were typical, yet soothing. Another reminder not much had changed in Elkridge. Thad nodded and waited until the stillness started to become uneasy. "I'd better get going."

"What about the meeting?" Bill looked to Rivers. "You're the training coordinator, tell him what's on the agenda, Black."

Rivers watched Thad like a hawk scanning the ground for its prey. "He'll come, or he won't. A man must make his choices."

A déjà vu chill ran up Thad's arms. One of his drill sergeants said the same thing. Over the years Thad had wondered how his life would have turned out if his dad hadn't made so many bad choices.

"Maybe I'll stop in another time." The way Bill was looking at him meant a lecture was coming, and he wasn't in the mood. Thad grabbed his bag of supplies to disguise his growing anxiety and backed toward the door. "Thanks, Bill. Rivers."

Bill walked around the counter. "You know where to find me if you need anything."

"Yes, sir." Thad gave him a friendly salute, then pushed open the door, laughing at the curmudgeon's annoyed expression.

He might be crankier than an old Buick, but Bill Mason understood. The Marine had brought his military discipline home to Elkridge, and used it to knock some sense into the high school football players. Fortunately, Thad was one of them.

Thad dropped the supplies in the truck bed by Custer's kennel. "Hey, bud. Want to go see Karly and visit all your friends?"

Thad didn't wait for a response, just slid in behind the wheel, and a few seconds later backed out of the parking space. Pulling into Helper Shelters dirt parking lot, he parked at one of the marked spaces denoted by a half-buried tire painted canary yellow.

He paused to slow his breath and let his

determination kick in. He pocketed his keys. He wouldn't tolerate any more of that polite "howdy-do, and here's a dog to train" crap. This time he'd get a truthful answer, one way or another.

"Stay." He opened the door of Custer's travel crate. "Good boy." He pulled a treat out of his jeans pocket and held out his palm. The dog lifted the nugget gently instead of lunging. "That's a good boy." Thad adjusted the dog's lead.

"Come," he motioned. Custer jumped off the tailgate, but went no farther. The attentive dog's stare gave him a jolt of pride. *Now that's progress.* He shortened the leash strap for the dog to heel and made his way toward the building.

He soaked in the sight of the old industrial shipping containers. The blue metal structures were lined up side by side, creating the inexpensive kennel framing just as he and Karly planned during their long-ago summer vacations. He was impressed, and a little sad. At fourteen, she'd shared her dream, and he hadn't been here to watch it grow.

Rows of wire fences surrounded the twenty-by-forty-foot kennels, and dogs could go outside or back into their holding pens through swinging doors drilled into the sides. A large, painted sign and old-fashioned lights, most likely also recycled, hung off the top of the first of six containers.

Just inside the customer entrance, the scents of borax, lavender, and vanilla wafted and twisted together. Karly ran an orderly business—not that he expected anything less. An oversized corkboard displayed the current month's schedule of training classes, thank-you notes, and pictures of adoption candidates. He stopped at the tidy reception desk.

"Karly?" he called out, then listened for a response.

When there was no answer, he moved closer to the reception desk and spied a small office in the back, jam-packed with file cabinets, a desk and a computer. It, too, was empty. He moved across the lobby and pushed open the kennel door marked with an employees-only sign. "Karly?"

A chorus of barks greeted him. He moved down the center of the wired cages. Custer trotted alongside with a look-at-me attitude while he ignored his former fellow inmates —the cocky bastard.

Thad averted his gaze, unprepared for the emotional tug. He hated seeing abandoned animals in cages. The shivers of fear. The mistrustful eyes. The tail-wagging hopefulness.

Halfway through the kennel area, he realized none of those traits existed for Karly's dogs. They were happy and healthy and well-adjusted, but that didn't mean he could leave Custer behind. He might have had reason to dump off the dog and let Karly deal with the consequences, but he couldn't force himself to do it.

"Damn dog." Custer looked at him from the corner of his eye, and he swore he saw the mutt smile. "Dog poop. That's what you are. A big ol' pile of steamy, lovable, brown crap. Don't you look at me with those aren't-I-cute eyes."

He yanked open the back door and stopped just a few feet inside the large open space, with the rollup steel door at the back.

There you are. He couldn't help but pause and take in the beauty.

Karly's legs were long and smooth as a gentle sip of bourbon, going down nice and slow, and just as hot. She never had a need for makeup or nail polish. Today, she'd pulled her midnight, shoulder-length hair through the back of her Rockies baseball cap. Her muscles moved and stretched and stirred some good memories.

Custer impatiently nudged his leg, wanting to visit his former trainer. At Thad's silent command, the dog sat close, this time not on his foot. He forced the images of his first and only love back into the mental tin can where he stored things he didn't want to think about. In fact, he just wanted apathy to take over so the rest of the world and his memories would just leave him be.

She dropped a forty-pound bag of dog food on the tailgate and went to move another from the back of the white pickup truck. When lifting the next load, she winced, and then carefully stretched.

Yep, same ol' Karly.

Never one to ask for help.

Always pushing too hard.

He released a frustrated breath. *Never pass a fault.* His unit's military motto, instilled into each soldier, and mentioned in every class session, field exercise, and battle instruction meeting. Commanding officers and trainers repeating the essence of doing it right over and over again. Check your equipment. Check your buddy. Stop and help.

When Karly rubbed her lower back again, he stepped out of the shadows.

"Let me help you with that."

She pivoted in his direction, then

dropped her arms to her sides. "Would you stop sneaking up on me?"

"I'm not sneaking. The dogs barking should have given you fair warning."

"I was thinking about something else."

Possibly the guilt you're feeling about lying to me?

He approached with Custer and tied the dog's lead to her truck's side mirror, then picked up the closest bag.

She waved him off. "I got this."

Nope. Not letting you brush me off. We have a score to settle. "Where do you store this stuff? And don't be a hardhead."

Hands on hips, she did her best to stare him down, but the military had trained him in the art of patience, to wait, quietly, and let the silence wage war. After a couple of huffed-out breaths, she pointed to the organized six-foot metal racks of pet bowls, towels, and other essentials. "You can put the food on the shelf over there."

He picked up the second bag, but probably shouldn't have. Every pebble and stick fragment embedded in his leg reminded him of the reasons he shouldn't play hero. His muscles complained about the extra weight. When he set the supplies where Karly had directed, he went back for more.

"You're limping."

Noticed that, did ya? "It's nothing."

The sentiment in her words indicated she cared, but she didn't. Not about him. Ten years ago, she'd managed to stick a knife where it could do the most damage. The scar had turned ugly and gnarled.

"Are you okay?" Her concern pushed him deeper into the angry cesspool.

Not even close. "It's nothing time won't heal."

He could do without the look of sympathy. In fact, he could do without a lot of things.

She lifted two bags on her second trip with a huff and a grunt. *Yep, just like always.* He hid his frustration and dropped the last two bags on the double stack. "Aren't you curious why I came by today?"

Her stunning amber eyes that were almost a perfect match to his turned his way. "I figured you'd get around to it eventually."

Fine. You want to play games, I'll play.

Karly wasn't the only one who could wield willfulness like a weapon. He could give her a workout, but not today. Today he wanted answers, and tightened his grip on his resentment. "Okay. It's been eating at me for ten years, and I need to know, why Brad Clairemont?"

"Why Brad, what?" The squinting confusion in her eyes made him pause. "He's the only veterinarian here in town. In order to run my business, I'm required to have a vet on record."

"I'm not talking about your business."

"Then what are you talking about?

"Are you going to deny it?" He leaned against the truck bed, working to keep years of bitterness from burning a hole in his stomach. "Two weeks. Only two weeks after I left, you started sleeping with him."

She gripped the tailgate until her

knuckles lost all color. "Who told you that? I've never dated, much less slept with, Brad Clairemont. Everyone knows he's a jerk."

Nice try. How about the truth? No way would he allow her belligerence to ease her out of an apology. She owed him that much.

"My sister saw you at Brad's house."

"Your sister?" Incredulity made her voice soar up an octave.

She pushed away from the truck, paced a few steps and then back, with a skeptical laugh, yanking on the end of the ponytail sticking out the back of her ball cap. "And you believed her? You believed the one person who was always trying to drive a wedge between us?" Her eyes went distant and glazed. A puff of air snorted from her nose. "After all this time…"

The sarcastic pinch of her mouth intensified his ire. "What the hell is that supposed to mean?"

"It means you're an idiot—a stupid idiot. That's what that means." She turned and pushed him, then again, a bit harder. "Go away. If you think I could have slept with someone just weeks after you left...just go away."

She turned toward the kennel area, but he latched on to her arm. "Oh, no, you don't. You don't get to walk away. I want an answer."

"You mean walk away like you did? And let go, you're hurting me." She ripped her arm back. "You never even called to tell me you were leaving. You just left."

"I would have if my dad hadn't smashed my phone." *At the same time he was busy busting my nose and cracking my ribs.* "I stopped by your house and told Kenny I needed to leave town—that I was joining up."

"Yes, you told Kenny. You didn't tell me." The fire in her eyes cooled and turned a shade of sad. "We had plans. We were going to move to Ft. Collins—get our degrees."

Your plans, not mine. "I still want an answer."

"You don't deserve an answer."

"Okay." He held out his hands, palms out.

"I'm sorry I left town without letting you know first." The apology sounded half-assed, probably because it was, but her expression and the way she looked at him, measured him—like he was a piece of trash—got in the way of honesty. "But I need to know."

"Fine." She threw the word at him like one of her softball pitches, fast and straight. Her jaw muscles pulsated. "Yes, I was most likely at the Clairemonts'. I was studying. Brad and I both needed to get our chemistry grades up to get into vet school." She wrapped her arms around her waist and paced a few more steps. "When you left, Mr. Krauss forced me to find another lab partner. When I said I didn't want one, he assigned Brad." Her eyes went from slightly suspicious to intensely dark. "I was determined to do the things we talked about. Get a scholarship to Colorado State. Finish vet school. Start my own clinic." Tears sprang from nowhere, and she closed her eyes. "It doesn't matter now."

Crap. I never thought. He locked his knees

to remain standing. The acid in his stomach surged into his throat. An ache sliced across his chest. "Kenny told me you didn't get accepted, but I never knew why. Karly, I'm so—"

"Don't." She waved him off. "Whatever you were about to say...don't. After you left, the bullying at school got worse. Some of the kids said I was the reason you left—that you couldn't stand to be with me anymore. I couldn't concentrate, and my grades tanked. I didn't have anyone to talk to." She picked at a scab on her elbow, then let her hands fall to her sides. "It doesn't matter. I have my shelter. This place is what I care about now."

"Karly..."

She raised her hands to ward him off, then pulled inward.

God, I'm such a jerk. He rubbed his temples, then stopped, letting the recrimination intensify into a headache. "I feel stupid for trusting my sister."

Once again, he'd managed to prove his dad right. He was worthless.

"Why didn't you fight for us?" she asked with a rawness that just about carved him in half.

"I did...actually." He cracked his knuckles one at a time, trying to buy some time, but the effort was futile. "My dad found out we slept together, so he decided to teach me a lesson. I figured if I just left—"

"You figured if you left, everyone would be perfectly fine, is that it?"

"No, that's not it." The self-loathing dug a little deeper. "My mom was always crying. My sister was hiding in her room. I had to do something. My dad never wanted me, and I figured—"

"You figured you had to fix things. You. Only you. No one else."

Strike one.

The hurt and judgment and condemnation he'd take, because, multiply those feelings by any number, and it wouldn't come close to how totally worthless he felt.

"You left me behind to deal with everything alone."

Strike two.

"Then"—her eyes bulged wider—"when you thought I'd slept with Brad Clairemont, you dumped me. Does that sum it up?"

Strike three. He suppressed the urge to tuck her into his arms, beg her to forgive him.

"Well?" she demanded.

He needed to come up with a response, any response. She deserved something. "We were going in different directions. You were leaving for college. What was I supposed to do? Your parents would have never allowed us to live together, and getting a job in Ft. Collins is almost impossible."

"A job. That's your excuse?" Her voice vibrated. "Or was it something else, like jealousy? I bet you figured once I got to college and was surrounded by all those college boys, I'd leave you behind, so you found a way to leave me first."

Strike four. It just keeps getting better.

"I needed you." Her chin quivered.

Strike five, the knockout punch.

"That's not true." He added a bit of tenderness to the statement, but she shot him a look that made his man parts shrivel. "You've always been very good at figuring things out."

"Forever. That's what you promised me."

The explosive IED blast that had ripped him apart was nothing compared to her bald statement. "I suppose you hate me now."

"I don't hate you. I've never been good at holding hate. You of all people know that."

"That's true. You could pop off like a champagne bottle cork, but in seconds the bubbles settled, while everyone else around you was still fizzing. I always admired that about you. I could stay mad for days."

"More like weeks."

Custer pulled against his lead in an effort to get to Karly. Thad moved to place a hand on Custer's head. "Shhhh. She's okay. Everything is going to be okay." *At least I hope so. I have to fix this.*

He scratched the dog's neck, while Karly's facial muscles tightened to hold on to her frown.

She held out her hand for Custer to lick. "Hanging on to anger eats at the soul. I was angry all the time after you left. At my dad and brothers for leaving me behind, and my mom for never listening."

He reached to tuck a stray hair behind her ear. It was such a natural instinct. He'd done it a thousand times before. This time, she jerked her head away with a glare.

"I...ah... I decided not to live angry anymore," she finished.

"I know you don't want to hear it, but I am truly sorry." *Sorry for the hurt. The lost time.* "I screwed up."

"That was ten years ago. I've moved on."

She wouldn't look at him, and her words sounded flat, passionless. She hadn't moved on. He could see what happened had crawled underneath her skin like a tick on a dog, and sucked her dry.

Today wasn't the day to ask for the details

about her dad, brothers, any of it. He wasn't going anywhere. In fact, he shouldn't have left in the first place. Not for the reasons he did.

He flapped Custer's ear, giving it a good rub. "I'll train your mutt. It's the least I can do."

"My mutt?" She shook her head, her forehead creasing to support her scoff. "No, Thad. Training Custer—that needs to be for you. You don't owe me any favors."

"You said you needed the money."

"There is that." With the light of determination in her eyes, she pressed her shoulders back. "I'm not getting the donations or fees I need to keep this place open. I'm running low on food. Heck, I'm running low on everything—cleaning supplies, paper towels… But I don't mean to burden you with my problems. I'll figure something out."

The set of her jaw and the decisiveness in her expression transformed her into the woman he remembered.

She'd always been an interesting mix of determination and insecurities, fearlessness and doubt, but he liked the new Karly even better. He hadn't been a part of watching her grow, like the pine he planted as a boy in his grandfather's garden. He'd always have that regret.

"I don't know much about running a business, but I can come up with some ideas. We could go for a coffee. Maybe you'd let me buy you a caramel latte as a way of saying I'm sorry."

A puff of wind lifted a tendril of hair that had fallen out of her cap. "You remembered. Lattes are still my favorite, but I don't think so. You've already apologized, and I've moved on. You should too. This town has grown since you've been gone, and has a lot more to offer."

"Like women, I suppose you mean." Custer looked up at him with those pathetic, sad eyes and mirrored how he was feeling. "It won't make a difference. Dating is not an option. I need time to figure out my next move." He unknotted Custer's leash. "You've got a good business going here, Karly. You should be proud. And, for what it's worth, I *am* sorry about the misunderstanding." *And for leaving. And for not being here for you.*

"Would you stop beating yourself up? The military should have helped you increase your self-confidence once you got away from your dad." A slight reddish tinge brushed the curve of her cheek. He'd always loved and counted on her honesty.

She could see his vulnerabilities—his flaws—and she never cared. The only person in his life who'd loved him as is. He hurt her —badly—and for what?

What kind of man hurt the ones he loved?

"I'll come by later this week to help you feed and wash some dogs."

"That's not necessary. I've already got volunteers scheduled. Plus, I'm sure you have better things to do. Besides, I wouldn't want you thinking there's something between us...'cause there's not. Training Custer is important to that little girl. She should be your priority."

He gave Custer the command to sit, and he waited for the dog to comply before turning back to look at her. "Do you remember that corn maze we visited in tenth grade? I got lost, and you had to come help me find my way out?"

"It was a hot day." Her eyes narrowed and her head tilted to the left. "By the time I found you, the sun had almost set, and we were the last ones out. Why?"

The day had been spectacular. She'd looked amazing in her jeans shorts. He could almost smell the coconut of her sunscreen, the scent of cornhusks drying in the sun. Somehow, he'd taken a left, and she a right. He'd called her name, again, and again, and again, but he couldn't find her. He ran, searching around each corner, taking a right and left and right again until he was out of breath.

The panic of that day welled in his throat.

Concern visited her face for a second before she wiped it way.

"Why, you ask?" He forced a smile because it was the right thing to do. "Because for the past several years I've been in that maze, working to find my way out. Right now I need to work through a couple of things. Feeding and washing a few dogs…it's what I need. I'll see you Saturday, Karly."

He gently pulled Custer's lead to get the dog's attention, and at his silent signal, the dog fell into step beside him.

He didn't turn back, although he wanted to. He didn't want to need anyone—love anyone—never again.

Besides, who would want to love the son of Raymond Lopez, a man who had enough DUIs to get locked up for eight months? No one in this town loved Raymond, and neither did he.

Too bad he couldn't find a big enough lock to hold the blasted memory box shut. Childhood, adolescence, adulthood…there wasn't anything good worth reminiscing about, except for the one bright light—Karly.

While his steps were uneven and unbalanced, regret was a steady roar through his veins. Sorrow with a ton of self-loathing piled on. He'd been such a fool.

Days like this made him want to go back. Go back to bombs and bullets and casualties.

Back to war.

He'd been expendable then, and felt even more worthless now.

CHAPTER THREE

Nothing matched the joy of puppy hugs and kisses.

Karly nuzzled the husky mix before setting the pup in the basin of water. The happy little guy had been transported in from New Mexico. The Colorado climate suited his thick coat, and she hoped finding him a forever home wouldn't be too hard. While her kennel was full, Karly couldn't resist accepting the full-of-energy, blue-eyed pup she'd temporarily named Krane, her namesake.

Her heart swelled, and tears stung her

eyes when she thought about how Krane had been hours away from being euthanized. Lavender and vanilla wafted through the air from the soap used to remove the dog's nervous scent gland smell.

"Karly?" Mara Gaccione appeared in the doorway. "Are you okay?" Buddy, Mara's service dog, led her into the utility room.

"Are you sure you're blind? 'Cause you sure see a lot." Karly lifted Krane out of the soapy water to give him a good rinse under the sink hose.

"Yes, I'm blind, not deaf. When I hear sniffles, I get concerned. Deciphering whether you have a cold or are upset isn't as easy, so I ask." Buddy moved in to take a sniff at Krane's behind, and the puppy turned to give him a nip on the nose. "Maybe my news will cheer you up."

Karly set the freshly washed puppy on the counter to give him a good toweling. "Don't tell me...you got a new car."

"Funny. Although, I did hear car manufacturers have developed a driverless car. Can you just imagine me driving a car? Everyone in town would run screaming from the streets."

"Don't you dare tell Lizzy Cranston. I'm surprised that old biddy hasn't bought a tank to run everyone off the road. As it is, she flips everyone the bird, even when she's the one who's run the stop sign."

Mara lifted her apron off the hook, placing it over her head. "For pushing eighty, she sure is a spry one."

"She's something, all right. Tell me... what's your news?"

The blush of excitement spreading across her friend's face provided a warning, but not quickly enough.

"Joe and I are pregnant." Her friend's voice lilted with excitement.

"Ohhh...that's...wonderful news." Mara's exuberant confession drove a stake through Karly's bruised and battered heart.

The turmoil she'd experienced the past two days after learning the truth about Thad's leaving broke through the dam of control and spilled. She couldn't speak. She couldn't breathe. The vast emptiness in her womb ached.

"Karly? Did I say something wrong?"

"No. No. I'm thrilled for you and Joe. Really. You both deserve so much happiness."

She rubbed her nose with the back of her hand and returned Krane to one of six holding boxes on the far wall.

Mara was having a baby. A child she could hold and love. Something Karly would never have.

"Give me a hug." Karly wrapped her arms around her friend. "You know what this means."

"No, what?" Mara arched back.

"I get to shop for cute little outfits. That's what." Karly squeezed Mara's arms. "If anyone deserves happiness, it's you two. Oh..." she turned on the tap of excitement, "...and we get to have a baby shower. We should have it here, and invite everyone. We'll get Jenna to make the cake. I bet if you give Gwen a list of stuff you need, she'll find everything on her thrift shop runs. She finds the most amazing things."

"Yes, but—"

"And I can come over and help paint the nursery. Brianne and I can get everything organized just the way you want it. I'm so thrilled for you. How is Brianne feeling about having a new brother or sister?"

"Not good. It scares her. She almost broke my heart when she asked me if we were still going to want her after the baby was born."

"Both of your lives changed after her mom hit your dad's car. Both of your worlds were shattered."

"I would hope by now Brianne would know, deep down, that we love her. She's as much my child as the one I'm carrying." Mara swatted at a tear hovering on the edge of her cheek. "Look at me getting all emotional."

"Why don't I stop by and take her out for lunch? I enjoy her company, and it might help her feel better. I'll assure her she's loved.

There are lots of people in this town who adore her."

Mara's chin lifted, and her eyes stared forward. "It might make you both feel better. You're sad. I can feel it."

"No. No. Not sad." Karly tried stepping away, but her friend held tight for a few more seconds before releasing her.

"Please, tell me what's happening."

"Don't mind me." Karly scrubbed the washbasin with a scouring pad, whirling in smaller and smaller circles, her arm moving faster and faster. *I've gotta stop crying every time my friends get pregnant. Just because I can't shouldn't matter. But, dang it, it does.* She blew out a long breath to push out the self-pity. "I'm just hormonal this week. I'll be fine."

"Are you sure that's all it is?" Mara placed a hand on her forearm. "When I stopped at Dreamy Delights to get muffins for Joe's staff meeting, Jenna said Thad finally stopped by to see you. How did that go?"

What the farts? Jenna's gossiping now? She

doesn't gossip...or does she? That's just plain dog poop.

Karly turned and sat on one of the transportation kennels and pressed her fingers into her temple to stop the sudden pounding in her head. "You're the fourth person who's asked me that question in the past two days. People shouldn't be so quick to hitch Thad and me together again, 'cause it ain't gonna happen."

"People care, that's all."

"And I appreciate that people care, but some people are just being nosy and should mind their own business." Anger bubbled up and out before she could flatten the feeling. "I wish my brother hadn't asked me to look in on him. I could have done an outstanding job of ignoring him."

"Yep, always the overachiever." Mara reached out to touch her shoulder and connect. "Don't be mad at Kenny. He feels responsible because Thad saved his life so many times."

"If Kenny hadn't fallen, then Thad

wouldn't have had to drag him to safety, and I wouldn't feel like I owed Thad."

"You stopping by Thad's wasn't just about Kenny. A couple of months ago, you played me a video from Thad's Facebook page."

Only because he hadn't locked it down.

"You've been checking up on him," Mara persisted. "Which means you still feel something for the guy."

"I only look when Kenny's tagged." Karly twisted her ponytail, wrapping it around and around and around her finger.

"Uh-huh." The skin tightening across Mara's mouth while it curled up at the ends didn't help.

Best friends can be soooo annoying.

"Okay. Have me arrested. I look sometimes, because I get curious, but it doesn't mean anything."

"If you say so." Mara reached for Buddy's ears and gave them a good scratch. "Everyone always thought you two would eventually get married."

"Marriage isn't for me." *At least not anymore.*

Mara huffed out a smirk. "I used to think no one would ever love me now that I'm blind, but then Joey came along."

"But you wanted to get married. I don't." *Or can't, might be more accurate. Who would want someone who can't have kids?* "I've got a good life. I'm surrounded by good friends, and I've got my fur-babies."

"You sound as if these animals are enough."

"There's something to be said for unconditional love."

"Yes, but in your case, you don't even get that. Not long-term, anyway. Your animals come and go every day. At least with Buddy, I get him for his lifetime."

She flicked away the idea like a flea. "I'll make it work."

"And, if you can't keep this place? Then what?"

Her morning coffee churned in her stomach with a surge of nausea. "I guess I'll just have to make certain I don't have to close my business. Besides, what else would I do?"

"That's my point. You can't work all the time. Is Thad the reason you stopped dating?"

No other man could play her heartstrings like Thad. The music he created was magical.

A surge of bitterness burned her throat. "He was my best friend, and he just left," *just when I needed him most. He destroyed my trust.* "Besides, there's no one in this town I'd want to date. All the good ones are taken."

"Yeah, you're right. I'd still be single if Joey hadn't returned." Mara fiddled with the strings on her apron. "Thad did leave rather suddenly. He just seemed to vanish."

"Can you believe he dumped me because his jealous sister couldn't keep her lying mouth shut?"

"What does Sarah have to do with Thad's leaving?"

"Nothing. But he dumped me later, as

soon as she told him I was fooling around with Brad Clairemont."

"Brad? Nooo. That's awful." Mara placed a hand over her heart. "Why would he believe such a thing? Brad's good at taking care of animals, but nice to people? Not so much. Everyone knows he's a jerk."

"Everyone but Thad." Karly rubbed her left ring finger where Thad's wedding ring would have been creating a happy, well-worn groove all these years. She'd expected to have a houseful of kids, animals, and love by twenty-eight. At least she had a bunch of animals to keep her distracted. "It boils down to trust. He just didn't believe in me." *Or my love.*

"Maybe. Maybe not. Guys can get some silly notions in their heads sometimes. Joe thought I wouldn't marry him unless he was rich. How silly is that?" The lines of Mara's face deepened with concern. "Pretty dumb, if you ask me." Mara puffed out an annoyed, protective breath on her friend's behalf, straight enough to hit a target.

"Thad and I were so close, we could almost finish each other's sentences. I thought he got me."

Mara took a step closer and placed her hand on Karly's forearm. "When emotions are running high, we tend towards the illogical."

"Or the stupid."

"Maybe you should give that trust thing another try. It's never too late."

Just the thought gave Karly a thumping headache. In high school, Thad was the first person to tramp into her half-awake brain every morning. Would he be late for school again, would he have finished his homework, would he pass her a love note in class? Every time she saw him walking down the hall, her heart did a hippity-skip and a cartwheel. She'd given him every ounce of love she had —even disobeyed her parents when they demanded she stop seeing him.

"It's too late for us. I forgave him a long time ago, but the trust just isn't there anymore."

"That's too bad." Mara's hand squeezed her arm, the sympathy warming Karly's skin. "That baritone, rusty voice of his makes my woman parts sizzle."

"Mara, you're married."

"Yes, but I'm not dead. If Thad looks anything like he did in high school, I'm surprised you're not taking advantage of what he's offering. You're both single. So why not?" Mara blushed. "Jenna said she'd make up a batch of her special dark chocolate frosting, if you're interested in smearing some on Thad and licking it off."

"Mara!"

"Well?"

Not going there.

Bonnie Raitt's "I Can't Make You Love Me" filled the room. *Isn't that just perfect?* Karly's breath oozed out in a stream of frustration. *Couldn't something other than that song have played? Really?*

"Tell Jenna I appreciate her offer, but I..." Karly reached in her back pocket for her vibrating cell phone. "Hey, Mom. What's up?" She took a deep breath, waiting for the perpetual judgment to begin.

"I just came by to see you." Her mother's voice squeaked it was so polished. "Where are you? Oh, there you are. Never mind." The phone disconnected before Karly said a word.

"Hello, Mara dear." Her mother patted her friend's arm like she was one of the animals in the kennel, then moved away from Buddy before Mara's dog could give her a sniff. "I came to talk to my favorite daughter."

"Ma, Mara knows I'm your only daughter."

"Yes. I'm sure she does. Mara, would you excuse us a moment? I have something important I need to discuss with Karly."

"Sure, Mrs. Krane. I'll get started on feeding the cats." Mara moved through the back door faster than Buddy could lead. Karly would have given anything to follow her friend out of the room and avoid hearing the inevitable constructive criticism that wasn't in the least constructive.

"Didn't you have a nail appointment this morning?" Karly replaced her phone in her back pocket, summoning her last remaining bit of pleasantness.

"I've got fabulous news." Her mother set her knockoff designer purse on the counter. "There's an opening at Elkridge Lodge for a part-time manager. I rushed over to bring you the job application."

Karly stared at the packet of pages with lines and boxes requiring information, the Elkridge Lodge and Spa logo emblazoned at the top. A bitter resentment shimmied down her spine, and she had to swallow several times to get her churning stomach to settle. "Mom. I have a job. My business takes all my time. I don't need another job."

"This job would be a steady income." Her tone managed to mix with a slight degree of irritation and an even heavier percentage of patronizing.

"I get by. I've never asked you for money,

have I?" She prayed for patience, knowing the repeating lecture loop was about to repeat itself again. Marriage and babies. That's what was expected of the only daughter of Karen Krane.

"I know you want to play and have fun," her mother continued, "but one of these days you'll have to wake up. This place doesn't make enough to provide you with comforts. You should be setting money aside for other things, like retirement."

Play? I'm working my butt off. And retirement?

"Mom, I appreciate—"

"You have to plan, Karly, hun." Her mother droned on about family and being fiscally responsible, even though Karly had never asked for a penny to start her business. Yep, she had a good grasp on what it took to keep food on the table, a roof over her head, and kibble in the animals' bowls.

"Are you listening to me?" Her mother's tone had taken on a persuasive passion. "You should take better care of yourself. Look at you." Her mother reached to push Karly's bangs to the side. Karly raised her hand to ward her off, hoping her mother didn't pull out an anti-bacterial wipe next.

"Just for once, Mom," she let the building resentment ease, "it'd be nice if you could be proud of me. Take a moment to see what I'm trying to build here."

"Karly, hun. I *am* proud of you."

The shocking statement numbed her brain. She didn't know what to say. She just stared at her mom.

"Don't look at me that way." Her mother glanced at her fingertips, then rubbed at a nail polish chip. "It's just that you work too hard. When will you have time to find a good man?"

Here we go again.

"The only thing guys in this town know how to do is leave. Look at Dad, Keith, Kevin, Kenny…they all left." *And so did Thad.*

Her mother's eyes jolted open, then eased. "Oh, honey. Trust me, life gets lonely. You can find one who will stick."

What if I don't want one who sticks?

Her mother played with her conservative gold loop earring. "Did I tell you I signed us up for one of those dating sites?"

Oh, jeez. What next? "No, you didn't. Is this one of those two-for-one deals?"

"Why don't you come over tonight, and I'll help you set up a profile."

"Really, Mom," Karly did her polite best to curb the welling frustration. "I don't need a man in my life."

"Every woman needs to find a man and secure her future." Her mother reached out to touch Karly's cheek. "When am I going to get my grandbabies?"

Never. That familiar sting in her eyes returned. "Would you settle for furry grandbabies?"

Her mother's eyebrows lifted. "I suppose you find that funny."

No. Just reality. If the topic hadn't been extremely serious, she might have laughed. "Puppies do have their appeal."

"Your response is so typical, and

becoming quite annoying." Her mother reached into her purse to grab her drama red lipstick. "I could have sold the house and moved back to New York, but I'd be too far away from you and the boys. It doesn't look like any of you are going to settle down anytime soon." She dropped the lipstick tube back in and retrieved her cell phone. "Kevin and Kurt will be in town next week to fix the back fence. Make sure you mark your calendar. And if you video chat with Kenny —tell him to call his mother. The only one he ever talks to is you. Now give me a kiss."

Karly dutifully leaned in and gave her mom what she wanted. She had learned to pick her battles. In her teens, she rebelled. In her early twenties, she defied. Now, she appeased...to a point.

Her mother picked up her purse and tapped the end of her sunglasses on her lips. *Oh, no. Now what?*

"Someone at the beauty salon told me Thad Lopez is back in town. I hope you're smart enough to avoid falling for his good looks this time. He did you and this town a favor by leaving."

Slowly, Karly stepped back and forced her frazzled nerves to calm. "You never did like Thad."

"Your father and I tried to protect you. Thad didn't come from a stable family, and he lacked in so many ways. You should keep well away from that man. He's nothing but trouble."

And one of the reasons you always found me lacking.

"I have to go." Her mother kissed her cheek, then proceeded to rub in the lipstick smear. "There, that's a bit more color. Don't forget. I'm having lunch with some of the ladies from the lodge, then I have a mani-pedi scheduled this afternoon." Her mother twirled and headed for the door.

Still trying to fit in with the wealthy crowd, huh, Mom?

"Mom?" Her mother paused and turned while Karly approached. "You can take this with you. I don't need it." Karly held out the application form.

"Maybe you should think about it. The job pays good money."

"I can recycle it if you would like." The rise of her voice and her rigid inflexibility caused her mother's manicured brow to rise. The silence loomed until her mother shrugged.

"You've always been such a stubborn girl."

You never hear me. Her frustration maxed out. "Since I've been on my own for a good seven years, I hope someday soon you'll see I'm no longer a child. I've grown up, Mom, even though I know you'll always see me as your baby."

"True. Very true. You should think about getting a haircut." Her mom's last statement trailed behind as she disappeared down the row of barking dogs.

So typical.

The husky puppy followed her every move with his big, sad eyes. "I bet you love me more than she does."

She closed her eyes for a moment to find her quiet place, a place where she didn't have to be the perfect daughter, sister, or friend.

A place she could just be.

Unfortunately, she couldn't imagine such a place.

CHAPTER FOUR

The strange crunching noise made Thad roll out of bed and drop to a crouched position. Half awake, yet fully aware, he scanned the now-silent room until he found the source of the disturbance.

"You gotta be kidding me." Custer looked like he swallowed a dog bone whole and dropped his head on top of Thad's half-chewed boot. "Those were my best pair."

Thad walked around the edge of the bed, grabbed his combat boots out from between Custer's paws and dropped them on his desk by the open window. The dog's tail thump-thump-thumped on the floor nervously while Thad released a morning fart, communicating his displeasure.

"You and I had an understanding. No chewing stuff." He dropped down to the bed, flopped onto his back, and hauled his hands down his face.

I feel like I've been run over by a tank.

A soft breeze moved the air in the room, bringing with it a scent of pine. The sun, barely awake, peeked over the horizon, wishing him a good morning, but he'd rather have pulled a pillow over his head and let the day slip past. However, the coffee pot called to him, and he rolled again to a sitting position.

"Maybe if I could sleep for more than twenty minutes at a time, I'd be in a better mood." Custer leaned into the bed, pushed his muzzle underneath Thad's hand, begging for forgiveness. "I guess I'd better take you out before you decide to destroy something else." Custer tilted his head to the side, listening.

Thad struggled into a pair of jeans and made his way to the kitchen to confirm the coffee maker had started to brew. The rumbling noise of a vehicle making its way slowly up the dead-end dirt road grabbed his attention. His mouth curved up while he grabbed a clean T-shirt from the top of his rucksack.

The old Ford stopped in front of his place as Thad opened the front door.

"Hey, Coach. Just brewed a pot of coffee. What brings you up this way?"

"I knew you'd be up this early." Bill Mason walked around the bed of his truck. "Tuesdays are always quiet, and my son-in-law is opening the store this morning. I came up to bring you the window you ordered, and to make sure you know how to use a level properly."

"If I don't, it's your fault." He scratched at his morning stubble. "You're the one who taught me to use one in the first place."

"True." Coach retrieved a large toolbox from the back of his old Ford. "Coffee, you say? Is it any good?"

"I doubt it."

The man's belly shook with a laugh. "I guess if I add enough milk and sugar, anything is drinkable."

Thad smirked, then glanced at the dog by his side. "Custer, mind your manners, and don't shove that nose of yours anywhere it doesn't belong." Custer moped to the corner of the kitchen, circled, then collapsed on the floor with a harrumph, telling Thad exactly what he thought of his orders.

Pulling an extra mug from the cupboard, Thad poured a cup three-quarters full, then pulled the milk, sugar, and spoon from their proper places and left Coach to do the rest.

"I see you got a new dog."

"Nope. Just on loan. Karly took it upon herself to find me a job, and brought me that furball to see if I could get him to mind his manners. Frankly, I think she just needed a place for him to stay, since her shelter has gotten a little crowded."

"He looks as stubborn as a mule."

"He is."

Coach pulled out one of two chairs at the old wooden table that had a wad of paper stuck under one leg, theoretically to keep it from wobbling. He leaned back and glanced around the ten-by-ten room. The elder might have had the easygoing, relaxed act down enough to convince most folks, but Thad had known the man too many years. His instincts were sharp as a glass shard, and probably picking up more than Thad wanted to reveal.

"We should get started," Thad purposely broke the silence, "before that sun starts to heat the day and make us both cranky and miserable." Thad tilted his head toward where the sun broke through the clouds.

"Cranky? Speak for yourself." Coach's arthritic hand lifted the mug to his mouth. "Dang, that coffee is hot." He thumped the mug, which boasted the slogan *Please wait while my sarcasm wakes up,* on the table. "I've never been cantankerous a day in my life."

Thad's brows hiked upward. "Is that so?"

"You always were a cocky kid."

"Come on. Admit it. I've always been your favorite." Teasing the one person who'd been more like a father to him than the father who'd given him his name felt comfortable. Easy.

The old codger scrunched his nose and mouth, and he snorted a laugh in response.

"I'd better remove that old window before you take off down the road with the new one still in the bed of your truck."

"You're learning."

It's nice to know some things never change. Thad headed out back. Coach showed up a few minutes later hauling a window, his breath a little short.

He leaned the new pane against the log siding. "You want to talk about how you got those scars on your hand and that limp?"

Sharp and observant. "Not really." The memory of a thousand flaming projectiles penetrating his skin made him wince. Thad picked up the pry bar to remove the old trim.

"Fair enough." Coach accepted the rotted molding while Thad removed the rotted boards from around the window. "What are the odds of me talking you into helping me coach football this coming fall?"

The sounds of whistles, the crash of helmets, the roar of the crowd, and the thrill of victory gave him a pump of energy, but his unsettled future put a kibosh on accepting the offer. "Let's talk closer to the start of the school year, when I have a better idea of what's what."

Coach picked up a stray nail from the ground. "There's some money in it. Not much, but some."

What is this? A pity party? First Karly. Now you? "Whose money? Coaching high school sports has always been a volunteer position."

"Now, don't go getting the wrong idea. The administration created a budget for the football team a few years back. You would be doing me a favor helping me handle the hostiles."

"What hostiles?"

"You know, the kids who think they can show up to games without practicing. Parents who are sure they know more than the coaches on the field. Administrators always on your back to watch the budgets."

When Thad tried hiding a chuckle and failed, Bill gave him the coach's eye.

"You think that's funny, do you? If you decide to take the job, you'll earn every penny. Those administrators can be quite stingy. Heck, they wouldn't even allow me to buy jockstraps for the guys who couldn't afford them."

Coach went quiet while he watched Thad remove the old sideboards. After a few minutes, he leaned over Thad's shoulder. "I brought an electric saw to cut out that frame if you don't have one."

"I found an old jobber in my grandpa's shed. Before you ask, I've got the nails, insulation, and sealing tape as well. I should be good."

"Seems like you know what you're doing. You finish up here. I'm going to relax, drink some coffee, enjoy the morning." He lifted the window off the ground. "This will be easier to install from the inside."

"I'll be in in a minute."

Fifteen minutes later, Thad set his toolbox on the counter. "That was the easy part." He brushed his hands down his jeans, retrieved a mug from the cabinet that said *Ask someone who cares* before filling it with dark roast.

Coach lifted a finger toward Thad's face. "Those black circles under your eyes tell me you're not sleeping. Do you have nightmares?"

"Nope. I've just never been a sound sleeper." He sat on the other worn oak chair.

Coach rotated the coffee mug in circles. "You know, some guys when they come back don't do so well. Flashbacks. Angry all the time."

"I might not be sleeping, but I didn't get insomnia from being in the military. I suppose you're assuming I have post-traumatic stress disorder."

"You're not sleeping, and those scars have a story behind them."

"Yeah, well. I haven't slept well since I was a kid. You knew my dad. Just because my childhood sucked doesn't mean I've got PTSD."

"Maybe you should—"

"Look. I appreciate what you're trying to do. I do. And I appreciate your concern." He gulped back the self-deprecation that would prove Coach had a point, which he didn't. "I already talked to the military shrinks before they allowed me to discharge." *For all the good it did.* "She reviewed the symptoms: intrusive thoughts, flashbacks, feeling disconnected, hypervigilance. I know the full list—trust me. A couple of guys I know lost their shit over there. It wasn't pretty."

Coach folded his arms, crossed his feet,

and leaned back. "Maybe you don't have PTSD, but—"

"I don't."

"But you're definitely avoiding life." He tapped his fingers on the reclaimed-wood table.

"Excuse me?" Thad pushed a thumb into his palm to relieve a throbbing ache, then leaned back in his chair. "I'm not avoiding people." *Well, not all people.*

He waved a hand, dismissing his indignation. "Some people call it numbing. Soldiers are trained to be tough. To suck it up. We don't talk about things."

"I talk." The words came out a bit faster and sounding more defensive than he'd like. "I've just never been one to splash my past all over the internet."

"Sure you do. By phone. Email. People can't see you that way. I know the tricks."

Stop pushing, old man. Why does everyone have to poke? "I just need time, that's all."

"Yep, I get it. When I came back, I

avoided family. Friends. Anything that would trigger the past."

He rubbed his fingers together like he was rubbing a stress stone. Back and forth, the motion continued, reminding Thad the subconscious habit had started when Coach quit smoking all those years ago.

"You're trying to get numb," Coach looked him directly in the eye. "Stay numb."

The truth sank in like a mosquito penetrating the skin. He tried squashing it, but couldn't. After a few seconds, the poison started to itch.

He'd been trying not to think. Seeking silence, a refuge from his failures.

"I'm good." Thad worked hard to make the statement sound legit. He didn't want people caring too much. He didn't want the burden.

"Good, my ass. Avoiding the things you love to do and the people you like, whether you believe it or not, will lead to depression. Isolating yourself, pretending everything is good, is worse than having PTSD. Avoiding living is close to not living at all. You don't want to go down that road. Trust me, son."

"Why does everyone act like I'm still in high school? I can take care of myself. The military taught me how. I'm just busted up a bit, that's all. I'll heal. I just need time." *Although I sometimes wonder if living this way is worth it.*

Coach's eyes narrowed, the same way they did when a player said something stupid. "The best solution is to keep busy. Get your body tired so your mind can rest. Work like you did every day on that battlefield."

Thad crossed his arms and leaned back in the spindle back chair. "A long time ago you asked me about my biggest fear? You wanted to know what I was afraid of."

"Yeah." He pushed his cup back. "Sorry, I can't remember what you said."

"I don't remember either, but I remember what you said, because it stuck." Thad picked up a measuring tape off the table, pulled, then let it recoil with a snap. "You said your fear was never being able to slay the past. You wouldn't explain what you meant, only that someday I might understand."

"Ah." Coach's whispered response didn't need any clarification. "There are certain things soldiers see or do or experience during a war that, unless they've been there, you can't explain to someone else. And if you've been there, there is no explanation necessary." He pushed his thumb into his shoulder to massage a pain.

"Exactly. I've seen things. Experienced things. Now I just need time to decompress."

"Yes, but in order to decompress, you need to fill your days."

"Is that what you did after you returned?"

"No." Coach lifted a spoon to stir his coffee, which he'd already stirred. "Don't do what I did. I had to hit bottom first. Take my advice, stay away from drugs and booze. There are no answers in the bottom of a bottle. And if you ever get to a spot where you want to dive deep into one or the other, call me. I'm here."

Thad looked out the hole in the side of the house, appreciating the offer, and even the unsolicited advice, though he wouldn't mind getting a little less of both.

"I had better get that window put in, it smells like rain's coming. Want to help?"

Coach rolled his wrist to look at his well-loved Swiss Army watch. "Weatherman said a storm was moving in, but I didn't believe him. He hasn't been right all week."

"Don't tell me you've turned into one of those old poops who sit down at the café talking about the day's weather, the national news headlines, eating pie, and drinking coffee."

The middle finger of Coach's right hand flipped up.

Thad chuckled and let the flippancy ease the tension tightening his neck muscles. "Well, then, it's official. I'll start calling you Grandpa."

"Might as well. The title fits."

"No kidding?"

"Last summer. That's why my son-in-law's helping run the business. The boy doesn't know a finishing nail from a drywall nail, but he's getting there."

Thad chuckled. "Sounds familiar. Remember the time you sent me to pick up some wood screws and I ended up bringing back a boatload of metal screws? You were hopping mad. You made me run a couple of extra miles at practice that day."

Coach's whole face shifted into a smile. "Served you right."

Thad gestured to the window. "What do you think?"

"You turned into a fine man. Oh, were you asking about the window?" Coach gave that old familiar wink, stood, and then gave Thad a gentle slap on the back. "I'd help, but I'd just be in the way. You know what you're doing. Just remember, you aren't alone. As a matter of fact, I just had a thought. Look up Chase Daniels. He runs a handyman business here in town. You might remember Ashley Bryant. They just had their first child, with another one on the way."

"Chase Daniels, huh?" Thad worked to glue the pieces of information together.

"Chase's best friend was killed by an IED blast, and he came here to find his peace." He chuckled. "I think he found more than he bargained for. Ashley's a handful."

"I can't believe the high school party girl is now a mom."

"People change. Sometimes life gives you challenges that make you even stronger. Better." Coach took a couple of gulps of his coffee and set the mug in the sink. "How about you stopping by my place next week to help me fix my deck?"

"Be glad to help. Just let me know when."

"I'll text you. I know how to do that now," he said before heading for his truck. "Like I said, don't stay away from town or be a stranger."

Stranger? That he was. He didn't know the guy inside his brain anymore.

"I'll see you soon." Coach wouldn't let him hide. In fact, he'd scratch at him until he was raw—vulnerable—exposed enough to surrender to the change life had forced on him. "Maybe we can get some breakfast on Friday."

"I'd like that." Coach started his truck. "Take care, son."

Coach completed a U-turn, and the truck backfired as it rounded the bend of the rutted mountain road.

Custer whined and licked Thad's palm. "It's okay, buddy. You're going to have to get used to those noises." He scratched the furry mane at the dog's neck.

Custer nudged him again.

"Let's go for a quick walk and see if we can't get you tuckered out so you stop chewing on my stuff, and while we're at it, get this leg to loosen up a bit. Then I need to see if I can get that window installed." He gave the dog a signal.

"No, not sit. That was get your halter. I-yi-yi." Thad reached over and snagged the nylon cords. "You are one stubborn-ass dog." *We're both too stubborn for our own damn good.* "Now I know why Karly put us together."

Custer stood while Thad attached the leash. "Just wait until I load you down. Then we'll see how funny you think you are, because one way or another, you're going to learn to help a little girl, and I'm going to help Karly get her money."

CHAPTER FIVE

The antics of the three dogs tethered together made Karly laugh. The large-breed dogs had grown restless in their pens and needed to spend some of that pent-up energy. Otherwise, she'd have several four-legged delinquents on her hands.

"Ready to go?" Karly walked along the dirt parking lot towards the trailhead. "Burt, you take the lead. That's it. Good dog. Maybe if I can get you guys settled a bit, I can find you good homes. I could use the adoption fee money."

The shepherd mix pulled and took off

running at a much faster pace than Karly wanted to set. She pulled gently on the lead while the team ran up the hill, and she settled into her long stride.

The first quarter of a mile on the narrow animal trail had only a slight incline, which then steadily increased as they raced past the wild grasses edging each side, along with clumps of aspen and evergreens adding shade. Her lungs hungered for oxygen, but she kept pushing. Farther up the trail, her favorite spot waited. Large boulders had tumbled down from the shelf above and settled, leaving the human trespassers to wend their way around the massive barriers. Yellow, red, and white flowers interspersed among the trees and grasses added color.

When they were almost to the giant metamorphic rock shaped like an Egyptian sphinx, Thad and Custer suddenly appeared around a cluster of trees leading from the western ridge trailhead, making her pull back on the leads.

She tugged off her earphones. "Holy crap.

I didn't see you coming. Where did you come from?" She didn't want to feel the quick leap of her pulse as he moved closer, or the little flutter in her belly.

"Just the other side of the ridge. I saw you from above and thought I'd say hi."

He moved like he had all the time in the world, and she stood there waiting, like she always had. Waiting for him to meet her after class, eat lunch, or reach for her hand. She just couldn't help feeling that tingling sensation whenever he appeared. His black running pants molded nicely around quadriceps and calf muscles. The offsetting neon yellow parachute jacket finished the image, and tugged on that old thread of desire. She closed her eyes to force the image to disappear, before opening them to focus on the dogs.

"I'm impressed." He moved a little closer. "Working three dogs at once takes skill. Mind if I join you? Custer could use some exercise."

"If you want." She pointed to the narrow

trail ahead. "Why don't you go first, and I'll follow? It will be easier with the dogs."

"You just want me to take the lead so you can look at my butt."

"That's not true." *I just wish you weren't so damn good-looking. It makes ignoring you really, really hard.*

That all-knowing grin, the one that bloomed like a flower opening, reaching for the sun, soaking up the rays, expanded on his face. *The jerk.*

"My muscles are tightening up," she said. "If we're going to go, we should get moving."

"Yep, I can certainly tell you're getting cold."

He turned and took off down the trail. She studied the front of her sports shirt. Sure enough, there were her nipples, hard and erect, giving him a salute. She sighed, adjusted the backpack carrying water bottles and dog supplies, and set off down the hill at a good pace to make him pay for that comment.

Only five feet behind him, Karly and the

dogs pushed him faster and faster until she spotted the abnormal pattern. He favored his left side. A half-mile farther and she could tell the pain had significantly increased, but he was still doing his best to stay ahead. He wouldn't slow down or stop. He wouldn't show weakness. She was about to call off the familiar rivalry when a rifle crack split the air on the ridge above their location.

Crap.

She fought for control of the dogs.

Thad dropped to the ground, but maintained his grip on Custer's leash.

He rolled behind a tree and searched the hilltop.

Seconds later, a trio of deer burst through the undergrowth, crossed the path, and raced down the other side. Thad pushed to a stand just as the excited dogs got the idea to chase some deer and wrenched Karly off balance. She lost her grip on the nylon leads. Her backpack shifted. The trail's edge disintegrated.

She fought to stay upright, but the gravel

on the hill's step edge slipped away and she lost her balance.

The sky.

The earth.

The sky appeared in a tumbling vision.

The air whooshed out of her lungs.

She grabbed for a tree branch, but missed and slid another couple of feet.

Suddenly, she came to a thudding stop next to a fallen tree.

Holy crap, that hurts.

The dirt-filled scrapes and torn skin along her forearms stung. She tried lifting her leg, but every muscle screamed in pain.

"Karly?"

A rush of snapping branches and rocks tumbling, spewing debris in her face, made her thrust an arm over her head. "I'm okay. I think I just twisted my ankle."

"Don't move." Thad's concern came through loud and clear. He slid around the large pine beside her, then came back up the incline to peer over the fallen log.

Stubbornness made her push to a seated

position and begin brushing the dirt and pine needles off to see if anything was broken. Her leggings were ripped in several places. She rolled her left ankle. Sore, not broken.

"Just some cuts and scratches," she said, to convince herself and calm the fear amplifying the adrenaline screaming through her.

"It looks like just a nasty gash." He eased back the ripped Spandex fabric on her shin to look at the bloody scrape, then pulled off his pack.

She couldn't help but notice how his hands shook, which divided her concerns. But as soon as he touched her, color returned to his face. His shaking calmed. His hands became steady.

"This will sting." He ripped open a sterilizing packet from an olive-green emergency kit.

Her muscles clenched in response to the alcohol-based antibacterial gel. "You weren't kidding."

Within a few minutes, he had the gash on her shin wrapped enough to stop the bleeding.

"Oh, no." She tried to see around the tall evergreens. "Where are the dogs? I don't hear them."

"They're not far. When you fell, the dogs took off and got their leashes tangled on a tree. I tied Custer to your group. They're together, just below the top of the hill."

"Good thinking." A stream of air let go and drained from her chest. "I'm not sure I'd be able to find them if they took off."

"Do you think you can walk?" He scanned every inch of her body, looking for an injury. "We need to get you safely up this hill."

You still care. I can see it. Yet the caring is different. Less demanding. More supportive. Mature. She bent her knee. The sting of torn skin zipped up her leg, but it was just a sting, not a pain. "I can walk. I just can't run."

"Let's get you back up to the trail first. If you can put weight on that leg, we take the next turnoff. It cuts through to the parking lot. It's a lot steeper, but it will save you a few miles."

She didn't want to trust Thad. Her heart couldn't survive his abandonment again. But fate left her no choice. Not today, anyway.

Thad stored the kit and handed her one of his water bottles and a pain reliever.

"Thanks." She accepted his offering, even if reluctantly.

"We need to get you up that hill. Why don't you get on my back?"

"Your back?" *Not on that injured leg.* "I'm not some sissy you need to hump out of here. I was clumsy enough to tumble down here. I'll figure out a way to get back up."

"God, woman. I've carried equipment heavier than you on my back."

"I can do this." *I can't let you that close to my heart.* She used the fallen log to push into a standing position. Just one step. *That's all you need to do, just take one step, then one step more.*

She gritted her teeth against the pain and focused on the breeze brushing across her skin, the green, spongy moss, the birds calling overhead, anything to keep her mind off her leg.

His reassuring presence, his silent support, and helping hand, helped her make it back to level ground. But thank goodness she didn't end up needing to wrap herself around all the hunkiness, or she just might have stayed there forever.

"Hold up here, and I'll get the dogs." He disappeared around a bend in the trail and then reappeared moments later with four dogs leading the way. Karly's relief came streaming out in one long breath.

Thad scanned the hill above them again, clearly worrying about the gunshot.

"It was just a hunter," she said.

The look on his face clearly stated he didn't buy into her theory.

"Let's get you off this ridge. I've got your backpack. You go first this time." He guided the pack of dogs off the trail to allow her to pass. "Bill Mason told me Ashley Bryant got married."

A glance over her shoulder told her what she expected. Never one to be a talker, Thad was trying to keep her mind occupied.

"Yes. Mara's married as well. She married Joe Gaccione."

"We played soccer together, but I never really got to know him."

She slid down the steep trail through a set of trees. "Tony Dijocomo finally married Gina."

"Tony and Gina. Wow. They used to fight like crazy. I remember a time Gina smacked Tony upside the head with a book."

"He deserved it for acting like he owned the place. He settled quite a bit after his parents died." She paused at a fallen tree to decide the best way around. "Kym took off with some Hollywood guy."

"That's no surprise."

"If it weren't for Mara, I think she would have been the first to take off. Mara shared a postcard Kym sent from Europe. Based on the pictures on her Facebook page, I think she's very happy." Karly lifted her leg to climb over the wide log.

"Good for her." Thad winced as he cleared the next fallen tree. He was definitely in pain.

"Thad, would you please tell me about the scars on your hand and why you're limping? I asked Kenny, but he said to ask you, and I'd like to know."

He studied the back of his hand. "It's nothing."

Nothing. "Hmmm. That's sad."

"What is?"

"We used to be able to talk about anything. Now there's stuff you don't want to talk about. It's lame that a misunderstanding and time could turn something special into something ugly. I'd like to be friends, at least." She stopped at the trail post. Thad moved next to her, holding his silence in a way that felt unbalanced. "Half a mile to go." She braced her hand on the next log and prepared to climb over.

"It was a homemade bomb." The

whispered explanation came out so softly it drifted on the air. "It doesn't sound like much, but it's amazing what pebbles and sticks can do to skin and bone."

She paused to sit on the log instead. "A bomb," she repeated, not liking how the words stung her tongue. "Is that why you got out?"

"Among other things."

Oh, Thad. Come on. You have to talk to someone. "Do the other things have something to do with how you reacted to that rifle shot, and why your hands shake?"

"You haven't lost your knack for prying."

Well, that hurts. We used to be so close you couldn't squeeze a dime between us. Not anymore, I guess.

"However, you've lost yours for being honest," she snarked before the guilt from his piss-off reaction pressed in. "I'm sorry. I guess I've been lying too. I'm still bitter about what happened. When you left, I had no one I could talk to. No one who understood me like you did."

She leaned down to place her hands on two rocks to slide her aching legs over the log and through the narrow gap. The dogs went up, over, and around, followed by Thad, who followed her lead.

"I said I was sorry."

Reflecting on his comment, she let the wind swirl around her and pushed blowing hair out of her face. "But not sorry enough to talk to me? You need to talk to someone. Why not me?"

His eyes grew distant, and the muscles in his jaw got a good workout.

"You don't need to confide in me if you don't want. It's none of my business." She braced herself against the nearest rock and waited for him to catch up.

He wanted to say something, she could tell he did, but suddenly looked away. "Talking about what happened over there doesn't come easy."

"The hard stuff is never easy." She gave him a smile and hoped the sentiment helped. "What do you find harder to talk about, the bomb specifically, or Afghanistan in general?"

"All of it. Being deployed, then being stateside. The difference."

"You're right. Seeing pictures isn't the same, and maybe I shouldn't push, but I'd like to think I'm still a good listener, even if I don't understand. Perhaps, after all we shared, we could at least try to be friends. I wouldn't want to waste the time we spent together growing up. No matter what happened over there, I know you're still a good man."

When his amber eyes met hers, he seemed to be more at peace. "Friendship, huh? I think I'd like that."

"Well, don't think about it too long, there, buddy." She gave him a nudge and a semi-laugh. "I just might change my mind."

"My mom tells me that's a woman's prerogative."

"After your dad died…" She unzipped her jacket to let the cool air ease her churning thoughts, and to give herself time for the words to formulate. "I got to know your mom better before she moved. She'd just finished with detox, and wanted to volunteer a couple of times a month at the shelter. Therapy, she called it. She didn't need to help at my place, but she did. She's a nice lady, and I'm thankful I got to know her. Did you visit her in Texas? I hear she has a new boyfriend."

"I did, and I met Paul." His face looked like he'd just bit into a lemon and he couldn't swallow. "He treats Ma good." He rubbed at his hand. "I think when she looks at me she still sees the bad stuff that happened. It bothers her that my dad and I look alike. I moved here to give her space."

Thad held the dogs back, while Karly navigated through another narrow passage.

"My sister met some Army guy and plans to get married next year," he said. "This is her second engagement. I don't think I'll hold my breath."

"You care about your Sarah. I know you do."

"Maybe she won't be as angry anymore. I hope she's found happiness. Mom says she's in love."

Love. The sentiment felt foreign, distant, like an apple on a top branch, out of reach.

Limping forward, she contemplated the boy she'd once known as well as the lines on her hand. "I've meant to ask. Why did you move into your grandpa's hunting cabin? It's barely livable. There are a few places in town you could rent." Her shoulders eased when the dogs grew restless, sensing the end of the trail.

"I've lived in worse. It gets cold, but it's rent-free."

"Free is always good."

The cloud of dust kicked up from Thad's feet was fitting, since he kicked up a lot of other things as well. She refused to feel sorry for him, but it didn't mean she didn't feel something.

"You're biting your lip." He squinted into the sun. "What's on your mind?"

Yeah, I gotta stop doing that. I've got my

feelings stamped on my forehead where you're concerned. "My mom called this morning. A friend of hers is starting to sell a line of jewelry. She thinks I should give it a try."

Thad shook his head. "Some things never change. Follow your heart, Karly. You've got a good business. Don't let anyone tell you otherwise."

There it was. His belief that she could do anything she put her mind to. She'd missed having someone in her life who believed in her, and in her dreams.

"Where's your truck?" She scanned the empty parking lot.

"At the cabin."

"You ran from there?"

"It's only six miles or so." He tipped his head back to study the sky. "I'll make it home before it rains."

"Come on. Let me give you a ride."

Thad stepped back and shook his head, then removed Custer's lead. "Thanks for the offer. Maybe some other time. You should get those scrapes cleaned right away." An odd expression flickered across his face. "Put some ice on that leg, Karly."

He released a quick whistle, then limped back up the trail. Custer ran ahead, circling back every few hundred yards to check on Thad's progress.

Why did it feel, every time they parted lately, like he was leaving her again?

She'd gotten used to being lonely, and doing everything she could to rise above the crap life shoveled out.

She didn't want to have to worry about him leaving her again, the way her dad and brothers had.

Why couldn't Thad have just stayed away?

CHAPTER SIX

"Want to see your friends?" Custer's ears picked up, and he shifted to look at Thad.

"You need some socialization, and I bet Karly needs some help with Adoption Day. Let's lend her a hand, or a paw in your case, and see how you react to strangers and other dogs."

Custer gave him a look before jumping off the end of the tailgate and pushing his shoulder against Thad's left side. "Yeah, I know, buddy. I'm a bit achy today. But I'll be okay."

He'd learned to live with the constant pain. The soul-berating emptiness, not so much. He missed the guys. The ones who had been with him on the last tour were supposed to deploy in another couple of months, and he wouldn't be there.

Not this time.

Not ever.

"Let's see what trouble we can get into, shall we?"

He grabbed a travel mug of steaming hot liquid, plus a freshly-made caramel latte and a bag of sliced banana bread. A conversation opener, maybe, but he wasn't stupid enough to think coffee and carbs would mend the past.

Armed and ready for battle, he and Custer headed around the building to the back supply area.

"Karly?" he called out.

There she was, elbow-deep in suds, but she didn't hear his approach. She returned the spray nozzle to the holder and released the dog's collar. Sensing freedom, the overweight mastiff mix shook, spraying the walls, the floor, the equipment, and Karly.

A full-throttle laugh, so rare, tumbled out of him before he could shut it down.

"And just what's so funny, Thad Lopez?"

"You should see your face." The annoyance in her eyes contradicted the expanding smile.

"What are you doing here this early? It's not even six yet."

"Custer got excited about Adoption Day and decided to come help."

"Is that right?" She reached for a towel to dry her face.

"Tell her?" Thad looked at Custer to back up his sorry ass, but the dog just sat down and looked rather bored. "You're no help." For a few seconds, he tried deciphering her mood. "I thought you might like a latte. Adoption Day has gotta to be a big deal, right?"

Her wary eyes met his as he approached. He extended his arm with the peace offering.

"Thad, I..."

"It's just coffee, Karly, and an offer to help. Nothing more."

That wasn't the truth either. He needed to stop lying to himself, and to her.

"Tastes like there's a touch of vanilla and whipped cream. You remembered."

There's not much I've forgotten. The flush in her cheeks showed his small gift hit the sweet spot.

"Since you're here and I'm wet, would you mind feeding the dogs? I've already fed the smalls." She gestured toward the far side of the room. "Food and dishes are over there. Instructions are on the wall. Just please go light on the food. I was late ordering my supply shipment. I had an unexpected repair on one of the skylights, and the cooling system in the quarantine trailer needed replacing. What I have needs to last until Monday."

Large plastic food bins and freshly sanitized dishes stacked against the far wall made it hard to miss. "You got it." He rubbed at the scars on his hand. "You know I can help with some of those repairs…if you'd like."

A host of expressions trotted across her face, and she looked like she didn't know whether to sit, stand, or fetch. Finally she threw up her hands. "Sounds great. I could use that kind of help."

He nodded. Websites and dog food and screwdrivers had to be some sort of millennial language of love. Who Knew? Women. He walked away before she pinned a Post-it to his shirt reading, "needs a clue."

For the next hour, he fed the dogs, cleaned the kennels, and fixed one of the door locks that kept getting stuck, all to the humming sounds of Karly going about her day. Her off-tune singing and the sweet way she eased the animals' fears created a peaceful atmosphere, something he hadn't experienced in weeks. Hell, he hadn't felt this way since he left.

Another hour passed, and volunteers started arriving to help families find their forever friend. He placed Custer in the communal play area and collected adoption applications until a boarding customer needing to pick up her dog sent him in search of the one person who didn't really want him around.

"Hey, Karly? Stella King's out front with her grandson wanting to pick up their dog."

She stood and pressed a palm to her forehead. "She wasn't supposed to be back from vacation until tomorrow. Would you please tell her I'll be a few minutes?"

"Tell me what you need, and I'll handle it."

Karly squeezed the back of her neck, her eyes going blank while her mind shifted gears. "She normally pays by check. It's forty dollars per day. Huckleberry is the miniature schnauzer in the third stall over in the boarding area. His leash is on the hook to the left, and his leftover food has his name on the bag."

Karly took a step toward the back door. He held up his hand. "I got this."

She hesitated. "You sure? You've done so much already."

"I'm good." He leaned to the left to see around her. "Looks like one of your furry buddies is about to be adopted."

When he turned back, she was blinking at the young girl with a kitten in her arms and parents hovering nearby, her eyes suspiciously moist. "Yep. And, thanks for the help." Her quiet tone matched the gratitude in her expression.

Something about the simple words put a spring in his step. He went out the back door to circle around the adoption center and quarantine house to the boarding containers, walking along the row of pets waiting for their families to come get them.

He picked up the excited schnauzer, and half- empty bag of food. The small terrier must have heard his master's voice outside, because he couldn't stop wiggling.

Connecting the leash to the dog's collar, Thad opened the employees-only door and set the oh-so-happy pup on the floor. Seconds later, the exuberant animal knocked the four-year-old over. The Norman

Rockwell painting scene, complete with a boy, a dog, and smiles, filled Thad with joy. A sensation he'd forgotten existed. He lifted the youngster and set him on his feet.

"Thanks, mister," the boy said in between doggy hugs.

"You're welcome." Thad handed the boy the end of the leash, and the woman standing nearby the leftover kibble.

"Why's your hand all gross?" The boy pointed at Thad's scars.

"Nicholas! What did I tell you about asking those types of questions?" The grandmother's eyes conveyed an unnecessary apology.

He crouched down next to the kid and pulled up his sleeve to show him the full extent of his injury. "Would you believe I was helping Superman save the world? There was this big explosion, and the Hulk and I had to shield Batman and Robin from the blast. We saved the day."

"That's cool." The boy's eyes flared as his

curious fingers skimmed over the leathery healing surface.

The boy's eyes brightened, and he turned toward his grandmother. "He's a hero, Nana. A real, live hero."

Not so much, kid.

"Yes, he is." Stella came to stand by her grandson's side. "You're Raymond's boy. Thad, correct?"

Here it comes. "Yes, ma'am."

"I'm glad you came home. I always thought you had a good head on your shoulders." She considered the mangled tattoo on his forearm. "Marines?"

Nope. I didn't follow my dad. "Army."

"Thank you for what you gave to our country."

He nodded and swallowed the uneasiness in his throat. Every day he reminded himself to push through the agony of working damaged muscles and ligaments, because at least he was still alive. Others hadn't been so lucky. Those who returned home with a flag draped over their coffin, those guys were the ones who gave. "Just doing my job, ma'am."

The kid looked up at Stella. "I'm going to be a superhero when I grow up."

"You're already my tough little man. Aren't you?" Stella lovingly ruffled the boy's hair. "Come on, Nick. Let's get Huckleberry to the car."

Watching the two walk hand in hand to the minivan made him think about calling his mom. Maybe he could send a card or schedule a Skype call. He'd sent her money, but what he could spare was never enough. The pressure to do more, be more, persisted.

"Thanks for your help." Karly appeared in the employee entrance looking completely exhausted.

"You're welcome."

"Volunteers are finishing up the paperwork, and we're about ready to call it a day."

"Are Adoption Days always this busy? I counted twenty families wanting to adopt."

"Yep, every first and third Saturday of the

month. Not everyone who came adopted, though. I like when people schedule appointments. I can spend more time with the family and get a feel for what type of animal would be a good fit. The animals are not as wound up, and it's easier for adopters to get to know the animals and their personalities."

"Did you get any placed?"

"As a matter of fact, we did. Four dogs, a cat, and a guinea pig."

"A guinea pig?" His you-gotta-be-kidding-me tone made Karly snicker. He'd forgotten how beautiful life could be when she smiled at him. The outside world disappeared. She created a bubble of happy and invited everyone nearby to come on in and enjoy her warm, safe place.

"You'd be surprised how many rabbits and rodents I get every month. Unfortunately, I have no extra kennel space. The little guys ended up in a ventilated storage closet I converted. The local elementary school borrows a different animal each week to help continue socializing the little critters. Just last week, one of the little boys adopted the box turtle I placed with his class. Some of the teachers have the kids write a story about the different animals. It's a good fit."

"Smart idea. You have a good thing going here, Karly. You really do."

"I'm doing my best. I wish everyone understood how much I care about these animals."

"Don't tell me." He shook his head. "Your mom again."

"How did you guess?"

Wasn't all that hard. "It's Saturday night, and I bet you don't want to cook. How about a pizza?"

"Won't happen."

The instant rejection stung like a flesh wound. Not deep enough to leave a scar, but deep enough to hurt. He followed her out of the metal container while she went about locking up.

She turned, her smile building slowly.

"The pizza shop in town closed. We could do Mexican or Chinese, or there's always calzones at More Than Meatballs."

Optimism whooshed in. "How about I pick up something at the store to cook?" he asked, not wanting to deal with all the whispers and sideways glances.

Her mouth started to curve up at the corners, then a twinkle of humor flashed in her eye. "You know how to do more than throw something into the microwave?"

He shrugged with a friendly smirk. "I've learned a thing or two while I've been gone."

"I'd like to see this."

He wasn't about to confess that baked chicken, hamburgers, and steak were about the limit of his culinary skills. "Are you good here? I could get the stuff and meet you at the cabin."

Please say yes. His nerves sent impulses across his chest and out to his fingers, the same sizzling feeling he got the first time he asked Karly for a date. He waited for her to finish her long internal debate, all the time holding his breath.

"Okay. On one condition—I bring the beer."

"I can live with that." His heart did a virtual fist pump, then settled. *Wait. Should I stay? Make sure she doesn't change her mind?*

Chill dude, Neon's voice popped into his head. *Settle your dumb ass down. She's fine.*

Karly's word was golden. She was just like his buddies in the Army. Someone he could always count on—especially when it mattered.

Neon was right. The title of dumbass fit. *Maybe that's why I'm still single.*

He walked beside her back to the main building to retrieve an exhausted Custer from the social time play area. At least Custer wouldn't have the energy to chew on his boots tonight.

He, on the other hand, wouldn't mind having a little nibble.

THE LINGERING aroma of medium-rare blue cheese buffalo burgers and deli potato salad mixed with the smell of pine from the outdoor fire pit. Karly relaxed in the Adirondack chair he'd recently sanded and repainted.

"I'm stuffed." She zipped up her purple fleece jacket and leaned back to look at the early evening stars.

The last of the sunset slashed oranges and reds against the purple mountain backdrop, and another small helping of contentment eased into his bones.

Thad picked up her paper plate and tossed it into the fire. "Do you want another beer?" He moved toward the ice cooler.

"No, I'm good." She lifted her legs and curled into the chair.

Her tight-fitting jeans hugged her curves nicely...not that he was looking. Who was he kidding? Tonight she attracted his attention like a deer to a rosebush. She was irresistible. Just like old times. She'd left her hair down and looked stunningly sexy. His heart kept sending off warning flares.

"If you're interested, I picked up some marshmallows for roasting. I forgot the chocolate, though."

"Maybe later. That burger was huge." Her mood turned introspective, quiet. She wrapped her arms around her knees and just looked at the stars.

"What just happened? You got all quiet."

She glanced at him, then gazed at the fire for a long, silent moment. "Just thinking."

He stood and unfolded one of the wool blankets he'd brought from the house and draped it over her, tucking in the sides. "Better?"

Gratitude and something more flickered in her eyes. "Thanks."

He crouched by the pit and added a couple more logs. Sparks spiraled into the night's crisp air and disappeared.

"The kitten that was adopted today reminded me of Juke."

He leaned and grabbed a stick to poke at the logs again and again, sending a riot of burning particles into the air. "When I saw the little guy, I had the same thought."

She tucked her forehead against her knees, shaking her head. "He was such a great cat."

"Was? You don't have him anymore?"

"After my dad left, my mom went on a cleaning frenzy. She didn't want the hair in the house. While I was at work, she took Juke to a shelter."

The sound of sorrow and something else in her voice made him drag his chair closer to hers. "But you loved that cat," he finally managed.

"I did." Karly wrapped tighter into a ball. "Anything that reminded mom of her old life, she sold or gave away. She barely even looked at Kenny or me. When he went to boot camp, I moved into an apartment. I posted notices on Craigslist trying to find

Juke, but I got no responses. He was almost four. If she took him to a kill shelter, I bet he didn't last more than a couple of days before he was put down. Most people want to adopt kittens." She lifted the collar of her jacket to hide her face, but her quiet sniffles escaped and expanded on the gentle breeze.

He itched to pick her up and haul her into his arms. Instead, he sat in his cold, hard chair a little less than arm's length away. "Yet you still talk to the woman."

"I told you before, I don't hold on to hate. Hate just makes the body sick, and I don't see the need. My mother won't change."

Custer, sensing her need, pushed his head against her leg. She scratched his soft ears and let the sound of the night fill in the gap. "I'm okay. Lie down." She snapped her fingers and pointed at the ground beside her. "That's a good boy."

A snap of a twig made Thad study the tree line, but this time he managed to stay seated.

"That's the third time you've about

jumped out of that chair. Is that a soldier instinct, or is it something more?"

"It's just my training kicking in." The lie was a small one, but left behind a great big mound of guilt. "It's better to be hyper-alert than unprepared when something pops out of the bushes."

"That's interesting." She stared into the fire.

"Okay, I'll bite. What's so interesting?"

"It's been a long time, and we've changed. I still have a pretty good instinct for when someone is not telling the truth. Do you want to try again? Tell me the whole truth this time?" She rolled her head toward him to give him that familiar look, the one she'd perfected. The one that looked into his soul, yet never judged.

"That's the thing about the truth. You might hear things that will stay with you forever. Things that can't be unsaid once they are out there."

"I'm assuming you're talking about your military experiences. You must have some good memories. You were in for a long time."

There it was, the open-ended statement, the one that hit him with the spotlight and exposed him. Instinct made him want to dig a trench and hide, but no matter how much training he received, she'd always find him. Suss him out. Make him vulnerable. "A few. It's just—"

"You don't have to explain." She waved a hand. "I get it. It's guy stuff."

He pushed from his chair. "Maybe we should go in. It looks like you're getting cold." He extended his hand to help her up.

She ignored his gesture and hunkered in. "Not until you tell me a story about your time away. I want to know about what happened after you left."

"Why?" He took a step back.

"Why not?"

She'd put him under a magnifying glass, studying each gesture and shuffle of his feet. When he licked his lips, a telltale sign, he almost groaned.

Well, hell. He got a beer out of the cooler. If he was going there, he needed to unclog the wad of regret stuck in his throat. He rolled his neck in a circle, then settled into the chair to watch the wind blow through the trees.

She waited. Like she always had. The silence squeezed tighter until he held out his hand again, palm up, and she placed hers on top. He closed his fingers and palm around her cold hand.

"There was this guy named Steve Plutton. We met in basic training. Everyone called him Pluto after the Disney character. Because he was always on the move. The guy had more energy than a portable generator." His puff of laughter echoed into the darkness. "One night, after we finished with an exercise, he got drunk. The bar was closing, and he decided he wanted to go for a swim. The problem was, there wasn't a pool open on base, and a taxi to a beach would have cost a lot of money. Unfortunately, there was a twenty-four-hour Wal-Mart close by. He bought one of those baby pools. Of course, he invited everyone at the bar to come back to the barracks. Most followed more out of curiosity than anything."

"Isn't that against the rules?" She released his hand to adjust her position.

"Yep. He didn't care. He ran a hose from the showers to fill the pool."

"What happened?"

"He got caught and ended up cleaning the bathroom with a toothbrush for a week." Thad snickered at the memory.

"Sounds like a fun guy to have around." She took a swig of beer.

Thad nodded, and picked at the label on his bottle. "The knucklehead became one of the best soldiers in the platoon."

"Where is he stationed now?"

"Ft. Sill National Cemetery in Oklahoma." Thad bowed his head.

"Oh. Oh, I'm s-sorry."

Custer got up and then collapsed at his feet, his head resting on his shoes. Thad drew in a long, deep breath and pushed his anger over the senseless death out with the air. "One minute we were on patrol together, and the next he was gone, and I was on the ground." He ran a hand over the back of his neck, his knee bouncing up and down like a sewing machine needle.

"That month we got orders to teach the locals how to remove mines. Every day we'd clear dozens, and the next morning there would be a dozen more in different spots. Steve was joking around, talking shit. He had just suggested we play Russian Roulette, that it would be safer, then, boom." He knew she wouldn't get the sick humor every soldier used to get through the day. "Ike and I were on point, and Steve was a couple of yards away. The sun was a bastard, and all I wanted to do was get back and take a cold shower."

"Whatever happened, it's not your fault, Thad."

He didn't want to hear her reassurances, her conviction. He shook his head to shake them off.

She reached for his hand and tugged on it. "No. Don't. You need to hear me. Steve's death is not your fault. If you want to blame someone, blame the person who planted that bomb."

The confusion. The blood. The gut-wrenching fear invaded his mind again while gruesome memories rewound and started playing from the beginning. Disoriented, he'd rolled, his trained instincts kicking in. He had to secure the area. Get to Steve. That's when he saw Ike. Steve lay just a few feet beyond. He closed his eyes to shake off the image. His left side began to ache as he remembered the hundreds of pebbles shredding his skin. "I should have found that bomb. It was my job."

She ran her fingers down his back. "How long until help arrived?"

"Seconds. Minutes. I don't know. I was pretty out of it."

She shifted, and tugged the blanket higher.

"I couldn't hear anything but this noise in

my head," he continued. "I was disoriented. Everything was moving in slow motion. Then I saw him." He choked down the taste of dirt.

"You saw Steve," Karly prompted.

"No, Ike." *Shit, I don't want to talk about this.*

"Ike? Who's Ike?"

"Ike was the best dog I ever had. We spent months training together to find bombs. Every look, whine, twitch of his fur was familiar. If I'd been watching Ike instead of listening to Steve..." Thad took a long gulp of his beer, then set it aside. Images of being on his hands and knees, a cloud of dust all around him came into focus. The feeling someone had set him on fire. Ike's eyes were open, staring at him. However, from mid-chest back, Ike's back end was missing. Thad swallowed hard to open his throat to breathe.

"He died, like your friend. He didn't make it, did he?"

"No. He didn't survive." Thad clenched

his hands, teeth, jaw—anything to keep the tears from falling.

"Oh, God. And I dropped off Custer without even asking."

He reached to squeeze her hand. "You didn't know." She squeezed back, but he wasn't sure who was giving and who was receiving comfort.

"It doesn't matter. You told me you couldn't train him. I just thought— I believed you didn't want to train him because of me." She reached to his face. "I want you to promise me something. You have to promise me."

He wanted to pull away. In fact, he should leave Elkridge. Let her live her peaceful life. She didn't need him, and all he was doing was making her worry. A tug of his shirt drew his attention.

"Look at me. I want your word. You don't hide from me, or leave, or do something stupid. You have to promise."

Leaving town wasn't what she was

worried about. He could see the uncertainty in her eyes.

"I can't make any promises."

"That's crap. I know you, Thad Lopez. I want your word. You want to leave, do something stupid again, fine, but this time you have to talk to me first. And I mean face-to-face, none of that wimpy note-leaving stuff." She tugged on his sleeve.

His throat clogged with emotion. "I promise. I'll come to you first." Custer stuck his nose under his arm and whined.

"I know, Custer. You're a good boy. Yes, you are." He tipped his head back and located the Big Dipper, then Orion's Belt. "Hell is empty, and all the devils are here," he whispered to the moon.

She gasped. "You hate Shakespeare."

He rolled his head toward her. "I don't *hate* Shakespeare, although I didn't want Mrs. Campbell to know. She was having way too much fun forcing us to play Romeo and Juliet in the school play. With you coming from the rich side of town, and me the poor —too ironic, don't you think?"

"Yeah, she did it on purpose, so did Mrs. Boyd. She made the Home Ec class make our costumes. Mine was a bit low cut, and my dad forced me to wear an undershirt. I was so embarrassed. I can't believe she wanted you to wear tights."

"My dad dragged me into the principal's office. He made it clear no son of his was going to wear women's clothes, as if I was the one who wanted to wear them in the first place."

Thad suddenly smiled, and pointed. "Did you notice Custer's bringing you presents? He doesn't like that you're upset."

Karly shifted to see the ground by the chair's leg. At her feet was a mound of pinecones.

"He started that a few days ago. When he thinks I'm sad or not feeling well, he finds a pinecone or a stick or something and brings it to me, but I've never seen him make a pile like that."

Custer lifted his muzzle to lick her face. "I'm okay." She scratched behind his ear and eased back into the chair. "I need another beer."

He got up to put another log on the fire, then fished a beer out of the melting ice. When Thad was halfway to the chair, Custer picked up one of the pinecones. With his ears back, he pressed his cold nose into Thad's empty hand.

"I'm good too." He leaned over to run a hand down the dog's back.

Karly tucked her fleece up over her nose. "Animals always know."

"Know what?" Thad sat and continued to rub Custer's chest.

"When we're sad or hurting, or when we need to play."

She looked adorable. Instead of handing her the beer, he leaned in. "You always knew what I needed." She licked her lips, and completely melted his resolve. He inched forward. "Are you going to let me kiss you?"

"Why are you asking? You never have before."

The lingering smell of her honey-vanilla lotion, the taste of barley, a gentle breeze blowing, the softness of her lips. He dipped his head, aiming for her sweet mouth, only this time it wasn't as sweet as he remembered. It was hot. Sizzling hot. When her tongue pressed in, searching for his, he encountered the bitter taste of hops, and the control he'd tried to master all night ceased. He dove headfirst into the deep end of the sexiest, wettest, most fulfilling kiss he'd ever experienced. His pounding heart questioned his objectivity. *What the hell am I thinking?*

He wasn't. *#BrainDrain.* That's the problem.

He lifted his head, his thumb still caressing the side of her jaw, as her head dropped back.

He could see her mind trying to engage, and when she gave up. She fisted his shirt and pulled him closer.

Oh, baby. My sweet woman.

When she broke off the kiss, her eyes opened slowly. Her mouth was trembling and still moist from the intimacy. She drew in a labored breath and stared at him. She touched her lips. "What-what were we talking about?"

He rolled his thumb unhurriedly over the tip of her erect nipple.

He eased back just a bit to rest his forehead on hers. "I've missed you."

She shifted and pushed him back. "We shouldn't be doing this."

"Doing what?"

"You and me. Things will never be the same. We shouldn't be doing this."

We'll see about that.

Every day, he used to wait to walk her home. He'd leave little notes in her backpack, and flowers in her schoolbooks, until she couldn't resist anymore. He could wait again.

"Is it time for marshmallows?" He took a step back. "I'll even burn one for you."

The corners of her eyes creased for a

second before flattening. "I'm okay." She drew into a tight ball.

"Whoa. Where did you go just then?"

She shrugged. "Last night, I was over at Mara and Joe's, and we were playing a game." She curled and propped her chin on her knee. "I just remembered one of the questions. That's all."

"What was it?"

"If you could change one thing in your past, what would it be?"

He sat on the arm of his chair, not wanting to be too far away. "And what was your answer?"

"I gave some answer, and Mara called bulldonkey."

He set his beer down. "Mara said bulldonkey?"

"No, that was my word, not hers."

"Ah. Thought so…so what was your answer?"

"After a lot of prodding by both of them, I said I'd have hunted you down and asked why you dumped me. Right then. I wouldn't have waited ten years." She stared at him for a long time. "Brad seems like an excuse. I'm still trying to figure out the real reason you stayed away."

With a finger, he swept her bangs back to get a better look at her face. He folded his hands in his lap, then looked at her. He opened his mouth to say something, but nothing came out. He swallowed and tried again. "I got scared."

He rubbed at the scars on his hand to ease the ache. "What did I have to offer? Boot camp. Basic training. Deployment. Your life was here." He shrugged. "Would you have agreed to become an Army wife if I had asked?"

"I'm not sure I can answer that question." She shifted and tugged her shirt cuff down to loop her thumbs into the finger holes. "Back then you didn't ask. Now things have changed."

"What's changed?"

She shrugged and looked away. "There are things I don't want to talk about either."

"Why not? Is it so terrible?"

"No, it just hurts too much, and no one here knows."

"Not a single person? Not even Mara or Kym?"

"Nope." Her whispered voice sounded far away, almost hypnotic.

Interesting. She curled her arms in tighter and folded them under her chin.

"You sure you don't want to tell me?" he asked.

She threw off the blanket and jumped out of the chair. "I have to go."

His alarm bells went off. He reached for her arm. "Karly?"

She pushed back, but he didn't let go. He stood and gently wrapped his arms around her. Reluctantly, she turned into his arms.

Please, tell me.

Her shoulders shook and breath hitched while her tears soaked through his shirt. He rested his cheek on the top of her head and held on.

Please, trust me, and tell me what happened.

You must already know my secret.

I still love you. Always have. Always will.

He closed his eyes to cherish the feeling of the woman he loved in his arms, because he was certain that if she was rested and thinking straight, she wouldn't go anywhere near him.

"Come on." He brushed his thumbs underneath her eyes. "Let's go inside."

"I should go home."

"That's a bad idea. You're tired. You've been drinking, and these mountain roads, especially at night, are not forgiving."

"I don't know."

"I'll sleep on the floor."

"No, you won't. You can barely walk without a limp most days. A cold floor won't help." She leaned her head against his chest. "Sleeping with someone... I just..." She stiffened and started to pull away.

"Nothing will happen, Karly, and if it did, I can promise you it wouldn't be as awkward, or fast, as our first time."

"You mean our only time."

"Okay, our only time. I just want to assure you I can keep up with the other guys."

"What other guys? Has your sister been exaggerating again?"

Wait a minute. He lifted her chin, and he could see her expression. "Karly? Are you saying there haven't been any other guys?"

She shrugged and looked at the ground, rubbing her foot into the dirt. "I just... I just haven't seen the need to date anyone else. Besides, who would date any of the jackasses in this town?"

Something wasn't right. The way she wouldn't look at him. The way she scratched at the side of her neck. "What are you not telling me?"

"I have my shelter. The animals require all my time and love."

"Try saying that again, this time looking at me."

She stepped out of his arms. "I need to go."

He took two steps and wrapped his arms

around her again. A pulsating pain knotted his gut. He'd done this. He'd permanently wounded her with his carelessness. "Please don't go. I need you to tell me what's wrong."

"I can't." The rawness almost choked her.

Her body went limp in his arms. "Come on. Let's go inside. Let me hold you."

She shrugged out of his arms. "Why don't you bank the fire?"

"Will you stay?"

"I'll stay, as long as you don't ask me any more questions."

Her melancholy was his responsibility. "If you ever want to talk about what's tearing you apart, let me know. I'll buy a two-liter bottle of margaritas. You won't feel a thing."

She cupped his face in her hands. "I wish you would believe me when I say you're a good man, Thad Lopez."

His heart stuttered as he tried to summon the energy to understand. "I need you to remind me of that every once in a while."

Her hands fell to her sides. "I don't think it will do any good. It didn't work before."

He lifted her chin so he could see into her eyes. "Things change."

Her mouth collapsed into a thin line. "Yes, change happens whether we like it or not. That's why we can't go back."

She walked, her feet smudging the dirt with each step, toward the cabin. He signaled to Custer to follow her, and the dog trotted to catch up, slowing when he reached her side.

What are you hiding? He wished she would confide her secret.

Because whatever she was hiding was a lot stronger than her mistrust of him.

CHAPTER SEVEN

Karly awoke slowly, drifting out of semi-consciousness. The nasty little men drilling holes in her temples made her groan.

Plus, someone had put a big rock in her bed, and it was poking her in the back. When the rock suddenly rolled over, her eyes popped open, and she inspected the intruding lump. The effect was dizzying, and the room began to spin.

Thad. Oh, no. What have I done? Another panicked groan released. "Why did you open that bottle of tequila?" She flopped a forearm over her eyes.

"I believe you were the one who challenged me to strip poker."

"I always won before. That was a stupid assumption."

"Especially since Army dudes play a lot of cards," the all-too-smug and sexy voice informed her.

He sounded way, way, *way* too chipper. Was that a wow-just-got-laid chipper? Or a nice-to-see-you chipper? Or a told-you-so chipper? She couldn't tell.

Her chest tightened. She flipped up the covers, finding bra and underwear still in place. Which didn't necessarily mean nothing happened. "We didn't... I mean... How did I get undressed?"

"One piece of clothing at a time. I see you got a tattoo. Nice."

Brat. She would swat him if only her brain could figure out where her arms were without triggering more stabbing pains.

He stretched, slowly, thoroughly, like a

cat waking from a nap. He rubbed both hands back and forth over the top of his head while glancing toward the bedroom window. "Looks like it'll be a nice day."

"How drunk did I get last night?"

"Wasted. You kept losing and taking shots." He brushed the tangled mat of hair off her face. "It was kinda funny, actually. Do you do that often?"

She squinted against the sunlight. "Not since I was twenty-one and swore I'd never get that drunk again."

He rolled out of bed and tilted the blinds to block a substantial portion of the light.

"Better?"

Yes. Freaking fantastic. Every ripped muscle in his torso made her want to run her hands across the waves. The side view of his white butt cheeks made her smile. When her scrutiny reached his jaw with its cover-model dark stubble, she nearly melted. His spikes of hair flying in every direction made her want to run her fingers through the short strands and play. He was casual about being naked in a way he hadn't been previously, and that was just plain fun.

"If you don't stop looking at me like I'm an ice cream cone you want to lick, I'm crawling back in that bed and doing some licking of my own."

Her sexy parts heated, but she couldn't allow him to get close. If he got close to her heart, she might abandon ship and swim on over to his side. She needed to find a life raft, and fast. Her eyes skimmed down his torso, and the empathy kicked in. Tiptoeing around his injury would just make matters worse. She sucked up some courage.

"I don't remember if I asked last night about your wounds. Your left side is one big scar," she murmured gently, to ease into the painful reality.

His eyes darkened. He leaned to pick up a pair of boxers and quickly stepped into them while she mentally gave herself another swift kick.

"Thad, I—"

"You always were one for telling it like it is. My scars are pretty ugly and hard to miss."

"Sorry. My question was clumsy. The scars are just a small part of you. I'm more worried about you as a whole."

She sat up and pushed the comforter back, but the room began to spin, and her stomach lurched. She swallowed acidy saliva. "God. Please let me get through this day, and I promise I'll never, ever get drunk again." She opened one eyelid to see if the room had settled into a stationary position.

His amber eyes studied her for a long moment before he moved to his duffel bag to retrieve a pair of jeans and a clean T-shirt. "I suggest you drink every drop of water in that bottle on the night stand, and then go back to sleep. I'll go feed and water your animals. There's no need to get up. Stay as long as you want."

"You don't need to do that."

"Who will feed them, then?"

She pulled her hands down her face. "I

guess you are. There are volunteers coming in, but not until later."

"Thought so."

Trying to remember what happened only made her brain ache more. *What did happen?* Surely she should be able to remember. Would it matter if something had happened? *Yes*, came the quiet answer. She'd want to remember every single detail.

"Thad? What happened last night?"

"Nothing happened, Karly, beyond us getting stupid drunk and having a lot of fun. Honest." He looked so amused she wanted to give herself a kick for asking the stupid question. "Now down that water and get some sleep."

Frustration slipped in between the pounding in her brain. "I'll take a shower and follow you in."

"Suit yourself. There are only about ten minutes of hot water. You might not want to stay in there too long." He pointed toward the clothes folded precisely on the nightstand next to the bed. "Your stuff's here, and the coffee's on a timer. It should already be brewed. Help yourself."

Thad turned at the door to stare at her. His eyes scanned over every surface, paying close attention to each nuance, like a best in breeds judge assessing a dog. What did he see?

Did he see a lonely woman who was tired of trying to please everyone?

Or the woman who was barely hanging on, trying to control a small-town business?

Or the girlfriend he left behind?

The jumbled feelings plaguing her for the past several days were magnified by the power of three.

He stood, silently staring, silently wanting. Wanting something she couldn't give him. Then he took a step back. "Maybe I'll see you later, Karly. Come on, Custer. Let's go."

She flopped back down on the bed. *What the hell am I doing?*

The earthy scent from his pillow aroused her senses and triggered her awareness of a natural need. She snuggled in and allowed the sensual dreams to pull her back into a deep sleep.

A couple of hours later, she got out of bed and grabbed her clothes, shoving her legs one at a time into her jeans. Within minutes, she was ready to leave, but paused to take one more look around.

There were no pictures. No books. Nothing personal. Like his childhood room. He'd kept his room tidy and limited to avoid his dad's ire, doing everything he could to remain invisible.

But you're not invisible.

"Oh, Thad. Please, no." She went into the bathroom. His organized shaving kit sat on the shelf, neatly packed. No razor or toothbrush sat by the sink. Shampoo was noticeably absent from the shower's cubbyhole.

Your dad's gone. There's no reason to be invisible anymore.

In the bedroom, his duffel bag sat in the corner, fully packed. She opened the top dresser drawer. Empty. The kitchen was the same. Dishes and pans neatly stacked. Thad had been in the cabin almost a month. Other than coffee in the pot waiting for her, the cabin looked like no one lived there.

Memories of conversations with Kenny surfaced. Little bits and pieces started gluing together. The developing picture wasn't a puppy-and-kitten type image.

Determination infused her as she reached her car. While she drove her truck back down the ridge, memories and a clear motivation surfaced.

No one else in this town understood Thad. What drove him. His needs. His desires. The childhood demons that lurked in his mind. Feeling inadequate—wondering if he should end it all—thinking others would be better off without him.

He'd always taken the blame for his father's rants and his mother's spiraling, medicated decline into prescription drugs, sleeping pills, anything to numb her. He'd been forced to raise his little sister, who hadn't appreciated having a substitute father, and made his life hell as punishment.

Karly pulled into the parking lot of the Tool Shed and tucked her hair into a baseball cap, then got out of her truck, propelled by determination.

"Hey, Bill. Got a minute?" Bill slid the pen he was holding behind his ear and gave her a friendly smile.

"Hey, pretty lady. What brings you in today? Do you need to order more fencing?"

She approached the counter, dragging her feet a little to give her time to think of a good way to pose her question. "I came to talk to you about Thad. I'm worried about him."

"If you're worried about him, why aren't you talking to him?"

"You know Thad. If he was a rock and you told him to roll downhill, he'd do everything in his power to push in the opposite direction."

"He's never been one to take direction. Hope he learned to take orders." Bill gave an uneasy laugh and shrugged. "What did you have in mind?"

"A job. The same stuff he did for you in high school. Stocking shelves. Running supplies. Anything to keep his days from being too long and empty."

"Don't you think he would see that as an insult? He's not a boy anymore. He's grown. Besides, I'm not sure he'd appreciate you meddling in his business."

Frustration made Karly cross her arms and lean against the checkout counter. "Anybody can see he's changed, but Thad is one of our own. He's been to war. Seen some shi—um...crud. He's fighting the invisible battles of his own. I can see it in his eyes. We need to do something before he does something stupid."

"I'll tell you what I said to him—talk to Chase Daniels. He might have some work for Thad."

"Isn't he working on building out Gwen Keebler's Thrift store?"

"Don't think so." Bill walked around the

counter to straighten sponges on an endcap. "Dale Bryant's doing the finish work. I think Chase's replacing the Bainbridge sisters' roof."

"Gotcha. Thanks, Bill. I'll head on over, see if there's any work for Thad." She took a step toward the door.

"Karly?" The concern in Bill's voice put a chokehold on her enthusiasm.

"When a man comes home from war, there's things he can't talk about. Things that make him feel guilt. Anger. Things he tries to hide deep inside, deep enough to forget." Bill leaned against the metal display. "Don't push him, Karly. There are demons that hide inside every soldier. When they come out, they are nasty, and lash out at anything that gets in the way. Those monsters help make a good soldier, but they're hell on wheels once the soldier is back home. If you get too close, you'll need to be strong enough to stand your ground."

"I'm not planning to get that close, but thanks for the warning, Bill. Besides, I'm stronger than I look, and Thad is someone worth fighting for. I know it. You know it. I want to make sure this town knows he deserves to be recognized. Did you know he was wounded? He has a whole bunch of scarring up his left side."

Bill approached her with heavy feet. "Not many people know this, and I'd appreciate if you'd keep it to yourself. I served six tours overseas. I almost made it home in one piece, but I was shot on the last one and sent home."

Her jaw hinged open. "I never knew."

"A soldier rarely talks about the missions he's been on, or the horrors he's seen. We talk about our friends, the funny shit we pulled, and reminisce about the ones who are no longer with us. We talk about the battles won, but never those where we got our ass kicked. When I was shot, one of my buddies hauled me out of the line of fire and was killed. Every day, I see his face and feel the guilt. He died saving me. When I went to see his parents, I could only tell his folks he died for a good cause. Every day since then, I've strived to live a good life, to ensure he'd be proud of the man I've become. To make sure he *did* die for a good cause."

The man's teary eyes and quivering lip brought tears to her eyes.

"You're the best, most generous man I know. Heck, you're a pillar of this community." She placed a hand on his arm. "You've provided equipment when the river flooded the town, dug cemetery sites when the ground was too frozen, sponsored several sports teams' uniforms, and there's probably a dozen things I know nothing about." She took a step closer. "You don't have anything to worry about, Bill. If your friend was standing here today, he'd shake your hand and give you a good slap on the back. He'd be proud. And if I was your daughter, I'd be proud too."

She squeezed his forearm. "Are you okay? I need to see Chase about a job for Thad, but I can stay if you like."

"Run along now. Just remember what I

said."

"I heard what you said, and what you didn't."

Bill nodded, blinked and hauled a rag out of his back pocket. "Stupid pollen. Gets me every time." He winked at her.

Something about this town raised heroic men, men who had no notion how much people appreciated them. "See you soon, Bill." She walked back to the truck and lifted herself up and into the driver's seat, mentally listing all the soldiers in town. For a town the size of Elkridge, the small community sure had more than its fair share. Most likely because there wasn't much to keep a person in town if a kid got an itch for more.

She drove the fifteen minutes across town and turned right on Elm Street towards Margaret and Patricia Bainbridge's home. The bales of roof shingles on top of the single-story house meant she found the right one. Getting out of the truck, she squinted against the sun, hoping to have a quick word with Chase. The shadowed figure sliding back the curtains told her no way would she escape with just a quick conversation.

Seconds later the screen door swung open. "Karly Krane, is that you?"

"Hello, Ms. Bainbridge. How are you doing today?"

"I'm just finished trying out a new recipe, pomegranate lemonade. Would you like to try some?"

"I look a fright. I haven't showered yet today, and am covered with dog hair." Custer's hair, not from the kennel, but the town gossip didn't need to know the particulars of the source.

"You look fine, dear. How I wish I could have been born in your generation. No makeup. No hair teasing. No bra."

"Ms. Bainbridge!" Karly's eyes popped open wider. "How modern."

"Oh, hush. Don't embarrass an old lady. Since I'm no longer teaching, I don't have to be as careful. Come on up. I'll even get out the bin of my favorite sugar cookies."

She remembered those sugar cookies. The flaky butteriness would just make a girl sigh.

Besides, Mrs. Bainbridge's lonely face looked familiar. Karly had seen something similar when looking into her bathroom mirror every morning. The urgency to help Chase suddenly took a back seat. She could spare a few minutes for her former seventh-grade teacher. After all, the woman had spent hours trying to help wrap her brain around mathematics.

"Sounds like a good idea on a day like today. Just a taste, though. I don't want to take more than my fair share from the boys on the roof."

"There's plenty to go around."

Listening to the staccato rhythm of nail guns stapling the roof tiles, she made her way up the gray cobblestone pathway to the freshly painted white steps leading to the front door.

"Why don't you take a seat, and I'll bring out a tray."

Karly lowered into one of the white wicker chairs with colorful flowered cushions faded from years out in the sun. She could hear a lawnmower in the distance, and spotted a robin in the elm. A few minutes later, Patricia, Margaret's twin, came out carrying a crystal pitcher, followed by her sister carrying the glasses and a plate of small square sugar biscuits that made Karly's tongue tingle with anticipation.

"Here we are." Margaret poured the pink concoction and handed her the glass. The zest of fresh-squeezed lemons and pomegranate circled on the gentle breeze. "There." She gave Karly a napkin. "Now, why don't the three of us put our heads together to see about helping Thad?"

Karly stared at the two women.

"Close your mouth, dear, or you'll let the flies in."

She leaned back against the flower print and took a sip of the tangy-sweet drink.

Maybe helping Thad wasn't going to be as hard as she thought after all.

CHAPTER EIGHT

"Karly, what are you doing?"

Her breath hitched, and she pivoted. "Thad Lopez, would you stop sneaking up on me?"

She hadn't seen Thad for two days but, oh my, he looked edible in those jeans riding low on his hips and a black leather jacket draped over his shoulders. However, the menace in Thad's tone made her cringe. Even the rescue dog standing next to her tucked his tail between his legs. "And to answer your question, I'm picking up poop. Want to help?"

"Don't play games. You know what I mean. I don't need your help finding a job."

"Oh, that. Well, it wasn't me, exactly. Well, I mean, I did stop by to see Bill, then he suggested I stop by the Bainbridge sisters—"

"Great. Now the whole town's involved."

The laser-focused anger emanating from Thad made her wonder if staying inside the gated kennel might be prudent. The pit-bull mix stared up at her while she took her time emptying the waste into a five-gallon bucket. Finishing the chore left her no choice. She lifted the latch.

"Not everyone is involved. Only the people who care. You know how this town is." Karly set down the pooper-scooper and bucket before turning back to the man who was spouting steam like a whistling teapot, boiling mad. "We just want to help."

His eyes narrowed, but he said nothing.

"You know how to use tools," she continued, steering around the caution signs. "Plus, Chase needs help. It's a win-win type of thing."

"A win-win thing," his jaw muscles ticked of time like a bomb counting down to detonation, "like tickling a meddlesome female until she cries uncle?"

"Don't tell me the military turned you into Mr. Grey. You're not into bondage and submission, are you?" She giggled and winked at Thad, hoping to turn his sour mood into sweetness.

"Karly." His eyes narrowed further, and he took a step closer.

"I'm kidding." She held out her hands to stop him. "No, really. I'm just joking."

The way he looked at her mouth, she'd bet a twenty he wouldn't mind kissing her into total submission. He could—without much effort. The fence clanged musically when she backed into the wire links.

His gaze followed hers and then shifted away. "Why are you trying to help me?"

"I told you before. Kenny asked me to, and this town supports the military."

He moved closer, pinning her against the kennel gate. "And?"

She studied his jaw, which pulsed as he gritted his teeth, along with the muscles in his neck. His shoulders were tight with tension, and he was holding back a tidal wave of resentment. She could feel the strain.

"Tell me the real reason." His tone was steady. Too steady. Like the silence before the rumbling of a storm.

"I…uh…"

He ran a finger gently down the side of her cheek and then brushed the pad of it over her mouth. She closed her eyes against the melting gold of his eyes. No longer numb with alcohol, she would remember how beautiful he was to touch. The precise lines of his muscles, his earthy scent, the heat of his skin. Her eyes latched onto his mouth, his tongue moistening his lips. "I…well…"

His hot breath against her skin weakened both her knees and the wall of willpower she had built against his ability to drag her in. He wanted her. She'd seen his need two days earlier.

"Why can't you admit you want me just as much as I want you?"

His announcement liquefied everything in touching distance. Not just her knees, but her hands, feet, head.

She fought off the feeling.

No matter what, she couldn't fall again.

Not for Thad Lopez.

He'd left her. He wasn't there on the worst day of her life.

A day tattooed in her mind forever.

But her hands had different ideas and reached for his waist. The heat emanating through his shirt could melt chocolate, and made her want to let her fingers roam. She slid her hands up his chest to feel the thrum of his strong, steady heartbeat through her fingertips, slowing her breathing, and synchronizing her rhythm with his tempo. He hadn't moved. Just let her explore.

He could be sweet, but she preferred spicy. She licked the corner of his mouth, and then took another nibble. And then gently sank her teeth into his chin. Beneath her hands, his muscles jerked.

She let out a heavy sigh. "I can't want you. You're dangerous to my health." *Besides, you need to be with someone else. I can't give you what you want. Not anymore.* She slipped out from between him and the fence and took several steps away before turning back.

He studied her, and then was holding her, kissing her, making her forget all the reasons why she needed him to stay away. His tongue pushed and tickled against her lips until she had no choice but to allow him entry.

Dangerous. Definitely dangerous.

He reached below the hem of her tank top, searching, skimming every surface, until he reached her bra and pushed it up, exposing her breast.

Ohhhh. Totally delicious.

He cupped her, his thumb creating the kind of intense desire she'd only experienced with him. Lifting the fabric, he took his time appreciating, and her nipples tightened and saluted him in response. He dipped his head and rested his mouth against her engorged nipple to blow hot air.

Then she felt his muscles vibrate. Ah. So she wasn't the only one feeling like the world had shifted off its axis. His soft moans of pleasure had a way of filling her mind and pushing every last excuse aside.

Oh, God. We can't be doing this. She gripped his hair and pulled. "Thad. You have to stop."

His hands slid up her sides.

"Tell me, Karly. Tell me you don't feel anything for me," he whispered.

She groaned and laid her head on his shoulder. "I can't."

"That's what I thought."

He lifted his head to angle in, but she took a step sideways. "If we could keep this casual, it would be one thing. But nothing between us has ever been casual. It's either all or nothing, and this time it has to be nothing."

She shoved her hands into the back

pockets of her jeans to keep from touching him, but his eyes skimmed down her front, so intense it felt like his hands were doing the skimming.

He released a breath. "You're not nothing. You're even more beautiful today than back then..."

"Thad. There's too much baggage between us."

"Okay. Let's have a garage sale and get rid of it all. No more baggage."

"This isn't something to joke about."

He took a step closer.

She held up her hands. "Don't."

"Don't what? Don't remind you of what it's like to get wet and slippery together? We're good together, you and I."

Her breath skipped with stolen memories of a hot summer's day at the lake. Take that memory, minus the teenage jitters, and she had a feeling she might enjoy sex more. A lot more. Yet their relationship couldn't go anywhere. On that fateful day, she promised herself never, ever, ever to take him back, because he didn't love her enough to stay. Fight for her. Love her. The crippled emptiness inside her womb pushed back.

"I won't start anything which can't have a good outcome. I need to concentrate on my business. It's what I love. The *only* thing I love. I don't have time to do anything else."

A stunned look crossed his face, then his expression sobered. "Tell me you don't want me. Want this."

"I don't. Well, I do. But what I'm trying to tell you is that I just need a friend right now. Nothing more."

Thad's frustrated groan practically vibrated the kennel fence when the front door chime sounded. "You had better go get that." He stepped back and gripped the wire fence.

"Thad, I... We still need to talk about what's going on."

He held up a hand. "I'm good. I just need a pack for Custer. I saw a couple of harnesses when I was here the other day. If Custer is required to carry oxygen tanks, he'll need to get used to carrying some weight."

Her mom's shrill voice sent tingles crawling down her spine. "My mom's here. Go out the back."

"Some things never change." His voice landed on the lighter side of menacing. "You had better jump, or are you waiting for your mom to tell you how high?" He hung his head. "I'm sorry. I...I shouldn't have said that." With a carefully blank face, he pushed through the back door.

You're right. Some things never change. We're good together, you and I. Too good.

"There you are. I heard voices. Whom were you talking to?"

"Just the dogs, Mom."

The door behind her swung shut, and she swore Thad had started barking, mimicking Custer. That idiotic feeling of emptiness sneaked back inside. "What can I help you with? I need to finish picking up after the dogs."

"I don't know why you insist doing such

disgusting work. You're the business owner. The least you can do is hire someone to help do the less-than-pleasant chores."

"I'll think about it. Is there a reason you stopped by?"

Karen Krane smoothed the hair off her face. "I was speaking with Vivian Newhall yesterday." Her lips pursed with pleasure. "She was telling me about this mobile fashion boutique. It's the rage." She ran her fingers lightly down Karly's arm. "With my selling ability, and your common sense, we could start a business together. Sounds like fun. Don't you think?"

Fun?

Shock kidnapped her air and held it hostage. The woman clearly had no idea. No idea she was ripping Karly's heart out and stomping all over her dreams.

"Tell you what, Mom. Why don't you go home and do some research? Find out how much it will cost to purchase a good used truck and commercial insurance, and the cost of merchandise, business cards, and signs. Once you have the information, we can discuss where to park the truck."

"It would be fun to work on it together."

"Have you discussed this with your accountant?"

"He'll just tell me I don't have the funds. I'm sure it's because he likes to keep the money in the account to earn his commission."

No, it's because you don't have the money to waste. "Maybe we should pass on this one. It sounds like a lot of work, and I'm busy here."

"Okay. I wish you would work in an environment that wasn't so...wasn't so, so dirty." Her mother retrieved her travel-sized bottle of hand sanitizer and squirted a mound in the center of her palm, then kissed Karly on the cheek. "You still need a haircut. How about I make an appointment at my salon? I'm sure there's an opening."

And, drive for an hour to get there? No, thanks. "Mother." Her frustration pushed its way out.

"No need to raise your voice, hun. I was

just trying to help." She turned, wiggled her fingers over her shoulder. "See you tomorrow night for dinner."

Karly's stomach rumbled, and she crossed her arms over her waist to ease the nauseated churning. Thad's spoken words came back. *We were good together, you and I.*

That's because you're the only one who gets me.

But she couldn't go there. Thad had always wanted a big family. He joked about raising a soccer team. After what he went through, Thad deserved to find happiness. He deserved to have a wife who could give him what he wanted—that soccer team—something she couldn't provide.

CHAPTER NINE

Karly's rejection stung. But Thad wasn't pouting. He wasn't. Well, maybe he was.

He'd stayed away from town for almost a week to train Custer. The progress they made astounded him. Custer's mulishness had given way on day two, and he took to following directions. The hard work and patience paid off, and gave him something to feel good about.

Today were the dog's preliminary trials. Thad couldn't tell who was more nervous, him or Custer.

He stared at his reflection in the bathroom mirror.

Failure. A non-passing grade would be just one more failure. Hell, he'd done everything possible to ensure his father's fists landed on him, not his mother or sister. When that hadn't worked, he'd figured he'd intercept some flying bullets, and when that hadn't worked, he'd volunteered to look for bombs.

Loser was the nickname his dad had given him.

His mom stuck with inconvenient.

His sister preferred pest.

The titles chiseled away at his self-worth. He'd tried once to end it all—to pull the trigger. Everyone would have been better off. But he couldn't do it. A little voice kept telling him suicide wasn't the answer. He figured the Army would see him to the end, yet here he stood, wondering how he still hadn't managed to move past worthless. He smoothed back his hair, hearing his father's voice reminding him to keep his hair off his collar.

"Custer, I think I'll let my hair grow." He rubbed his chin. "Maybe grow a beard." The dog tipped his head to the side, as if trying to piece together what Thad had said. "Come on, boy." He moved his hand to get the dog's attention. "Let's get your trial over with. Karly needs her money. Fetch your leash."

On hearing Thad's command, Custer padded to the door to retrieve his halter. "Good boy. How about being an overachiever today, and getting a passing grade on all your elements? A little girl is counting on you."

Thad secured Custer's halter, grabbed his wallet, several bottles of water, a gear bag, then met Custer at the truck. He lowered the tailgate. "Up." Custer entered the oversized kennel and settled in, while Thad shut the wire door. "Good boy."

He sucked in a slow, refreshing breath of cold, crisp mountain air, and let the early morning mist settle on his skin. The smell of pinesap mixed with the clean, fresh air. Overnight, the grass had turned silver from the moisture clinging to the blades. A mourning dove called a greeting to her nearby mate. The combination calmed the voices in his head and allowed him to function.

He backed out of his gravel drive.

Driving over the bridge into town on his way to Cuppa Joe's, he couldn't help but look toward Karly's business.

That's odd. His gut tightened.

He took his foot off the accelerator. *There are lights on. Where's Karly's truck?*

Pulling alongside the buildings, he shut off the engine and opened the door to listen. The dogs were agitated. Something was off. From under the seat, he retrieved the plastic handgun case. Once his firearm was loaded, he moved to the side of the building.

Sweat made the grip slick.

Stay calm. Breathe.

His breathing became shallow as he made his way to the corner to peer around the building's edge past the fence line. Too exposed. He ran to the opposite building and placed his back against the steel wall.

Time slowed, and his mind flowed back to the Helmand province, near the capital of Lashkar Gah. His unit received orders to help Afghan forces look for a band of rebels. The sounds and smells and tension.

Sweat beaded on his forehead.

Readjusting his grip on the firearm, he inched his way toward the storage area at the back of the adoption center. Agitated dogs and the pounding of his heart in his ears were the only things he could hear.

Rounding the edge of the building, he made his way to the back door.

A bitter smell drew his attention. *A hand rolled cigarette butt.* He crouched lower to analyze a fresh set of footprints in the soft dirt beside the door. *A midsize male, one-eighty, maybe. Size nine or ten shoes.*

Fury fueled his protective gene. If anything happened to Karly, he'd hunt the bastard down.

Leaving the evidence intact, he tested the steel door and pushed it open an inch at a time.

Around the counter, the storage area was nothing but a dark hole. He'd give anything for his thermal night vision goggles. He made his way through the kennel slowly, clearing each section, then the office, making a full-circle sweep.

Sounds of footsteps halted his movement. Aware of the space, he slipped behind a supply rack.

The scent of vanilla hit him before the storage lights flickered on. He removed the bullet from the chamber of his gun and stepped forward.

"Jesus, Thad. I saw your truck. How did you get in here? And, what are you doing with that gun?"

Thad gazed toward the back entrance. "The back door was open. I saw your office lights on and decided to check things out."

Thank God you're okay.

She stared at the back door like it dripped

with blood. "I locked the door last night before I left." Her eyes widened, and she rubbed her arms, even though the temperature inside was stable and warm.

"Did you call the sheriff?" Her voice quivered.

I was too busy making sure you were safe. "I wanted to be sure there was a need before I made the call. You or someone else could have forgotten to lock the door." *I'll make sure it's locked from now on.*

"Neither Mara nor I would ever forget to lock the door." Her eyes ripened into round circles, her tone stiff. She pulled her hair into a fist and started twisting. "We need to call the sheriff. He needs to know about this."

"I'm not sure what he will be able to do." Thad engaged the safety on his gun. "But if you call, tell him there's evidence of a smoker who wraps marijuana in his tobacco." Her face paled to the color of tapioca pudding. "What just happened?"

"You sure it was marijuana?" The

squeaked, fearful question upped the pressure in his chest.

"Positive." He touched her forearm to get her attention. Her eyes were dilated, although she was doing her best to keep the panic contained. "All kinds of people in the military have vices. Tobacco. Alcohol. Pot. Pills. You name it. You get to know the signs."

Her muscles trembled beneath his hand. She crossed her arms and started to pace. "Then the sheriff will want to know."

"Why? I didn't see anything broken or damaged. It might be some neighborhood kids wanting to see the dogs." The excuse sounded lame, even to him, but he'd say anything to calm her fears. "You might want to see if anything is missing first."

"I expect nothing is missing. That's why we have to call Joe."

"Who's Joe?"

"Joe Gaccione. Mara's husband. He was elected sheriff after his brother was killed.

There's a guy who's been stalking Mara. He smokes cigarettes laced with marijuana."

This wasn't good. He braced a hand on the nearest shelf. "Since when does Elkridge have stalkers?"

"Since a couple of years ago. And things have gotten weirder since."

"What's Gaccione been doing about it?"

"He's made several arrests, but Mara doesn't believe any of the drug dealers they've arrested are the guy who's been following her around. She's certain the stalker is linked to her brother-in-law's murder." Karly moved toward the door to study the lock. "How did he get in? We've been so careful. I was starting to think Mara was wrong, that Joe had arrested the stalker."

What the hell's going on? Elkridge has stalkers and murderers?

The hairs on his arms stood to attention. "If that door was locked, a professional picked it. There are no marks on the door or signs of forced entry."

Her head whipped in his direction. "Oh, God. That's not good."

"You're shaking. Come here." He engulfed her in his arms, half expecting to hear her teeth chatter. He scanned the room to make sure he hadn't missed anything. "You need to install better locks and a security alarm."

She pushed from his arms. "Yeah, and who'll pay for the extra security equipment? It could cost thousands."

I would if I could.

"At a minimum, you need to get better locks. I didn't put my life on the line for this country to have some asshole running around scaring women and killing people in my hometown. Bill Mason might have a better lock lying around. I'll talk to him. We'll think of something."

She ran her fingertips under her eyes. "It's just that…"

"What, Karly?" He rubbed his hands up and down her arms slowly, to get her panicky breathing to slow. "Just because I was stupid all those years ago," he softened his tone, "doesn't mean you can't depend on me, trust me to help when you need it." He lifted her hand and brushed a kiss across her palm, then curled her fingers inward. "I told you before. I'm not going anywhere. Not again."

"You've said that before." She tilted her chin back, and he pushed a thread of hair behind her ear. Her eyes searched his. The barking had faded, and his mind quieted. Only two people existed. He leaned in. He closed the distance. He wanted her, wanted this—then she shifted and took a step back. He dropped his head.

"I need to go check on things. Make sure nothing is missing." She pointed over her shoulder and took a couple of steps backward.

"Yep, check on things." *#RunAway.*

"I'll call Mara. Tell her we might need to cancel her class this afternoon."

"Why? Don't you need the income? There will be enough people here to make sure nothing happens."

"There is that." The caution in her voice sent up a flare. He'd love to know what was skulking around in that pretty brain of hers. Nibbling on those sexy lips might rattle something loose.

Her eyes darkened like an aged whiskey. He took a step toward her, wanting to touch, caress.

In seconds, she disappeared through the door faster than a dog wanting to play.

Guess the preliminary trials are going to wait.

He stood there a while, contemplating her reaction, before finding something to do, because there was no way in hell he would leave her alone in this place.

A HALF AN HOUR LATER, Karly found him checking one of the dog's paws that looked red and raw, while Custer looked on.

Custer licked and sniffed the other dog with a high-pitched whine. "He'll be okay." Thad patted Custer on the back.

Karly knelt and touched the pitbull's hind leg. "I freaked out the first time I saw Barley's feet. When he gets bored, he starts licking, and it causes skin irritation. That's why his pads and feet are red. I need to take him for a run." She leaned against the kennel door. "Do you think Custer is ready for his prelims?"

"He's gotten through everything fine the past few days. It'll be interesting to see if he'll follow someone else's commands."

"Let's get this done. I want to take some of the dogs for a run. I was wondering if you'd be willing to come along. I'm not feeling all that safe since there still might be a stalker out there."

"Sounds good."

Karly's proposal provided relief from the turmoil boiling in his gut. He'd expected her to push him away again...or worse, ignore him, and was glad she finally reached out.

Thad let go of Barley's paw and ran a hand down Custer's flank. The dog danced away. "Custer's agitated and distracted. This should be interesting."

"Let's start with the basics." She leaned down to scratch under Custer's chin. "See how he does. If we get through the list, we can mix up the testing, see how he does with the unexpected. Since we don't know what a child will do, let's push him to see how he'll react. I'll go get things set up." Karly pushed through the back door.

Thad ran his hand down Barley's back. "It's okay, buddy. We'll be back shortly to take you for a run." The dog's ears perked up as Thad pushed to a stand. "Ready, Custer?"

When Thad entered the back room, she had indeed prepared. She'd built an obstacle course full of things Custer wouldn't be familiar with.

"Ready?" Karly lifted a clipboard off the wall and handed it to Thad. "I'll run him through the checklist. You assess what he's learned." She put on her training apron, which she'd filled with treats and whistles and klackers.

"Look." She got Custer's attention with a command. "Come."

For the next twenty minutes, Custer progressed through the checklist—leave it, drop it, sit, lie down, stay, wait...then he moved into the unknown. Jumping up on a box, going under a table, around a pylon, and through a tunnel.

Karly's work with Custer looked effortless. Her commands and reactions were flawless. She stayed in rhythm with the animal. Each verbal and non-verbal command was timed perfectly to help the dog perform his best. The way she interacted with animals was the same way she interacted with people. She listened, a rarity in this world, and the reason he'd been in love with the woman for all but ten years of his life. He might have fallen in love with her sooner if he'd figured out she was pushing him into mud puddles because she liked him.

She ran across the open area toward

Thad, stopped and turned. "Custer, come."

The dog trotted up to her, watching her hands, waiting to claim the beef nugget as his prize.

"Sit." She pulled out a treat. "Good boy." She rubbed the slobber on her jeans. "He needs more practice with the command wait, and he's reluctant to go into tight spaces."

Thad handed Karly the clipboard. "Do you think he'll still pass? I want you to get paid."

"*We*...so *we* can get paid." She studied the dog. "Do you think you can get him comfortable with the space issue in a couple days? I've already put off the Carsons once. They have an opening in their schedule, and want to retrieve Custer on Thursday."

Custer waited patiently for instruction. "Honestly, I didn't think he'd do as well as he did. Focusing on a couple of items shouldn't be a problem."

"I wish you would have more faith in yourself and your abilities."

The confidence the Army had built brick

by brick surfaced. "I have confidence in myself. It's others I'm not so sure about."

"That's true. Look at me. I was the closest to you, and you still believed I'd do something to hurt you."

"The military changed most of that. I learned to depend on others." Thad took a step closer and brushed her bangs aside. "But, you're the only one I learned to trust with my heart."

"But never fully." For a second there was a flicker of sadness. The need to let go of the pain. To be together without the push-pull. She leaned down to pet Custer. "What do you say we go for a run, big boy? There are a couple dogs next door who need some fresh air. Besides, a good run cleanses the soul." She fluffed the dog's ears. "I had dinner with my mother last night. You know how that goes."

"Yes, I do." He embraced the change of subject and transitioned his thoughts to Karly's mother. He'd like to give Mrs. Krane a how-to book on motherhood. The only thing she understood was overbearing control—control that ground her children down until every ounce of confidence had disappeared, or the kid rebelled. Luckily, Karly had created a diamond-encrusted suit of defiance.

The tension in Karly's shoulders and the shadows under her eyes supported his assessment that Mrs. Krane's interference had taken its toll.

"Do you have anything to run in?" He pointed at her jeans and flip-flops.

She huffed a laugh. "Half my wardrobe's here. I'm always here, and I need a change of clothes just about every day."

"What are we waiting for? Dogs are fed and watered—no worries there. How's your leg? Is it healing?" Thad bent his leg at the knee, stretching the thigh muscle. "Mine isn't too bad today. I stretched it good this morning, so I should be good for five miles or so."

"My leg's fine. I should be able to keep up."

"Let's take it slow. We're not in any rush, and it's nice out." *And I want to spend as much time together as I can squeeze into the day.* "Let's problem-solve while we run. Between the two of us, we should be able to come up with an inexpensive way to secure your place better. I'll get my backpack."

Karly unlocked the front door to let Thad out. "Lock the door when you come back in, would you?"

"Sure. I'll only be a minute." She nodded and disappeared.

On his way back in, he spotted the office door ajar. Moving to close the door, he paused. Every male part went on high alert, the ooh-la-la kind of high alert.

Karly hadn't gone to the bathroom to change. Nope. Through the crack in the door, he got a three-inch view from head to toe.

Well, lookie there.

He should change, but how does one take their eyes off perfection?

She had an efficient way about her that

most days he appreciated, but not today. Today, he wanted to expand time. Her long legs slid easily into running shorts that ended mid-thigh. The tangerine-colored racer-back shirt slid down her torso. The tattoo on her leg again made him curious. A drunken indulgence, maybe? Twisting up her hair, she shoved the ends into the loop of a baseball cap and opened the door.

"Oh. Hi. The restroom is down the hall if you need to change."

"I was just enjoying the view."

A wave of red flushed her face. "It's usually only Mara and me here, and she's blind."

"It's not like I haven't seen you before." He glanced toward her thigh. The blue-gray design on her skin was now covered by black and neon green running strips. "I meant to ask you about the tattoo."

"Oh, that?" She touched her leg just above where her shorts ended. "I got it in Vegas. A couple of us girls went there for my twenty-first birthday. It was supposed to be a crane standing on the back of a turtle, but it didn't turn out the way I expected."

A note of regret hummed through his cells. The memory of their milestone birthday plans played the sad tune. "We have a saying in the Army. A good tattoo ain't cheap, and a cheap tattoo ain't good."

"That's a good saying." The blush gave way to relief.

She made him want her to uncover those bits voluntarily. The voluntarily part being the biggest obstacle. The anticipation was killing him. He opened the front door. "After you."

"How come you only have the one on your arm? You talked about getting several."

He took the leads of three of the five dogs, deliberately placing Custer in her group to see how he'd do. "I found an artist who could pull off one of those 3D tats. It would have covered my whole back, but we couldn't get the drawing right, and pretty soon I was deployed again, and the timing never worked out."

"What design were you working on?" She turned toward the trail next to the river, and the dogs, alert to her slightest move, automatically headed that direction.

He hesitated. His chest tightened and his mouth dried out, because she was the only person on the planet who might understand the imagery.

Letting her step into the dark room in his mind, the place where he hid his moody, imperfect images, wasn't a good idea, but then again...

"It was a robotic skeleton, like the Borg in *Star Trek*, only the tattoo was a view from the inside, and it covered my whole back."

She glanced his way. "I bet it's like that drawing you did our senior year—that mechanical heart—with bits and pieces scattered across the bottom." She reached out to touch his arm. "Do you still feel broken?"

Damn her. She wasn't supposed to remember. She wasn't supposed to be able to see inside him. "When you're trained as a soldier, you're trained to think, act, react in a certain way. Like a robot."

She shook off his explanation. "But that's not why you're attracted to that drawing. You've always believed you were damaged in some way. I remember you saying you were expendable—that if you disappeared, no one would notice. But it's not true."

He gripped the leads tighter and pushed forward. Too bad he wasn't running a marathon. He wanted to feel that burn—the pain of pushing past exhaustion. Damn it, he wanted to feel something besides inadequacy.

She caught up with him a half mile later. "What are you doing?" she demanded, trying to catch her breath. "Was that your idea of running away?" she puffed out.

He slowed to a trot, but didn't dare look her way.

"Hey." She gave him a nudge. "You can never run far enough to get away from yourself. Believe me, I've tried." She allowed the dogs to fall into a pack.

He wanted to avoid the sympathy that was sure to come, but she surprised him.

She pulled at his arm to get him to stop, then tapped him on the chest. "You've spent years trying to convince everyone around you, even yourself, that you're not worthy. I'm not exactly sure what you think you aren't worthy of, but you've worked hard at it. Don't you think it's time you put all that effort into more positive pursuits?"

His heart picked up the pace. "Why do you care how I feel?" *I need to know.*

"Because, Thad Lopez—you are a person worth caring about. That's why. Some day you need to find a way to believe it." She took a step toward the trail leading up to a spruce and aspen covered grove. "Come on, soldier. Let's run. I want to see what you got."

I don't got a lot, since I don't have you.

She could split his chest open easy enough. Then again, she was the only person who could figure out how to put the pieces back together again.

CHAPTER TEN

"You can cancel more classes if you feel the need, but I won't send families away who want to adopt." Karly huffed out the frustration, hitting Mara right between the eyes with her unintentional resentment. "It's been two days since Thad found the back door left open, and everything seems back to normal."

Karly tossed a bill onto the heaping pile of invoices she was struggling to pay. "Mara, I'm sorry. I'm just frustrated."

Mara crossed her arms and leaned back in the office chair on the other side of Karly's desk, if you could call it a desk. The work area was made out of a wood door and two filing cabinets, and the door handle hole held a plastic cup full of paperclips. Her jerry-rigged desk worked, but her jerry-rigged life didn't.

"Joe is not just my husband, he's the town sheriff. If he thinks we should cancel classes, we should at least give it some thought."

"I know. I know. You're right. I don't mean to be defensive. It's just that Helper Shelter is my home. I built this place so I could feel good about my life—to be happy. Why would someone want to destroy that? There's nothing here for them to take except unwanted pets even I can't find forever homes for." She gulped down her frustration rather than bursting into tears. "And most of the time, we can't even give these precious critters away."

Mara gently threaded her fingers through Buddy's fur. "Joe asked me to cancel classes for a week or two."

Karly's gut seized with panic. Dog

training classes brought in dearly-needed cash flow. Without the classes, she might as well just board up and lock the doors. She picked up a metal clip, squeezed it open and let it snap shut again and again and again.

"Do you think it's truly necessary?" Karly asked with a hitch in her voice.

"I know we need the money. Honestly, I don't see the need to cancel classes."

Karly blew out a relieved breath and let her clenched fist open.

"Besides," Mara added. "I'm only here half an hour before the training classes start, and there's a ton of people around. I'm more worried about you coming in early, or staying late to feed the animals."

"Oh, please, don't say that out loud. My mother might hear you and be down here in a heart-pounding minute to put the first nail in the 'out of business' sign."

"Thad seems to be coming around a lot lately. Maybe the two of you can work something out so you won't need to be here alone."

More Thad time—that's exactly what I don't need. "Please don't go there."

"Why not? You said yourself he's good with the animals."

Yes, but he's not good for my heart. "That's all I need. A testosterone-driven male running around with a loaded gun. I'll see if I can change the schedule to make sure there are two people here at all times. I don't have the funds to pay for help, so I'll just have to get more volunteers."

"Which reminds me." Mara shifted uneasily. "Joe asked you to have Thad apply for a concealed weapon permit, or he'll have no choice but to charge him with a misdemeanor."

"Me? Isn't that his department's job?" The whine in Karly's voice was clear as glass, and she didn't like the sound. In fact, she was feeling rather self-centered lately, and hated being needy.

"It was a rather odd request. Joey's been rather preoccupied lately. Something is going on that he can't talk about. Before we were married, he told me being a sheriff's wife wouldn't be easy sometimes, because there would be things he couldn't discuss, but I didn't know the secrecy would bother me as much as it does."

"Is your sixth sense telling you something isn't right?"

"Maybe." Mara's blindness had honed her instincts to a razor-sharp edge. Shaking her head, she signaled Buddy and got up to leave. "I'd better get out there and start teaching puppy basics."

Her friend's almost caustic expression made Karly chuckle. "Come on, at least the puppies are cute."

"I can deal with puppies, it's their parents I can do without. Buddy, let's go train the humans how to manage their little ones."

Karly cringed when Mara ran smack into the door. Her helper instinct escalated, but out of respect for her friend, she stayed in her chair. If she could find even half of Mara's courage, she might just believe she could face any challenge life threw at her.

Karly's cell phone rang. Noting the caller, the desire to let it roll to voice mail was tempting, but it would only ring in another fifteen minutes. "Hello, Mom," she sighed.

"Karly, hun, I have the best news. I was talking to your brother this afternoon, and he told me there is an office manager position open at his company. You would be perfect for the job. Just think, you'd have insurance and benefits."

Good thing she was already sitting down. "Mother. You're meddling again."

The same way Karly was meddling in Thad's life. *Oh, no.* She rubbed her temples. *I'm turning into my mother. That can't happen. I won't let it happen.*

"Wait. There's more." Her mother's trill of excitement wound Karly's coil of self-berating resentment tighter. "Since Kevin's roommate moved out, he's been struggling to pay the rent. He said you could move in with him."

I doubt it. He wouldn't be struggling with rent if he didn't eat out all the time, and go to bars twice a week. He would love to have a cook, a maid, and someone to help with rent. No, thanks.

"Let me get this straight. You want me to apply for a job in Denver and live with Kevin, the brother who tossed me down the stairs when I was nine and cracked my head open."

"Oh, honey, that was so long ago. He's changed a lot since then."

Yes, he has. Now he'd do the job properly, and toss me out his twelfth-story window. She rubbed her head, cycling through and discarding a selection of sarcastic replies. None of them would get her mother to back off and let Karly live her life.

"Just in case, you should make an appointment to get your hair trimmed and highlighted."

"I'll think about it," she said, hoping next week her mother would have forgotten all about the job in Denver, although the odds of her mother forgetting anything were not in her favor.

"You should look professional for your interview."

If I go for an interview. "I'm set, Mom. I had my hair done yesterday."

"Did you tell your stylist to cut it the way I recommended?"

"Sure did." *The dog shears worked great.* If her mother only knew.

"Good. Well, I had better run, hun. I'm playing bridge with Vivian Newhall this afternoon."

"Have fun playing cards." She rolled her eyes, thinking her mother and Vivian were a perfect pair. The only problem was they both wanted to be the Queen of Diamonds. However, her mother never could see she held a losing hand. She hadn't yet learned to avoid playing games with cardsharps.

She placed her phone on the desk, then brought up the schedule on her computer to calculate how many more boarders she needed to book in order to make the bank loan payment and the annual kennel license due at the end of the month.

She pulled at the pocket of her flannel shirt, to peek in at the sleeping gerbil who looked forward to a stint in Karly's body-warmed pocket like a trip to a day spa. "Looks like I need to get my newsletter out. Generate some new business, or start panhandling for donations. What do you think?"

The gerbil stretched and yawned and curled into a tighter ball.

The face of pure bliss gave her a moment of pleasure. "Okay. A newsletter it is."

PROPPED against Karly's office doorframe, Thad observed quietly. Her pouty frown contradicted her loveliness. She'd wound her hair in a ball and secured it with a pencil, exposing her long, kissable neck. The temptation to nibble and caress was almost overwhelming. He took a step into her office. "Talking to yourself again?"

"Do you enjoy sneaking up on me?" She saved her work and closed out the computer file. "Where's Custer?"

"I'm giving him a day off. We went back to the park yesterday to practice. He did an excellent job dealing with the kids, swings, and slides. The kids wore him out." Thad slid into the seat across from her.

"The Carsons will be here tomorrow to pick him up. Are you sure he's ready?"

"Don't look so worried. He'll do fine." *At least I hope he will.* "What has you looking like you just ripped the head off your favorite Beanie Baby? You still have that purple bear?"

"There's a saying about old friends."

"Keep them close?"

"No…don't make them your enemy. They know you too well."

Damn, he loved her confidence. It was downright sexy.

Memories of their first kiss, of the first

time he collected enough courage to tell her he loved her, of her face while they made love, came tumbling back. "Anything I can help with?"

"I'm updating my business plan. I have to figure out a way to increase my cash flow. The sheriff wants me to cancel some training classes, but I can't do that and still pay the rent. I'm trying to figure out how to get in more donations, or get a grant."

"Is there anything I can do to help?"

"Find me a bucket full of money?"

He pointed at her computer screen. "I was looking for the Helper Shelter Facebook page, but didn't see one."

"That's 'cause I haven't had time to set one up. Twitter, Instagram, Snapchat, who has time for all that?"

Time? He did. He released a heavy sigh. "At minimum, you need a Facebook page. It will help potential customers in neighboring towns discover you. I could set one up for you. If you send me pictures of the rescue animals, I can set up your page. It might bring you a bit more traffic. Plus, you can post and link to other pet-finder sites."

"Since when did you learn how to use a computer?"

He pulled at an ear, wondering how much he should say. She had unfulfilled dreams of going to college. He barely got the school's principal to sign off on his diploma before leaving town. How would she feel if he admitted to getting his degree online? Would it crush her? Maybe. Maybe not. He didn't want to take the chance of hurting her feelings.

He brushed a hand over the top of his head. "The Army has a lot of high-tech equipment. Learning how to use computers is part of the job."

"I could use the help. If I don't figure out something fast, I might have to take my brother up on his offer and move to Denver."

Denver? The idea sucker-punched him in the gut. "Kevin is the one who lives in Denver."

"How do you know?"

"Kenny must have told me." He hated the idea, and no doubt so did she. "Kevin's the one you don't get along with."

"You're right, but soon I might not have any choice. Both my mortgage on this place, and the rent on the apartment are due."

"There's empty space in that back trailer. You could fit a bed in there." *Or come live with me.*

"Can you imagine what my mother would say?"

"Fair enough." He moved around the edge of her desk and leaned in to grab her mouse. "Let me show you something." He pulled up a website he'd found while at the Cuppa Joe's. "Look here. The shelter lists supplies needed so people can donate toys, bedding, office supplies, or anything else the shelter needs. And, see here? There's a calendar plugin. Volunteers can sign up for dog walking or cat socialization. On this page, the shelter advertises food drives and dog washes, and then streams the information to other social media sites with a click of a button. The workflow is done automatically. There's less work for the web administrator."

"The huh?"

"Web administrator. The person who maintains the site."

"You learned this in the Army?" He gave her a little shrug, surprised to realize she wasn't pushing him away. The way she looked at him gave him a cold beer on a sunny afternoon feeling.

"The Army taught me some. A couple of the guys in my unit were masters at metadata tags, SEO, and RSS feeds. They taught me a lot."

"I have no idea what you just said, but it sounds impressive."

"Once you get a hang of the stuff, it's kind of cool, actually."

He pulled up another website. "I did notice one thing. You're boarding, running training classes, grooming, fostering, and adopting for all types of animals. That's a lot, and maybe why you're overwhelmed. I couldn't find another shelter doing all of those things. I know you love the animals, but if you go out of business, you won't be able to keep doing what you love, and what will happen to all the animals?"

"What do you have in mind?"

"You've got a ton of volunteers, and everyone here loves being able to contribute. What about deciding what part of the business you're most passionate about, and then partner with other people in the area that have compatible businesses."

"There are a lot of fosters and groomers close by."

"Exactly." He wanted to hold her attention and a whole lot more. "Let me show you one of the websites I built for a buddy of mine. He took these amazing photographs—*National Geographic*-worthy. Willie's wife is helping him sell them online."

His fingers shook as he typed in the URL. Seconds later the site appeared. Willy's memorial to Steve Plutton, his military brother and friend, flashed up on the screen. Thad quickly clicked through to the picture portfolio to avoid the face he still missed seeing every day. That, and the guilt.

The rolling slide show of a little Afghani boy laughing and playing in the streets brought back some more palatable memories of helping villages carry water, giving out chocolate to the kids, playing a quick game of kickball.

"These are amazing. Says here these were posted two days ago?"

He pushed back from the desk and stared at the screen. "Yeah, I heard Willie was stateside. I should give him a call."

A warm hand folded over the top of his. "Does he take any pictures of dogs or cats? I'm always looking for pictures."

"I can ask." He leaned in to close the browser window. "We sorta had a falling out. He and Pluto were good friends, and…well… Willie blames me for not finding that bomb."

Her breath hitched in sympathy, a sentiment he didn't deserve. "We settled this. Steve's death is not your fault. You didn't plant that bomb."

He stepped back, but she held on to his arm. He studied the computer screen, wishing, hoping he could see his good buddy, see his wise-cracking smile, hear another one of his pitiful jokes. Pluto had been the jokester—always playing around, willing to take things as they came. Not Thad. He had to push. Push hard toward the invisible line. A line that, if crossed, would mean he'd be able to feel something positive. Anything. But he just couldn't find that invisible line.

He failed Steve. Just like he failed his mom and sister and Karly.

He'd failed a lot of people.

By staying.

By leaving.

By existing.

He'd give everything he had to trade places with his buddy. To avoid having to tell everyone how sorry he was. If given a chance, he'd give his life without a second thought. Regrets were the reason he couldn't sleep, or eat, and was always tired. Dead tired.

He inhaled his sorrow. "I know it's not my fault. Willie just needs someone to blame."

"Don't do that. Not with me," she said with a bitter annoyance fueling her voice. "You and I both know you believe Steve and Ike's deaths were your fault. I can say it's not your fault every day, all day, and still, the only one who needs to believe is you."

He gazed into a face full of worry. "What do you want from me?"

"I want you to stop taking responsibility for things that are not your fault—things you can't control. You didn't make your dad the way he was. He had a choice. He chose to be an alcoholic."

"It is my fault. If I'd kept my mouth shut, done as my dad told me, he wouldn't have started taking it out on my mother and sister."

She waved her hands, making circles that made no sense. "Your dad is the one who did the hitting. It's not like you purposely walked into his fists. We all feel guilt, but we have to let it go."

He pushed back from the desk, refusing to listen. "It's not that easy."

"Nope. It's not. But it is possible to embrace it, make peace with it, and move on."

Her face revealed concern, the same expression his buddies had while they loaded him into the medevac helicopter.

"Can we talk about something else?"

At another point in time, she might have pushed, tugged, even carried him back from the self-berating line. She'd make him face his nemesis—taunt him, no doubt—and be by his side every step of the way. Another screw and bolt twisted into place on his broken heart. She made him feel whole, yet he still wasn't steady or working properly.

His chest tightened with a burning desire to hold her in his arms. The need wasn't sexual. He wouldn't mind going there, but it wasn't what his need was about right now.

He wanted to feel something good.

Something new.

Damn, he wanted to feel anything but regrets.

He turned and drew her to him, his hands sliding over her hips. "God, you're beautiful."

Her eyes widened. His fingers shook as he slid his hands up her arms to touch the soft skin on her face. *My beauty.* Her eyes searched for his intent, then she softened and wrapped her arms around his neck, meeting him halfway. *There you are.*

She lifted up on her toes and pressed her lips to his. Need pulsed through him. Hunger gripped him, like a predator on the hunt. Patiently watching. Waiting to devour. He pulled her against his chest, wanting to feel every inch of her heat. *I've missed you.* His thumb brushed against the vein in her neck to feel the way her heart pounded in rhythm with his.

When she pulled back, he tightened his grip. "No. Don't go." Her golden eyes searched his while her breath steadied, and his knees weakened. He touched her jaw, and wordlessly she pressed her cheek into his palm.

His whole being roared with desire. "Karly? Do you know what you're doing to me?" The low, gruff question didn't require an answer. She kissed his palm.

Oh, man. Do that again.

Her hand cupped his face. "I'm making you forget."

No. You are making me want to remember. He wanted her in every way possible. But not here. Not in her office, or on a desk with an open door. No, he wanted her in a mountain valley, the summer sun heating their skin, surrounded by beauty.

"This isn't…"

"Shhh." She placed a finger over his mouth, and then replaced her finger with a kiss. She pressed in, and he groaned. Wanting more. Much, much more.

He tightened his arm around her waist. Her tongue eased inside and sought his. He let her explore, play, take what she wanted.

She kissed him more deeply, and his heart opened wider. His hand drifted lower and around, and splayed across her stomach, then slipped lower. She wrapped a leg around the back of his to press them together.

He should stop her. Stop this...yet he couldn't.

He didn't have the strength to move away. He couldn't leave her. Not this time. Not again. He lifted her shirt to trace the line between her shirt and running pants, skimming over her soft skin.

Another groan—this time hers.

She vibrated against his hands, her skin damp. She was his. His woman. Not that he could ever own her. No one could. But for these precious moments, she gave herself to him. He possessed her mouth. The feel of her nipples rising to his touch thrilled him. Her little whimpers of pleasure encouraged him to explore. He wanted to feel her flesh under his hands. He slid his hand lower and pushed her against the wall.

He wanted to make her soar.

Lowering his head, he placed his mouth on her breast, sucking on the crinkled skin to make the nipple expand. She gasped before she could stop the sound.

"That's it, Karly," he murmured. "Tell me what you need."

She dug her nails into his back. "More," she thrust out on a sharp exhale.

"More?" he asked again, as a thrill sizzled down his spine.

"Yes. More, damnit."

With a groan, he pressed his mouth to her neck and slid his hand south, down to give her more. He slid his hand inside her panties. His fingers opened her folds and touched juicy flesh.

"Open for me." He nudged her thighs. While his fingers sought the warmth, her hips pushed forward. "That's it."

Her breaths were coming in quick blasts, her groans pure, exquisite torture.

"Thad…"

"Say my name again." He nibbled his way to her mouth.

"Thad. Thad. THAD!"

Ah, heaven. His fingers circled faster and faster and faster, driving her to the edge. Her body jerked and trembled. He played. Speeding up. Slowing down. Making her climb higher, until he dangled her over the edge, her muscles pulsing again and again.

He held her while she struggled to catch her breath. *Bliss. Pure bliss.*

She shoved shaky fingers through her hair, then wrapped her arms around his shoulders.

"Thad, I—"

"Karly?" Mara asked, opening the door wider. "You there?"

Karly pushed on his chest, staring at him, and then turned. "Yes. Thad and I were just discussing his ideas about social media and how we can get more business."

His full-blown hard-on ached, and for the first time he was grateful Mara couldn't see.

"Hi, Mara." Seeing the red blotches climbing Karly's neck and cheeks gave him a thrill. "Yep, social media. That's what we were discussing. I'm sure you ladies have things to talk about." He rubbed a thumb gently over Karly's mouth before taking a step back.

Mara took another step into the office "Thad. Before you go, I'm singing at Mad Jack's on Friday night. Why don't you stop by? Karly will be there. I'd appreciate the support, and it would be fun having you there."

"He doesn't like crowds." Karly spoke a little too quickly for his liking.

"I'll be there. What time?"

"Jenna's meeting me there at 6:30. Why don't you join us?"

"Sounds good, Mara. I'll see you Friday. Karly, I'll meet you at the park tomorrow. Don't worry, I'll make sure Custer's handsome and ready to meet his new owner."

"Don't be late."

"Five minutes early is ten minutes late in soldier time. You're just going to have to trust me." *Something you're not good at doing.*

He walked slowly back to his truck, not wanting anyone to see the bulge in his pants. Then again, what did he care?

He just might kiss Karly in front of the whole town, because there didn't seem to be anything either of them could do to change the way they felt about each other.

CHAPTER ELEVEN

L ife was certainly getting back to normal—if there was such a thing as normal.

Walking through the park, Custer pranced, almost like he understood the importance of the day.

Thad leaned to pat him on the side. "Hey, buddy, you need to be on your best behavior today. This is your chance for a forever home, and to help a little girl who needs you. You can't be stubborn." Thad checked his coat, which was still damp from being washed and clipped. "You can do this." Thad reached the playground in time to see Karly arrive.

"Hey." She let Custer smell her hand before giving him an affectionate ear rub. "He's looking mighty handsome today." While she leaned in to pet the dog, his heart sighed. She looked edible in those tight-fitting jeans that cupped her rear end so perfectly. The sherbet orange T-shirt didn't hurt, either. This afternoon, he might take her to find a nice, sunny spot and have a lick.

She stood. "Don't look at me like you want to nibble on something. The Carson family is supposed to arrive any minute."

#Busted. "What did they say when you called?"

"Not much. I've answered most of their questions already. The Carsons are just excited about meeting Custer. I also told them I brought a kennel and a few supplies for them to take home."

Custer sat silently beside Thad, looking mighty pleased. "You were right about him. He's a good dog."

She nudged his shoulder with hers. "He had a good trainer."

For the first time in months, the praise in her voice overruled the hypercritical negativity that normally shredded his thoughts. He pinched a dog hair off her cotton shirt. "Thanks."

"Thad, there's something I need to tell you."

"They're here." Thad pointed over her shoulder at the gray minivan pulling into a handicapped parking spot. "Let's talk later." Thad wiggled his fingers to get Custer's attention. "This is it. Ready to meet Lily?"

Custer stared at him, waiting for his command. Was that sadness he saw? Did he understand today was their goodbye? Or was the expression just a reflection of his own sense of loss? Letting go had never been easy. But unlike Ike, at least Custer had a chance at happiness.

Thad took a step forward. "Heel."

Both Custer and Karly fell into step beside him. Walking across the lawn, he dragged his feet until he saw the little girl with ribbon-tied ponytails.

Her blond, curly hair matched Custer's, only it was a bit longer and floated in the breeze. A blue T-shirt, jeans, and a pair of white tennis shoes with pink flowers on top perfectly fit his image of a little girl named Lily. Even though she had an oxygen tank dragging behind her, her smile was as brilliant as the sun.

"There's Cuth-ter." She jumped up and down, clapping her hands.

Custer brushed up against his leg and let out a nervous whine. Thad gave the leash a gentle tug. "It's okay," he encouraged in a quiet, soothing tone.

He stopped a few feet from the little girl and crouched beside Custer, wrapping his arms around the dog's chest. "You must be Lily. Would you like to meet Custer?"

"Cuth-ter." She held out her hands and wiggled her fingers in a come-now way.

Custer licked Thad's face, then pranced on his front paws. He leaned forward, straining against the lead. "Okay," Thad gave the command.

Lily raised her hand to touch Custer's fur. Custer inched forward. After only a brief touch, she pulled back. A squeal of giggles splintered the tension. "Soff. Dog soff." The glee in her eyes exploded like a bowl of confetti.

"Let's see if we can't get Custer loaded, shall we?" Thad gave Custer the command 'stand' while he loaded one of the oxygen tanks Mr. Carson brought along. "That's a good boy, Custer."

"Good boy, Cuth-ter." Lily patted the dog on the nose.

The interaction provided a reassuring comfort. "Are you ready to try this out?"

Lily patted the dog's back and walked ahead, and thankfully Custer followed.

"You must be Thad. I'm Tom Carson, and this is my wife, Pam."

"Nice to meet you. You've got a beautiful kid." Thad gestured toward Lily, who was untangling her plastic tubing from around

Custer's legs. "Let's see if we can't get them down the slide together, shall we?"

Tom glanced protectively toward his daughter while Pam choked back a sob. "I can't wait for her to be able to play like an average little girl."

"That's the goal." Thad took a deliberate step towards his newly-found purpose.

Lily climbed up and over, slid down, swung high and low with a rainbow of expressions, all the while telling Custer he was a good boy. She dragged her feet along the sand to slow her swinging movement and tottered toward her parents.

"Can we keep Cuth-ter?" Her eyes danced with hope.

Tom looked at Pam, and both nodded at the same time. Lily hugged Custer. The dog blew a breath in her ear. "Wait till you meet my best friend, Mary. She's nice."

Lily walked to Thad and yanked on his jeans. "Mith-ter. Thank you for my dog."

Thad knelt down. "If you take good care of him, he'll be a good friend. Just remember to let him rest. Dogs need to sleep more than we do."

Custer came to lie at Lily's feet, and she tugged on the edge of her navy blue T-shirt which declared "I'm adorable," written in sequins. She touched Thad's nose with her finger. "Don't be sad."

Kids saw much more than most people expected. He attempted a smile. "I'm not sad."

"Yeth, you are."

Maybe he was, but he didn't want the world to know. He forced his mouth to smile. "I'll be just fine. Don't you worry about me. Karly has a whole kennel full of dogs who need a new home. I'll find another pup to train."

She poked at his hand, running her fingers along his scars, rotating his hand to see the other side. "Maybe your new dog can help get you better. Like Cuth-ter. He'll help me."

Kids and animals. They had a gift of seeing what jaded eyes could no longer sense. "Maybe. Or maybe I can train another dog to help someone special, like you."

"Momma tells me I'm special all the time."

"It must be true, then."

She giggled. "C'mon, Cuth-ter. Let's play."

"Hold up a minute. We need to help you learn to talk to Custer. He only knows a few words, and you need to know what they are so he can understand what you want."

She giggled and shrugged her shoulders almost to her ears. "Dog's don't talk. They bark, silly."

"You're right. They bark, but they also listen and do what you want them to do if you give them the right command. Watch." Thad held up his hand, and Custer followed his movements. "Up."

Custer stood up on his hind legs.

"Sit."

Custer nudged his hand and sat.

"Good boy." Thad pulled a treat out of his pocket. "This is his latest trick." Thad balanced the treat on the dog's nose. "Leave it." Custer's eyes never left him, and he started to drool. When a drop of saliva hit the tip of his hiking boot, he smiled. "Okay."

With an upward jerk of his muzzle, Custer launched his treat into the air, and less than a second later, it disappeared in one gulp. Lily's scream and hand claps followed. Custer's ears went flat, and he nudged Thad's hand. Thad snapped his fingers, getting Custer's attention. The dog sat, watching, waiting.

"Lily, do you want to try?"

She thrust her pudgy little hand out, palm up, to accept the treat. She lifted her hand to place the treat on Custer's nose, but it fell into the grass. The dog was the first to reach it.

Lily moved to wrap her arms around her dad's legs, and peek at Thad and Custer from behind the wall of safety. "He ate it." Her lips trembled. "He didn't wait."

Thad dropped into a crouched position and tugged on the hem of her jeans to get her attention. "Yeah, Custer can be stubborn sometimes. I bet he's just like you. Do you always listen to your mom and dad?"

"Yesssss." Lily blinked and pulled inward.

Tom tapped his daughter's shoulder. "Lily, is that true? We tell the truth, don't we?"

Her blue eyes sought his. "Noooo."

Her mouth puckered into a pout.

A joy tiptoed through his soul, coloring everything happy as it went along. "Custer is still learning. He sometimes has bad days and doesn't listen. You just have to make sure he practices his commands like you practice your alphabet, every day. You have to promise to practice every day."

She twisted the end of her T-shirt around her finger. "Okay."

Thad held out his hand, and she gave it a slap. "Are you ready to learn the rest of Custer's words?"

"Yaaaahhhhh." She screamed and jumped up and down, clapping.

Thad caught a glimpse of Karly. He'd expected to see happiness. What he saw was more in line with regret, maybe sorrow. The interaction with Lily had triggered something raw, and she was doing her cheery best to fake it, but he knew her better.

He wanted to pull her into his arms and squash the sadness forever, unfortunately now wasn't the time.

For the next ten minutes, Thad helped Lily learn Custer's vocabulary. He repeated the steps over and over. Holding her attention was a challenge, but he managed to coax her along until she got them right. He gave Lily a hug for learning the lessons and stood.

Oddly enough, his leg didn't hurt as much as it did most days. "I can't thank you enough." Tom held out his hand to Thad.

"Glad to help."

Pam placed a hand on her husband's shoulder. "We should get going. We have a long drive."

"I'll help you get the kennel and supplies loaded." Karly wrapped her arm around Pam to provide comfort while the women moved toward the parking lot.

"When Pam came up with this idea," Tom lowered his voice to almost a whisper, "I thought she was crazy. Seeing them together, playing…" Tom blinked, and his mouth began to tremble. Red tinted his cheeks while he knuckled away tears. "When she was born, we almost lost her."

"And, look at her now." Thad shifted, shoved his hands into his pockets and rocked back on his heels. "She's able to move freely, and will have a dog to make sure she doesn't get in trouble, or maybe it's the other way around."

"Yes. Yes, she'll have time just to play and be a kid."

"Let's get you on your way." Thad placed a hand on Tom's back. Only a few minutes had passed, but Thad connected with this father. He was a good one, unlike his dad. Thad would make sure when Karly had their first, he'd be a good dad.

Tom held Lily's hand while they walked

to the parking area. Thad could barely comprehend the pain and suffering this father endured while watching his daughter grow and struggle. He hoped he'd been able to help in some small way.

After a small, tired tantrum, Lily relinquished her hold on Custer and allowed her new best friend to get into his kennel.

"Drive safely." Karly stepped back from the Carsons' driver's side window.

Thad raised his hand while the specially equipped vehicle backed out of the parking space. Neither Thad nor Karly moved until the car signaled left and turned toward the interstate.

"Seeing Lily play with Custer makes me want to have kids."

Karly shivered and rubbed her arms. "The insurance check should arrive by the end of the week."

"Was this really about the money, or finding me work?"

"It was about saving animals and children.

The look on Lily's face was priceless." Karly turned back toward her truck. "It's the reason why I started matching animals and families, there's nothing more satisfying."

"What do you say to a juicy hamburger over at Mad Jack's to celebrate?"

Karly hesitated. "Not today. I have paperwork."

"But you wanted to tell me something."

"Oh, that. It can wait."

She wanted to have lunch. He could tell, but something stopped her. "You sure?"

"I'm sure. I'm supposed to help my mother paint one of my brother's old bedrooms. She wants to redesign the room, and make it an office."

He gave her a nudge. "Lunch would be more fun."

"I agree. However, I'd be interrogated relentlessly about why I canceled. It's just easier to go."

"Since when have you done the easy?"

"Since I've gotten older and wiser." She

took a step back. "You go celebrate. You deserve it."

It wouldn't be any fun without you.

"See you later." She turned toward her car.

He walked backward a few steps, watching, waiting for her to turn back.

She never did.

CHAPTER TWELVE

"This isn't a date. Shop fidgeting. It's not a date," Karly mumbled for the fortieth time.

She opened the door to Mad Jack's bar and walked into the crowded pub. Spotting Mara, she headed toward the stage, but Jenna caught her attention.

"Karly, you look awesome." Jenna leaned in for a hug. "Ready for your big date?"

This town is way too small. "Hey, lady. Looking good yourself."

"Where have you been? You haven't

stopped by lately for your double-fudge or pecan nuggets."

"You know what running a business is like. Every second of the day gets eaten up with a thousand different things."

Jenna reached up to play with Karly's gold loop earrings. "Love these, and look at you, sporting your skinny jeans, all tight and sexy. And you're wearing my favorite boots. Very nice."

She wiggled her toes in her western ankle boots. "Haven't worn them in a while."

"They're just the thing you need to wear to get laid."

Karly choked. "What did you say?"

"You heard me. Thad's in the back looking all scrumptious. Word is you two have some catching up to do. I hope you wore your good undies."

"It's not like that. We're learning to be friends. That's all."

"Friends. Uh-huh." Jenna leaned in and lowered her voice. "If he doesn't have his hands all over you by the end of the night, stop by the bakery tomorrow. I'll load you up with sympathy treats."

"That won't be necessary, 'cause this isn't a date."

Jenna stepped back with a wave of her hand. "Whatever you say. Either way, you look scrumptious."

"Thanks. How is your bakery doing?"

"Business is booming." Jenna's face got that happy puppy look Karly loved. "Grant's helping with the marketing and running the store, which gives me a lot more time to do the creative stuff."

"That's wonderful. I'm so happy for you."

The envy bug sneaked in and nipped her with a sting of jealousy.

"We should catch up soon. I've missed seeing you. You should come over for dinner. Grant is working on a new meat rub for wild game."

Jenna's face reminded her of one of the cupcakes in her cases, teeming with gorgeous, sugary bliss. "That sounds fantastic."

Jenna bit her lip and hesitated. "If you want, we can make it a double date."

A loneliness choked off her air. Mara, Kym, Ashley, Jenna—all her friends had found their happily ever afters. She couldn't go there. Fate had mapped out her future. She'd had her one chance at motherhood and blew it. Life wouldn't include wedded bliss.

She forced her face into the bogus smile she'd perfected for her mom, and anyone else who suggested matrimony. She couldn't let anyone see the excruciating pain of never being able to go there. Her dreams to marry, make a home, raise kids, had been obliterated even before she graduated from high school.

She pushed the searing hurt back. "Let me think about it. If Thad's busy, can I come alone?"

Jenna grabbed her hand. "Of course. Any of your friends are welcome."

Her friend's sentiment placed a temporary Band-Aid over the wound. "Sounds good." She turned toward the stage.

"I had better wish Mara luck before her set starts."

"Yes, of course. See you soon."

"Soon." She reinforced the phony smile and made her way through the tables to the stage.

"Are you all ready for your set?" Karly scanned the roomful of locals eating appetizers and watching sports reruns. "It looks like you drew a big crowd tonight."

Mara pulled her guitar closer to her chest. "Don't say that. I'm already nauseous. I'm good at pretending I'm only singing to a few."

"You sing here every week. How can you be nervous?"

"You get up here and pour your heart and soul into a piece of music, and then have to listen to some stranger criticize your work. There's always one in every crowd."

"There must be some ordinance against being mean. You're Joe's soft spot. Have him arrest them."

"Yeah, like that will happen."

Karly leaned back to see around a few bodies. "If I'm not mistaken, that's the sheriff at the end of the bar."

"Yeah, he managed to get the night off. Brianne is doing a sleepover at my sister-in-law's place, so maybe I'll get lucky tonight. This is our date night. We haven't been able to have one for awhile." A smile stretched like sweet taffy across her face. "He showed up a few minutes before Thad. Maybe it's your lucky night, too."

Karly's stomach did that wonky whirl again while she surveyed the crowd. "Speaking of Thad, I'd better go find him. Jenna said he's back by the exit."

That nervous, jittery feeling made her reach for her phone to have something in her hands to play with. The jitters started soon after her morning coffee, and had lasted all afternoon, especially while she tried on outfit after outfit, none of them creating the casual yet sexy look she wanted to convey. This wasn't a date, but it didn't mean she didn't want to make an impression—remind Thad of what he left behind.

Mara placed a hand on her forearm. "Would you do me a favor?"

"Of course. What can I get you?"

"I'd really like my business partner to have fun tonight. No thinking about work, or the past, or anyone but you. You're always thinking about taking care of your animals and volunteers and business, and tonight? Tonight I want you to think about yourself."

Wow. Didn't see that coming. "I'll try."

Mara squeezed her arm. "Now go find Thad."

Stationing himself next to the exit made sense. He always hated crowds. And people drinking always reminded him of his dad, and made him want to stay out of the way. Karly squeezed Mara's forearm. "Good call." Karly leaned in for a quick hug. "Stop being nervous. You'll be great. I'll be back in a bit."

Passing the pool tables and dartboard lanes, she nodded and waved to friends, but kept going.

Then her breath stalled.

There you are.

He sat very still. Silent. Waiting.

This is a bad idea. Turn around. Leave.

Her body wouldn't listen. He sat in the booth, one arm on the table, the other across the back of the leather booth. His faded blue, long-sleeved T-shirt showed off his muscular chest and arms, and she wasn't the only woman in the bar who'd noticed. But the look on his face when he saw her said she was the only person who mattered.

She glanced at the table. "Did you order a drink?"

"I'm good."

His gaze started at her reluctant smile and continued down her lace-trimmed tank, and past her faded jeans. His mouth curved slightly with a knowing smile—he was fully aware she'd dressed for him.

"Well, I need one." A petite blonde stopped by their table. "Carrie, would you bring me a shot of the house tequila, and some chicken nachos with a side of guacamole? Oh, and a couple of plates. We'll share." She slid into the booth before she lost her nerve.

"Thad, would you like anything?" Carrie wrote down the order on a pad then looked directly at the gorgeous man.

Startled, he shook his head. "No. Thanks. Just water for me. It looks like I'll be driving."

Carrie smiled in the notice-me kind of way, and Karly considered yanking on the girl's ponytail. *How rude.* Carrie shoved a couple coasters and silverware packs on the table, and dangit if she didn't lean in just enough for anyone who was looking to get a full view.

Karly kicked Thad in the shins.

"What?"

"You know what."

She slowly unwrapped her napkin, biting back the dozens of things she wanted to say. "One shot of tequila won't get me drunk."

"Isn't there a song about tequila and clothes falling off?"

The Joe Nichols song rolled through her

head. "Don't try to be funny. It doesn't work."

His chuckle annoyed her, but only because she wanted to laugh along with him. She studied the crowd, trying to avoid the happy, tingly warmth invading her system.

"Who was that?" He pointed to the waitress. "How did she know my name?"

A jealousy spider crawled under the table and started nibbling on her toes. "That's Carrie Robertson. Judge Robertson's daughter."

"That's little Carrie? Is she old enough to be serving liquor?"

"She just turned twenty-two last month."

"Really? I never thought I'd say this, but even the cheerleaders look young." The jumbo screen reporting sports highlights caught his attention, but only briefly.

"You and I are the same age." Karly's statement drew his gaze. "Do I look old to you?"

"No. You look like a four-layer cake.

Scrumptious. Edible. Too much to eat in one go. You need to be savored."

A slow, erotic heat rolled up her legs and ignited a fire in her belly. She hadn't been fishing for compliments, but doubted any guy on the planet could top that one.

Not knowing what to say or think or do, she ignored him and started to climb out of the booth.

"Don't go. I didn't mean to make you uncomfortable."

She chided herself for giving him mixed signals, and being so wishy-washy. It had been a long time since she'd felt comfortable with anyone. He fit her like a nice, comfortably worn pair of jeans—snug in all the right places.

But she could never give him a family. Kids. He wanted children. Always had. But did he still? She wanted to ask. Wanted to tell him. But why? It wasn't like they were going to get married. Heck, she didn't even fully trust he wouldn't leave again. "I don't know what to do around you anymore."

"It's that baggage thing again, isn't it? I still think we should have a garage sale, sell the whole lot for a buck. It isn't doing either one of us any good."

Her shoulders eased. "These past few weeks...seeing you, being with you. I didn't even realize how much I've missed just being able to hang out with someone without being judged."

"I get what you mean. Transitioning out of the military has been hard. People seem to have expectations I'm not sure what to do with."

"You must miss your friends."

He straightened his napkin flush with the table, then stared at his silverware. "That, and I miss the adrenaline rush. Being out there. Being on edge. Worrying about only one thing...keeping everyone alive." He refused to look at her. "I crave it," he murmured. His thumbs started pounding a nervous cadence on the table, and his face flushed.

"A lot of guys sign up for the reserves," she offered as a solution.

He shook his head. "I'm done with the military, or more accurately, the military is done with me. The reserves would drive me nuts. If I went back, I'd go back as a contractor."

I figured you would leave again. A corset of fear squeezed her chest. "You would do that? Sign up to be a contractor? Isn't that dangerous?"

"It's good pay."

"I'm sure it is, but you joined the military the first time because you were wanting to escape from your life here. I worry that you won't ever have a life if you keep running. You used to dream about building a cabin, training dogs, hunting, climbing the fourteeners in the state. What happened to those dreams?"

"Here you go." Carrie set the food and Karly's drink on the table. Karly reached for the shot and downed it in one go. The alcohol burned its way down to her toes. She plunked the inch-tall glass down on the table.

"Do you want another?" Carrie asked.

Karly met Thad's gaze. The desire for another drink was deflated by his assumptions swimming in his eyes. "No. Water will do. With lemon, please."

When Carrie walked away, Karly pushed the nachos in his direction. "Then again, there is something to be said for not growing old, for throwing yourself in front of bullets, and almost getting killed by a bomb. You'd never go bald, or have the need for glasses or dentures."

"Karly?"

"Don't mind me." She waved a hand in front of her face, trying to shake away the conversation. "It's just I get these dreams. It's like a thriller movie, or maybe more like a horror film. You're always in them. Always in some kind of fight for your life."

The tequila worked its magic and kicked in the numbing process. Too bad she couldn't have a second or third to complete the job, because there was no way she could allow him to take her home, and she desperately wanted to feel his arms around her, remind her what life used to be like.

"Want to play some darts?" She stuffed a big bite of the cheesy chicken mess into her mouth, then licked her fingers. "Do you still like to play?"

"I do." He selected a chip, but managed to put it in his mouth in a far more dignified manner.

The delicious warmth of the shot, plus a load of carbs, did amazing things for her confidence. "Why don't we play? If I win, you wash the dogs for a week."

A slow, sensual smile crossed his face. "I think you can do better than that." He licked his thumb and then picked up his water glass for a long swallow.

"Okay. If I win, you have to update my website and do that social media stuff you were talking about. For free."

Thad released a slow laugh and stole the

nacho chip she was aiming for, right before she picked it up.

"What do I get if I win?"

She scooped up a dollop of guacamole with a new chip. "Your choice."

"My choice? Karly, when it comes to you, I've never had a choice. You stole my heart in grade school, but I was too stupid to figure it out until we were in junior high. By high school, I was doomed."

"Doomed. Huh. That pretty much describes what we had. We were two kids fighting the world together."

"Our parents sure didn't make life easy." He licked his fingers one at a time before pulling his napkin out from under his silverware. "I loved you. Hell, I still love you, but this," he waved his hand back and forth between them, "whatever this is...isn't working. You keep pushing me away, for reasons I'm not totally sure of, and I'm not..."

"Not what? Good enough? Is that what you were going to say? I hope I haven't given you that impression." She set her forearms on the table and leaned in. "The reason we can't be together has nothing to do with you."

He stared at her for a long moment. "It sure feels like it has everything to do with me."

"There are good reasons we can't go back." *I don't trust you to be here when I need you.*

"I need to know what is so terrible that we can't start over."

She shoved the plates back and then shifted her gaze to meet his, surprised to see a glint of hope on his face. "Fate deals some interesting cards." She watched the muscles in his jaw pulse, and studied the eyes that missed very little. "I need to tell you something." She reached across to him just as a shadow fell across the table.

"Karly. Thad. You need to come with me." Sheriff Joe's official duty tone of voice sure didn't produce warm fuzzies.

"Is everything all right?" She sat back

against the leather fabric, questions and worry clouding her mind.

"I just got a call. Several, actually. Someone's released your animals. They're running all over town."

Karly shoved out of the booth and rotated in a circle, not sure what to do first. "Do you think this has something to do with the break-in?"

Joe shrugged, his eyes narrowing, becoming cold. "It might. I'm heading over there now. Ernie's already there."

"I'm coming." Thad stood and rested his hand on the small of her back. The soothing support calmed the explosion of adrenaline galloping through her system.

"Sheriff," Thad leaned closer, "if your dispatcher can relay the incoming calls from residents to our cell phones, Karly and I will pick up the animals. It will only take us a few minutes to strap kennels into our truck beds."

Joe gave Thad a nod. "The military taught you to think on your feet."

"I know how to prepare, plan, and engage. With help and an organized plan, we should be able to get all the animals back safely."

"Sheriff?" Chase Daniels appeared from the pool area. "I just heard what happened. I've got a truck. Need some help?"

"Do you know how to catch a dog or a few cats?" Joe raised a brow.

Chase chuckled. "I've got some buffalo jerky. That should do the trick."

"Unless someone wants to order a dozen hamburgers to go," Thad added. "Everyone loves Mad Jack's burgers—dogs and cats included."

For a few seconds, there was silence as the four of them looked around the circle, then Joe started to smile, then Chase, then Karly.

"Let's get started." Joe turned toward the exit.

The uninhibited confidence on Thad's face made her melt. At that moment, he just about dissolved all the reasons she had for keeping him at a distance, except for the one. The one, insurmountable reason. He'd hate her when he learned what happened.

She needed to concentrate on her animals, and their safety. A cat might get hit by a car, or a dog drown in the river, or never being able to find the rodents. She was responsible.

Whoever was behind sabotaging her business was doing a good job, but she wouldn't allow them to hurt the innocent.

The animals were her responsibility.

CHAPTER THIRTEEN

T had drove down River Creek Road, having loaded his last two escapees in the kennels. The rapid temperature drop gave him a bit of a chill. He scanned the neighborhood to see if his headlights triggered the glow of another animal's eyes.

Poor Karly. She must be going crazy.

The night air circulated through the truck's cabin, producing a subtle white noise, giving him a chance to think about possibilities. A few weeks ago, he didn't think he had any, but Karly changed that.

He'd been wrong to let her go. She was

stronger and more flexible than he realized. She just might have learned to be a soldier's wife after all. He could deal with whatever life threw at him, but only if Karly was in his life.

For whatever reason, she loved him. She might not have said it directly, but she'd demonstrated her love in little ways. She'd fussed about his leg, tried to find him a job, defended him, just like she did in high school. She might be the only one who loved the real him, not a reflection of what others thought of him. He never understood why, but she loved him, dents and all. She needed support, and he'd be there, because sooner or later her family members would let her down. They always did. And no matter what it was she was hiding, he could deal with it.

When he arrived outside of Helper Shelter, she was the first out the front door.

"I've got a total of five in the back," he said, leaning out before shutting off the engine.

She reached out to touch an arm.

"Thanks." She shined a flashlight in the kennels. "I'll mark them off the list." She hurried back inside.

Her touch seemed insignificant, yet was so casually intimate it made his pulse beat double-time. He backed into the nearest parking spot. Several volunteers raced out to help unload the animals. Karly returned with a clipboard and highlighter. "Finding the rodents and lizards will be almost impossible. They may be gone for good. We're still missing a cat and four dogs."

"Maybe this is fate's way of helping you decide how to consolidate your business. Maybe boarding and dog training is what you need to focus on."

"Those are certainly the most profitable parts of my business."

"We just need to figure out how to get enough money to keep you going for now."

"Right now, it's not about the money. I need to do what I can to make sure these animals are safe. I don't know how I'm going to ever thank all these volunteers."

"They love these animals, as much as they care for you." *We all love you Karly. I wish you could see that.* He studied the tree line. "I'll get a flashlight and see if the last of the bunch might be close by."

She moved next to him while he unlocked his tool case. "You're exhausted. There are already a dozen people out searching. I can't ask you to do any more. You've done enough."

He studied her face. *Nice try. I'm not falling for you sending me home.*

If they hadn't been at the bar together, she would have called everyone, but him. He knew that, and he hated knowing it. The fact was, he knew her.

He lifted a flashlight from the metal case. "Tell you what. I'll join the search crew, and we'll start a grid search. At the end of two hours, we'll call it a night, and start the search again at daylight—and that includes you. Deal?"

"No, I need to stay here. The animals are

upset. A human presence will help keep them calm."

"Mara called to check on my status. She told me Mrs. Gaccione, Brianne, and the sleepover crowd decided to set up tents in the back. There are more than enough hands to help calm the animals. Mara's your business partner. Let go for once."

"But—" She lifted that perfect, stubborn chin. "Why are you doing this?"

He dipped his head and gently placed his mouth on hers for a slow, healing kiss before pulling back. "Do you have to ask?"

Seconds had passed before she released control. "Thank you," she said quietly, this time without a smidgeon of defeat or failure.

Heck, yeah. He'd take the small win.

In the dark of night, the streetlights from the bridge and her building reflected off the tears of relief shimmering in her eyes. He'd had bullets whizz over his head, bombs go off next to him, and planes fly so low they shook the ground he walked on, but nothing terrified him more than the way she had wrapped around his heart, refusing to let go. He wanted to be the man she saw when she looked at him.

She stared at him for a good long while before she took a step back. "I'll round up a few more folks so you can brief them on that grid search thing you want to do."

Halfway around the building, several volunteers emerged from the tree line, and people poured out of the building. Many he didn't know ran over. "We found them," echoed on the night's breeze. "We just need a couple more halters and leashes."

Several women grabbed what they needed and headed off. "I guess they don't need either of us after all."

"Maybe not me." Thad wrapped a hand around her back. "You. We all did this for you."

She looked around at the people working with the animals, helping settle them, giving baths to those that needed them, doing whatever was necessary to help her business.

"I can't believe these people just showed up."

"I can. This is Elkridge. People help each other."

"But…" She sniffled, and her lip quivered.

He shoved the flashlight into his pocket, and opened his arms wide to invite her in. She only hesitated for a minute before walking the two steps into his embrace. Her shoulders trembled, then began to shake as the building tension released and converted into liquid emotions.

The evening wind picked up, but he shielded her from the gusts that swirled around their intertwined bodies. The skies were clear, and the moon had risen. The building allowed them to stay in the shadow —to enjoy their own little corner of peace.

Ten years ago, Thad wouldn't have appreciated this moment. A hug was taken for granted. A loving kiss brushed aside. A soft word spoken ignored. Not anymore. He'd seen the short side of life. A life snuffed out in an instant.

Slowly, her emotional vibrations eased and became still. Karly wiped her nose with the sleeve of her fleece jacket. "I don't know why I'm crying. You come back to town, and I turn into a weepy wimp."

"I wouldn't classify you in the weepy wimp category."

"No? What category would you put me in?"

"I would put you squarely in the seriously strong category."

She adjusted her baseball cap, then played with her ponytail woven through the back. "Strong? Me?"

"Don't like that one, huh? How about beautifully brave?"

"Now you're patronizing me."

She stood there with her pouty expression, her hair rippling in the breeze, studying him with those purposeful eyes, and he wondered if he'd ever seen anything more beautiful. She thought he was here to help her, but in reality, every touch, smile, or friendly poke helped him heal.

He took a step closer, carefully backing her up against the building. "Never patronizing, but maybe a bit more honest than you want to hear."

"But—"

"Don't fight me, Karly. Don't fight this." He lowered his head to remind her of all the reasons she was good for him. He pressed deeper, and then finally her hand fisted his shirt and yanked him closer still, her grip urgent. She released a growl of frustration, wrapped her arms across his shoulders and pulled, circling her legs around his hips.

Yes. He pushed her up against the metal wall to let his hands explore. She kissed his neck and nipped his chin with abandon.

His legs weakened, and he locked his knees, pressing harder against her.

"Thad?"

"I'm right here. I've got you, babe."

The heat between them exploded, with hands and arms moving in different directions, fighting to memorize every inch of skin.

"You might want to take that PDA someplace else," Sheriff Joe's voice conveyed a hint of sarcasm, "before I have to write you both a ticket for indecent exposure."

Thad pressed his hands up against the building while Karly slid her legs down off his hips, hiding her face.

"That's a good idea," Thad said, not taking his eyes off her, a chuckle lodged in his throat.

"No, it's not." Karly pushed on his chest, but he wasn't willing to let her go, not yet.

"Tell you what," Joe continued. "Mara and I are going to stay with the kids. You two take off. Get some...um...rest."

"I can't just leave." Karly started to duck under his arm, but the absence of her heat made him realize what he wanted. Screw it. He wanted her now.

She took two steps before he tugged on her arm, spun her around, and threw her over his shoulder. She landed with a soft oof.

"I'll take you up on that offer, Sheriff. Mighty obliged."

Karly slapped his rump. "Let me down."

The sheriff laughed. "And drive the speed limit. I don't want any more calls tonight. I have six youngsters wanting popcorn, pizza, and a movie. My sisters are setting up a projector even as we speak."

"Yes, sir."

"Sheriff." Karly kicked her feet before Thad could wrap an arm around them, blocking her. "You need to arrest this man, for…"

"Karly?" Thad stopped to adjust her weight. "Do you want me arrested, or do you just want to see me in handcuffs?"

When she pounded on his back, Thad started laughing. He gave her a smack on the butt, and that quieted her for about three seconds. At the truck, he set her down next to the passenger door. "Do you want food, shower, or bed?"

"We've had food."

His brow lifted. "That leaves shower or bed."

She lifted on her toes and bit his chin, then eased back. "Why can't I have both?"

"See? That's why we're good together. Get in."

In the truck, she still looked a bit dazed, and he had no doubt that, once they were at his cabin, she'd fall asleep in less time than it took him to shower off. He took her hand and drove the few minutes to his place in silence. She just sat, unmoving, as he shut off the truck's engine.

"Would you have rather gone back to your place?"

She shook her head and then looked at him. "No. I'm just tired."

"You're way beyond tired."

"No. I mean I'm emotionally drained. We've had this push and pull thing going for a few weeks now. Tonight reminded me that anything can happen. Just once, I'd like to be with you without my worries interfering. Do you think we can get through tonight without all the tugging back and forth?"

He reached over and drew a line with his

finger down the side of her face, under her jaw and then down her throat. "I've always believed you could do better than me. You can do anything you want, choose any guy in this town, yet you've always chosen me. I don't understand why. Maybe that's why I've always struggled with what goes on between us. Tonight, I won't question why. The answer is yes. Yes, Karly, I won't fight this. You make my nightmares go silent. That's a good thing."

She looked at the cabin. "Then what are we waiting for?"

"Wait here. Give me two minutes." He shot out of the truck, opened the front door, and went in the house. He lifted the emergency candles from the cabinet and placed them around his room, lighting them as he went. After he put the third candle on the side table, the front door opened.

He turned. The moonlight flowing in from the windows outlined her silhouette. She looked like an angel. He drew a shaky breath and reached out to take her hand.

"This is your dance, Karly. I'll follow where you lead," he said, giving her an opt-out card. "There is shampoo in the bathroom cupboard. I think it's the kind you like. Plus a clean towel and a new toothbrush."

"You bought me shampoo?" She searched his eyes. "Did you think you might get lucky?"

"Call me optimistic. I also have condoms in my nightstand drawer."

A weird expression crossed her face, then evaporated just as quickly. "I want to make the awful things that happened today go away." She reached for the edge of his shirt to lift the cotton fabric over the top of his head. "I want you, under the covers, right now, Lopez."

He grabbed her around the waist and started to walk her backward toward the bed, toward paradise. "That sounds like a perfect plan."

CHAPTER FOURTEEN

Thad kissed her shoulder, and Karly yanked at the top button of his jeans.

She wanted him naked, fast.

He skimmed out of his pants. She threw off her shirt. The bra came next, then socks. She molded her body to his, trying to cling to his skin like plastic wrap. Tight. Perfectly sealed.

Making him lose control.

Making her mind stop thinking about all the reasons she shouldn't be doing this.

When he slid her cotton hipsters to the

floor, pure joy surged through her limbs, and fought back the plague of doubt.

He made the years of resentment and loneliness melt away, and she tried desperately not to worry if the feeling would last, or if she'd regret being with him in the morning.

His muscles bunched when he picked her up to place her in the middle of the bed, and then crawled onto the bed slowly.

"Are you sure about this?" he asked, his voice rough. His need clear.

She closed her eyes, beating back her indecision. "I'm sure," she said, with confidence she didn't quite feel.

Her heart began to churn with raw emotion while he kissed her belly. His glorious, warm, muscular mass made her female parts eager for more. He nuzzled her throat, working his way across to her mouth, then back down to her breasts.

"You are so beautiful."

Joy crowded out any other feeling. "So

are you." She ran her hand down his side, sliding over the ridges of his scars.

She arched to meet him. He cupped her bottom to pull her core against the most mouthwatering erection, then he kissed her.

"I need you, Karly." She couldn't mistake the urgency in his voice.

"I need you, too," she echoed, this time believing the words. "Make love to me."

Twining her arms around his neck, she made her point by pressing her mouth against his, pressing hard, with a little bit of sloppy.

"I'm taking my time. The first time was a little rushed."

She bit his cheek. "No you're not. I want you now. Right now." *Before I change my mind.* She kissed him hard, wild, releasing the sexiest, most erotic sounds from him she'd ever heard. Her breath came in short bursts.

"Karly," he whispered and buried his fingers in her hair. "I want you. I want this."

Thad ignored her commands. Apparently more interested in ticking items off his own agenda, he slipped his fingers between her thighs. Her core burned, and she wiggled and pressed harder against his fingers. He licked and kissed. Every tiny caress magnified the sensations cascading throughout her entire core. He was hot. She wanted more.

"Thad…please."

He shifted, pinning her to the bed, and rolled on a condom.

"Hurry!"

She shivered, needing his warmth to wrap her in ecstasy. He pressed his mouth to her throat while one of his hands caressed her nipple. She cupped his face until their eyes met. "Now, Lopez."

There was no air between them as he slid a thigh between hers.

"Now?" He murmured the words before kissing her hard, demanding her attention. And as soon as she returned his kiss, he pushed into her. Mutual gasps of pleasure punctuated their joining. She was ready, but he eased her back down, only to build her up again.

What was it about this man, who could make her want things she'd never believed possible? She closed her eyes to savor every sensation, but then she wanted to watch him. Connect. See the moonlight dance across his skin. Let his body tell her things he never could say aloud.

He pushed in, deeper. Every thrust coming harder, faster. "Thad. I know you don't like people telling you what to do," she gasped for air. "But if you don't hurry up…"

"You'll what?" His breath was hot and warmed her neck.

She wanted more. "You'll regret it," she declared, with clear intent.

"Yes, ma'am. I aim to please." His eyes turned dark, and he thrust hard. "Is this what you want?" He pulled out almost all the way and thrust again.

"Heck, yeah."

The ride was exquisite. She went up and up and up. A dozen more thrusts, and she exploded like pop on a hot day, thoroughly, completely—a sugary sweet mess.

He arched back, his need taking over. A minute later he jerked his release on a groan, then he went limp and collapsed.

Her chest heaved while she struggled to catch her breath. He slid his hand under the nape of her neck and gently lifted her mouth to his.

She expected him to roll off and braced for his absence, but he remained. A soft rumble started in his belly, then turned into a full-fledged laugh, and she shoved his shoulder.

"What's so funny?" She turned his head to better see his expression.

He held his weight on his elbows before he tucked and rolled to the side, resting a leg over her hip, keeping their bodies connected. Her forehead rested on his chest. Her breath brushed his skin, followed by goose bumps. He buried his face in her hair.

"That was…that was awesome."

Awesome didn't describe the feeling, but

there wasn't another word that was better. She nudged him with her elbow. "Can we do that again?" she murmured. "Only, this time we do it at my pace."

"Are you trying to kill me?" His teeth sank lightly into her shoulder.

Shifting upward, she kissed his ear, then the little spot under his jaw. He hissed his excitement.

"Two can play that game." He returned the gesture by pushing away, flicking his tongue across her nipple, then blowing.

"You've learned a thing or two."

"Hold on, let me get rid of this." He pulled a tissue from the box on the dresser and disposed of condom number one. "Give me a minute, and I'll show you a few more tricks."

"No." She giggled at his reaction and pushed him onto his back, riding him to the top.

He tried to touch her, but she forced his hands above his head. She kissed and nibbled him again even harder than the last time. "My turn."

She took her time licking, teasing, her moves bolder and bolder, until he had time to recover. When he stiffened again, satisfaction zipped up and out, stimulating every cell. She reached for another condom and rolled the rubber sheath in place.

She shifted, putting her hands on his chest and slowly lowering onto him. When she rose onto her knees, he thrust his hips up just as she pressed her weight back down. His hands circled her waist while her core tightened, and she rose again. She threw her head back, relishing the dreamy, giddy experience of making love with the man she loved. When she lifted, he gave her a hard thrust, forcing her to gasp his name. Her thighs tightened against his sides. He held on while she rode him hard, their breaths panting in sync, making everything else in his world disappear.

She wanted to mark him.

No matter what happened between them, she wanted him to remember this night— this one night, never to be repeated—

because the shields she'd put in place to protect him, to protect his heart, were weakening. She needed to be strong enough to walk away.

She threw her head back and screamed into the night, as he pooled his energy to give her what she wanted and thrust into her core, once, twice, before her inner muscles began to spasm and she collapsed onto his chest.

She lay still, listening to his breathing and the beat of his heart slowly dial back to a normal rhythm. His hands slowly moved up and down her back.

She savored the smell of his sex musk. Gently, he rolled her to his side, efficiently disposing the condom, then framing her body with his arms, chest, and legs. He hauled the blanket up from the foot of the bed, tucking her in while her heartbeat slowed.

When his breathing evened, and his body grew heavy, she kissed his chest and whispered, "I love you, Thad."

The idea wrapped around her like a summer's breeze. She loved him. She always would, but it didn't mean they could ever be together, in the real sense. He'd hate her when he discovered what happened.

She just wanted a bit more time before she had to let him go.

CHAPTER FIFTEEN

Karly woke up stiff. She'd slept hard...then realized she wasn't lying on a bed. She was sprawled on top of Thad.

She didn't dare move. Her cheek was plastered against his chest, and her legs were so intertwined with his, she'd never be able to untangle the mess without waking him. She opened one eye. The room was a disaster—a teenager's room on steroids. She closed her eyes with a grimace.

"It's all right. I'm awake," he rumbled, sliding a hand up her back, gently caressing.

Her insides trembled with the memories of her wildest fantasy, only the dream had been real. Her sensitive female parts were proof.

She gave in to the inevitable embarrassment. "Please tell me I didn't snore or drool."

"Okay, if you want me to, but your snore is rather cute. I like it."

She used his chest as leverage to roll to the right. "No one likes snoring."

His arm circled her back, keeping her from going too far. "I like yours."

The sexy vibration of his voice and the memories of their lovemaking made her insides quiver. Her heart pulsed. Her body temperature climbed.

"What time is it?" she asked.

"Why? Are you going somewhere?"

He slid his hand down to her lower back, lifting her up within reach of his mouth, placing little kisses on her nose, lips, chin, anywhere he could reach, aiming for a repeat performance.

"Mmmm, Thad?"

"Not yet."

He slid his tongue across her mouth, tasting, tempting her to let him in. An onslaught of tingling sensations sang through her core. He could make her come alive in ways she'd never thought possible. It was like Fourth of July fireworks, Christmas lights, and New Year's confetti rolled into a single thrill.

"What do you mean, not yet?" she pushed away

"Too late."

His hand skimmed over her shoulder blades.

"You are so frustrating. Why won't you answer my questions?"

There was that push and pull again.

A slow, sexy-ass smile lit his face. "I was hoping we could have a slow start to our day. As soon as your brain wakes up, it's all business."

"When you own a business, I'm afraid it's

all work. I'm constantly thinking about feeding, washing, placing the animals. Speaking of which, I should make sure the girls got all the puppies and kittens back in their cages."

"I'm not talking about Helper Shelter." He placed a hand on her hip.

"You're not?"

"No. Helper Shelter is a part of you—an important part. I'm talking about the sterilized version of you, the one you showed to your dad, mom, and brothers. The side of you that would rather appease and avoid conflict than fight for what's right. You tiptoe around the issues so you don't have to hurt anyone's feelings. Like now. I bet you're thinking of ways you can leave, but you'll stay, just because you think it's the polite thing to do. Just once, Karly, I'd like to see you live without regrets."

Damn you. You know me too well. "Well, that 'all business' you talk about has gotten me this far."

"I get that. In boot camp, the instructors pushed until I was completely exposed. I could draw on fear or anger or resentment, whatever they threw at me, until they pushed past my defenses. For some, it can get ugly. Civilians can go all their lives without getting comfortable with the uncomfortable."

"What is your biggest fear?" she asked while drawing small circles on his chest.

He turned to look at the wall, then the ceiling, his jaw working out a response. He released a long-held breath and looked straight into her eyes. "Not having the confidence to stand my ground when the shit went down."

"The day I left, my dad beat me because our parents didn't want us to be together, but there was more. I only told Kenny part of the story."

"So tell me all of it."

"My dad had been out drinking, and was still pretty drunk when he got home. He woke my mom and demanded she make him some eggs over easy. Because she was still half asleep, ma broke a yolk. When I heard the shouting, I crept downstairs. Sarah was standing in the hall, begging me to do something. Anything."

"What were you supposed to do? You were barely eighteen."

"Protect the innocent. The only crime my mother ever committed was not leaving her abuser." Thad put a forearm over his forehead while his words got smaller and smaller. "He beat me from one end of the house to the other. The last punch I ducked, and he hit the doorjamb. After that, I took off. I ran. I didn't stand my ground."

Her heart ached for the boy, but she wanted to weep for the man. All these years he'd felt responsible. She reached toward his face, but he turned away.

"He put my mom in the hospital that day. Don't feel sorry for me. It's misplaced. The Army drilled me until I could stand and shoot while bullets and bombs went off around me."

"Is that supposed to scare me?"

"No, just the opposite. I won't run anymore. I know my limitations. The Army pushed me until I figured out which side of the line I wanted to be on. I chose to be the guy who wouldn't run, when shit was going down, I would take it."

She lifted onto her elbow and slid her arm around his neck and kissed him with a slow I'm-going-to-take-my-time kiss. Letting go, she tugged on his arm, making sure he was paying attention.

"No regrets sounds nice."

"There don't have to be regrets. Not between us, Karly."

She lay on her back, intending to pull the covers up, hide, escape from the scrutiny, but then she remembered. Thad didn't judge. He might get jealous, want her for himself, but he never judged her. He always took her side. Always. "Then you'll have to help me learn how to live that way. I can't change overnight. We need to take it slow."

"I can do that."

"What do you say we go feed the dogs, and then get started on updating my website and working on that social media stuff you were talking about?"

"You'll seriously allow me to help you?"

"Uh-huh," She slid her finger down the side of his face, over the sharp early-morning stubble. "Right after you show me last night wasn't a one-off."

He lifted his head and took playful aim at her finger with a snap of his teeth. "Is that a challenge?"

No regrets, she chanted. "As a matter of fact, yes."

She squealed when he flipped her onto her back, then silenced her surprised gasp with a kiss before making his way slowly toward her belly, licking and caressing and kissing his way along. He took his time, because he always took his time, and she let him. His fingers played with her folds, teasing her until she writhed with need. The sizzling sensation balanced on a knife edge between good and bad. Since she was sore from the previous night's lovemaking, the intensity made her gasp. She reached to push his hand away, but he held her wrist and continued the in and out, back and forth until the feel was too exquisite to ask him to stop.

"Please," she whimpered.

Her muscles quivered with each small touch, stroke, and kiss.

He temporarily changed the rhythm, then slid two fingers deep, sending her up that sensual ladder until she reached the top and exploded. As she slid down the other side, she sank into the mattress. She couldn't move. Her bones had melted into mush. He slowly made his way back up and stretched out beside her.

"Now that's what I call a morning wake-up call," he said in a raw, husky voice, telling her she wasn't the only one affected by the morning's activities.

"Oh, baby," she managed to whisper. "And you've got my number. Now, it's your turn."

She leaned in to show Thad a thing or two, but a familiar chiming ringtone filled the room. Karly pushed away and she scrambled to the end of the bed and scrounged through a pile of clothes on the floor.

"Mom. What's up?" She managed to ask before sliding off the bed and landing in a sprawling heap.

"Mom? Mom? You there?" She rubbed her head. *Ouch.* "Yes…I'm fine. No. No, need to stop by. I'm on my way to the kennel to… um…feed the dogs. Don't worry. I'm fine. Lunch. Today? Well, I…sure. I will be there at ten. Yep. 'Bye, Mom."

Thad's face suddenly appeared above her head as he peered over the edge of the bed. He brushed the hair off her face.

"Don't say it," she warned.

"Don't say what? That you give in to your mom every time?"

She let out a slow, unsteady breath. He

kissed her forehead and then pushed off the bed. Her gaze rolled up his gorgeous body, skimming over his scars, pausing at the message board and the clearly posted sign showing he wanted her in the worst way. Her mouth pooled with longing, and she licked her lips.

"I'm going to take a cold shower. I suggest you do the same. Especially if you need to deal with your mother."

"Want to come with me? Use some of those military moves to fend off my mom?"

"Now, that would be torture. And here I thought you liked me." The scrunched-up funny face she gave him made him smile. "How about I stop by after I help Chase estimate a job? We can review ideas for your website and Facebook page. How's that sound?"

"Sounds like the business."

A spark lit his eyes, then his white, semi-crooked teeth made her wonder. "We could always go out to Rivers Bridge. I could pick up some subs. I have blankets. We could hang out."

Her imagination took over, and her muscles began to heat.

"I think we had better stick to the business plan. It's safer that way."

"You sure about that?"

"U-huh." She managed to say, before he pulled her closer for a kiss.

CHAPTER SIXTEEN

Three days later, Thad was still trying to conquer the guilt for feeling joy while his best buddies had died because of his carelessness.

Holding Karly in his arms, feeling her respond to his touch, was still the only thing he wanted to think about.

God, Karly was such an adrenaline rush.

Chase Daniels even recognized the recent change and gave him crap about his just-got-laid glow. Thad had seen the goo-goo effect on other guys and had refused to believe it would ever happen to him.

But it had. Karly had recaptured his heart. The thing was, he didn't want to take it back.

Driving up the ridge into the sun to meet Karly for a run, he caught his goofy smile in the visor mirror. His skin felt stretched from smiling so much.

After parking his truck next to Karly's and noting the Sheriff's SUV, he hopped out and made his way around to the trailhead. He spotted Karly up ahead in her usual running pants and pink short-sleeve shirt. Au naturel had always fit her like a stylish pair of wraparound sunglasses.

He increased his pace when Karly suddenly pointed at the ridge, tossed her hands in the air, then leaned a bit too close to the sheriff. By the time Thad arrived, the air sizzled around them like lightening had just struck the ground.

"I don't understand." Karly tugged on the leads of three dogs, who were milling around, ready to run. "This trail has never been closed."

The perturbed crispness in Karly's voice couldn't be ignored. Thad nodded to Sheriff Gaccione and the other woman with him, then stopped beside his irritated beauty.

The stranger took a step forward, but Joe gave her a look, and the tall woman backed off. Based on the look on the woman's face, she was used to giving orders, not taking them. Thad noted the pin on her jacket. DEA. *What's a drug enforcement agent doing in Elkridge?*

"Karly, Thad, this is Gabrielle Dalton. I've invited her up from Denver to audit and observe. She's going to help with some training over the next couple weeks."

"Gabrielle, welcome to Elkridge." Karly managed a smile, but Thad could see brewing disappointment behind her flash of white teeth.

The sheriff pointed a thumb over his shoulder. "A mountain lion's been spotted on the ridge. We're closing the trail as a precaution."

"A mountain lion?" Karly leaned forward

to pet one of the rescue dogs. "That's strange. Have you contacted Animal Services?" The Australian Shepherd mix whined anxiously, watching Karly closely for the signal to run. "I haven't seen any tracks or signs of a big cat." She turned to Thad. "You don't think that's what the hunter was shooting at, do you?"

"Hunter? What hunter?" Joe asked before Thad could respond.

"Someone fired a rifle while we were running a couple of weeks back," Thad replied, then hesitated, thinking Karly wouldn't appreciate him adding the details of her tumble downhill, taking a moment to revise his statement. "Whoever fired the shot scared some deer across our path, and caused a problem with the dogs."

"Which trail?" The question shot out before Joe could ease his emotions back into his usual casual calm. "No one has a permit to be shooting off random rounds at deer or otherwise."

Thad had seen the expression on the

sheriff's face before. Concern. Frustration. Resolve. Joe didn't hide his feelings any better today than he had in high school. Thad did another sweep of the ridge. "We were on the upper ridge, the one connecting to the trail just behind my cabin. Come to think of it, we probably should have called in the shooting."

"I agree." Curiosity deepened the lines around Joe's eyes. "But why do you think so?"

"I've lived in this area as long as you have. I don't know of any hunter up here carrying a lighter caliber rifle, say something like a .223. Hunters prefer the larger caliber, just in case they run across a bear or moose or an aggressive elk."

Karly's eyes widened. "You don't think that guy was after the mountain lion, do you?" She studied Joe. "I've read articles about local poachers selling pelts on the black market."

Joe finished locking the metal gates to the Lonely Ridge Trail parking lot. Karly looked downright gorgeous in her flurry of frustration. The DEA agent-slash-observer didn't seem impressed.

"The cat was just spotted a couple of days ago, so I think he's fine."

"That's good. He can still be relocated before the park service is forced to put him down."

Good? Thad wouldn't use that descriptor. While working in the military, he'd learned to spot a liar, and the sheriff was weaving a mighty fine tale. Something was going on, but he didn't want to upset Karly.

Thad took a sip of water and handed the bottle to Karly. "Looks like we need to find someplace else to run," Thad said to take the pressure off Joe to come up with any more excuses. Then again, he wouldn't mind a few more answers himself.

"There are a couple of trails behind my place," Thad glanced west in the direction of his cabin. "The path is not as well groomed, but we should be able to run a good five miles before it gets too rocky."

Thad caught an odd expression crossing the sheriff's face before Joe locked it down tight. *Just as I thought. It's not just this part of the ridge you're worried about.*

"Why don't you use the River Creek trail?" Joe suggested. "The path by the river is popular."

"It's popular," Karly picked up the conversation thread, "and tends to be muddy and full of people. That's why we like to run these trails. It's easier with several dogs, and baths aren't required afterward. Plus, rescues are not entirely predictable when it comes to dealing with other dogs. I wouldn't want to risk something happening."

Joe shifted and gazed at the opposite ridge. "You could always go over to Mountain Ridge Road. It's got some nice logging trails."

"We could, but the round-trip drive adds an extra forty minutes to exercise outings." Karly unwound the leash from around the sheepdog's prancing paws. "You sure we can't run on this trail?"

"It's not a good idea."

The Sheriff tried, again and again, to come up with options. Karly shot down every single one of them. The harder Joe tried, the more the hairs on the back of Thad's neck stood up and took notice. He got the impression more was going on than the sheriff wanted to share, and the DEA woman looked positively hostile.

Thad ran a hand down Karly's tense arm. "There is no sense standing around getting the dogs," *and you,* "all wound up. Let's load the dogs. After that, we can decide where to go. Nice to meet you, Gabrielle."

The relief on the sheriff's face was easy to read. "Thad." Joe reached out a hand. "If I remember right, you left school early to serve in the Army."

"I was there for ten years." Joe held his hand longer than necessary. He was probing for something. Thad shrugged. "Why, do you have a job opening?"

Sheriff Joe gave him a touché kind of smile. "Might be an opening soon, if the budget is approved," Joe added as an afterthought. "Be careful on your run. You spot anything, let me know."

Thank goodness Karly let her irritation put a cramp in her attention span. She'd already zoned out. Thad, on the other hand, was paying close attention, not only to what the sheriff said, but what his body language contradicted. The DEA agent was also a virtual whiteboard of information.

Interesting.

Thad scanned the ridge behind them and saw a reflection flash in the sun. The odd shine that drew his attention. Sun glasses? A rifle scope? A cell phone? Whatever it was, nature didn't produce it.

Someone's watching.

Thad took a step to put himself between Karly and the flash on the hill. "Karly, why don't you load the dogs, and I'll catch up with you in a minute." Karly's frustration turned into an accepting nod and she took the dogs back to her truck parked on the side of the road.

Thad continued to monitor the hillside where he'd seen the anomaly. Without taking his eyes off the ridge, he asked, "Sheriff, speaking of rumors, did I hear your brother was killed a couple of years back? A poacher or something?"

Both Joe and the DEA agent followed Thad's line of sight, squinting against the sun's rays. "My brother was murdered on a logging road just on the other side of this ridge. Why do you ask?"

Murdered? Mysterious break-ins? Mara being stalked? What were the odds?

Thad kept his posture casual so as not to cause alarm. "Mind if I ask how long you intend to keep this trail closed?"

"For now, indefinitely." Joe rested his hand on his utility belt and shifted his weight as he relaxed. "Your help would be much appreciated. It's my job to keep this town safe."

"Probably a good idea. Someone's up there now, watching. During our discussion, I saw another flash of light, like the sun reflecting off metal. My guess is a rifle scope." Thad held out his hand, and Joe readily accepted the gesture. "Sheriff. Gabrielle. Watch your backs." Thad forced his face into neutral to avoid showing aggression or weakness and took a step toward the trucks. "I'll make sure Karly finds another trail to run on."

"Have a nice day," the DEA agent's eyes narrowed as her dark face went rock hard. Her tight pixie curls might have made her look stylish if it hadn't been for her don't-mess-with-me expression. She'd been around. Seen things. Possibly experienced things. He wasn't about to deliberately put himself in her path.

Thad took one more good survey of the ridge. The area was only a couple miles from his cabin. He'd give it a once-over, get an idea what was lurking in his backyard. He didn't like surprises.

"Have a nice day, ma'am." Thad made his way toward the parking lot.

As he drew closer, he noted Karly had

finished loading the dogs. "I was thinking—"

"Now that's another problem," Karly turned his way. A glitter of a laugh made her eyes shine in the morning sun. "You thinking."

Thad loved the way Karly's eyes sparked when she teased. The familiar expression made his thoughts rotate from concern to contented. He rested his arm on the truck bed ledge. "I was thinking," he began again, this time on a lighter note, "I haven't run the trail by the Elkridge Cemetery since I've been home. I know it's on the other side of town, but why don't we check it out? See if it's as good a trail as I remember."

"Do you remember when we used to go up there to kick back, look at the stars, play some music?"

"Those were good times." Happy warmth encouraged his muscles to ease. "Remember when Jason Newhall threw up on his grandfather's grave? For the next week he was paranoid his grandfather would haunt him for the rest of his life."

"Oh, oh, oh...and the time Camilla Gaccione convinced her sister, Anna, she only needed to yield at stop signs that have white borders around them?" Karly laughed. "Anna got a traffic ticket on her way home for failure to stop."

If he could capture Karly's essence and stuff it in a vial to carry around with him, he would. He planned to figure out how to make her smile last for an eternity. Being in her company made him feel something other than the darkness. She brought him to life. Hope.

Thad picked a piece of dog fluff off her shirt. "I also remember the night we decided to give each other our virginity."

"I was so nervous I couldn't stop shaking, and you called it off. We fell asleep holding each other under the full moon. The next day our parents were freaked out. I was grounded for a month, and forbidden to ever see you again. I laughed when my mother took me to see her gynecologist that week." Karly's lips eased into a sheepish smile. "You should have seen mom's face when I insisted the doctor verify I was still a virgin." Karly stepped on a rock and rolled it around underneath her running shoe. "I was so mad at my mom, I didn't talk to her for a week."

Thad reached out to touch her hand. "Back then, I don't think either of us got what we wanted." Karly intertwined her fingers into his. The rising body heat blew the doors wide open, and his hand tightened. "I know. You trusted me. That's all that counted. Trusted me until I blew it. Karly, I'm sorry." *#Truly.*

"It's okay. We both wanted things to turn out differently."

"I want to earn your trust again."

She released his hand and took a step back. "I forgave you a long time ago, and I'm working hard on the trust thing. It will take time, but I do want you in my life, it's just…"

Thad pulled her into his arms, his mouth seeking, connecting, exploring. He poured every ounce of sorry into that kiss, hoping she felt his apology.

When he eventually arched back to take in much-needed air, she followed him for only a second before lowering her head.

"Oh, boy." She tucked her chin in. "We should get out of here."

Yes, we should. That shooter's no longer in sight, but I don't want to take any chances. However, that little smile of hers meant something different.

"What's going on in that head?"

"I think my clothes are about to fall off, and that's not good. I haven't even been drinking."

"Not good, huh?" He brushed a thumb across her soft, creamy lips. "I thought you liked getting naked with me."

She looked up, her eyes opening wider. "I meant not good, in a way that all that yumminess shouldn't be on display here, out in the open. Anybody could show up."

A sizzling sensation crept through his system, igniting each cell as it went. He leaned in and nuzzled her ear. "My cabin is not far. Just on the other side of that ridge."

Her hands slid up and pushed. "Tempting, but…"

"But you still don't trust me."

"When it comes to sex, oh, I trust you. When it comes to my heart, I'm still working on it." She took a step back, then another, and another. "Let's go for our run. Then maybe later we can take a shower and see where it goes." She winked, her eyes sparkling with a playfulness he missed when it got buried under her worries.

"I could kiss you again, maybe change your mind."

"Thad…"

"I'd prefer not to have to beg."

"I don't want you to beg." Her gaze held his for way too long for someone who'd decided against giving him her heart.

"Yes, you do." He took a step closer.

She gave him a shove and, like a lightning bolt, was in the driver's seat, started the engine, and backed away. Twenty yards away, she stopped her truck and studied him again before completing a U-turn.

"You coming, or what?"

"Absolutely."

He stood for a long time, savoring the look on her face, listening to the wind move through the trees. He hadn't come back to Elkridge. He'd come back to her.

"Well, what are you waiting for?"

You. Somewhere deep inside she cared, although she was stubborn as on over-packed mule—and she wouldn't ever change. Not that he wanted her to. Everything she'd done, dropping Custer off, trying to find him a job…it had all been to show him what they had wasn't lost.

Then again, maybe he was just a fool.

It wouldn't be the first time he'd made a fool out of himself.

Life rolled in circles. He just needed to figure a way out of the groove, because this time he wouldn't repeat his mistakes.

He eyed the ridge.

Nothing. Not one thing would keep them apart, ever again.

CHAPTER SEVENTEEN

Karly laughed when the hundred-pound shepherd nudged her aside as she placed his food bowl on the floor. "Brutus, mind your manners." She rubbed the large male's stiff ears. The smaller border collie mix ignored the food. He was more interested in busting out of the place.

"Hedge, I'll take you for a walk later."

A menacing growl and focused stare from Brutus made her turn.

"Hello, sweetness."

Karly's heart pounded in her ears. "How did you get in here?"

The man on the other side of the kennel gate laughed. The low, menacing rumble made the hair on her arms stand on end. He looked like a gangbanger. A heavy chain hanging out of his back pocket. Low-riding, loose-fitting jeans that potentially hid a gun, knife, drugs, or just about anything else.

"Who are you?"

Even when he smiled, the demonic, tattooed face told her he wasn't interested in adopting an animal. In fact, he wasn't interested in doing anything she wanted to help with. He wrapped his fingers through the wire fence. "Now, isn't that an interesting question?"

She eased away from the gate. "What do you want?" The demand emerged as a parched squeak. She couldn't swallow.

Brutus stood in front of her, growling, snapping his teeth, but his behavior didn't frighten her. He was doing what he was bred to do: protect.

Tattoo man retrieved a gun out of the

back of his pants. "I came to play." His mouth twisted into a snarling smile.

Karly moved toward the back wall and glanced at the dog door. She'd never fit. "I don't want to play."

"That's too bad." He aimed the gun at Brutus. "Come out now, *coño*, or I shoot the dog."

No. She held out a hand. "Don't shoot." Her mind raced to find options.

Tattoo man rotated the gun sideways, his index finger resting on top. "Come on, then. I don't have all day."

Karly moved to the gate. "You promise not to shoot?"

"I promise." He took a step back. His black and yellow tattooed face reminded her of a serpent's head... fitting, since his blood must be pure, unadulterated venom.

She lifted the gate latch and, as she started to swing the gate open, she drew upon every ounce of willpower she could find and slammed it wide open, knocking him back.

Run. Her mind screamed.

She fought for air.

Pop. Pop. *Brutus, nooooo.* Pop. *Hedge!*

The screaming cries of the dogs nearly destroyed her.

What have I done?

Blood pooled around Brutus's head. Both dogs lay on the floor, unmoving.

When the stalker took a step in her direction, she yanked the container of dog food over and bolted for the front door.

Boom-boom-boom. Her heartbeat pounded in her ears.

She grabbed the front door handle and pushed. *Locked. Key? Where were the keys? The office.*

Her feet slapped against the linoleum floor while she pulled the phone out of her back pocket. She tried to run and dial at the same time, but messed up, hit the delete key and tried again.

Tattoo man's cackles thickened the air around her, making breathing and moving hard.

Grabbing her keys, she turned. All she could see was a wall of man in the hallway. She raced into her office and locked the door. She tried again to phone for help, but the cell slipped out of her hands and hit the floor.

Grief over Brutus and Hedge nearly drowned her, but the handle of the office door jiggled.

Window. Get out. Now.

Dragging the chair over to the filing cabinet, she stood on the chair seat.

Pop. Pop. Pop. Bullets splintered the door.

She shoved with all her might to push open the window, but it wouldn't budge. Her hands shook as she tried the latch again. Just as the window gave way, a hand closed around her ankle.

"Let's play."

"No." She kicked back, "Stay away from me."

Another hand grabbed her other leg and yanked hard.

Her grip on the window slipped.

A scream welled from her core, but she lost her balance, bounced off the chair, and collapsed on the floor, the breath knocked out of her.

Tattoo man grabbed her hair and gave it a painful twist. "No more running."

"P-please let me go."

"Don't worry. I'm going to let you go. In fact, I'm going to make you disappear."

Disappear?

He crushed her phone with the heel of his boot. All hope of rescue was gone. Terror paralyzed her, body and mind.

"Come on. Let's go play."

He hauled her to her feet. With his arm around her neck, his gun to her head, she didn't dare move. He pushed her toward the back entrance.

"Please don't hurt me. Where are you taking me?"

His hot breath made the skin on the back of her neck shrivel away from him. "I'm taking you to paradise."

She gagged, swamped by the foul odors of tobacco and licorice on his breath.

Noooo. This can't be happening.

"Move! That way."

The back door was coming up fast. *Don't let him take you.* The defense instructor's instructions came back. *Fight. Kick. Punch. Anything to get away.*

Two steps away from the door, she mentally prepared. She could do this. She would survive.

A prick on her neck made her swat at the sting. She looked behind her.

"Easy there, *coño.*"

"What did you just do?"

"I sent you to paradise."

The room dimmed.

Legs turned to water.

Can't swallow.

No... Oh, God, no.

CHAPTER EIGHTEEN

T had had reached his limit. He needed a Karly fix. He drove to Helper Shelter and parked in front. For only a split second, he thought about leaving, 'cause she mentioned something about feeling smothered the day before, but...

"Oh, what the hell?" He opened the truck door and slid out. Maybe he could help Karly clear her desk for the day—the fun way.

He headed for the entrance, but he spotted Mara. She was holding onto the metal fence on the side of the building. Buddy stood behind her, the canine's body nudged up against her back legs, his stance rigid and tense.

"Hey, Mara? It's Thad." He called from twenty yards. "Are you okay?"

As he neared, she focused her phone at him. Her tear-streaked face answered his question.

"Joe," she said, her mouth trembling, "Thad just arrived. What do you need him to do?"

"Tell him to stay with you. I'm two minutes away," the sheriff's voice growled from the phone.

"Okay." She pulled her arms closer to her chest, the phone's camera still connected to her husband.

In the distance, Thad could hear the sirens coming from the ridge. The frantic barks coming from the kennel drew his attention.

Just past Mara's shoulder, he spotted the bumper of Karly's truck. An ominous feeling swelled and started to cut off his air, and his vision narrowed, turning gray at the edges.

He fought the effect and forced himself to focus on the present.

His eyes centered on Mara. "Where's Karly?"

"I don't know. I think he took her." Mara's hands shook, her voice small and lost.

His heart slammed against his rib cage and pounded with anger. "Who? Who's taken her?"

"The same guy who's been stalking me. When I got here, I smelled him and called Joey."

"Stay here. I can see the emergency lights. Your husband's almost here."

The voices in his head quieted. His breath evened. His senses became hyper-sharp as he ran toward the back and entered through the storage area, scanning, assessing, processing. He didn't touch anything, only absorbed the placement, smell, details of the evidence. His mind played a possible scene. Karly entered through the back, but someone had been waiting for her. He could smell stale cigarette smoke.

Oh, God, Karly I warned you. I should have insisted on better locks.

The kennel room door, normally closed, was open. Thad lifted an animal catch-pole off the shelf. Slowly, he opened the door with his foot. At a quick glance, it looked as though Karly had opened one of the kennel gates to slow the intruder down, or she had to open the gate to get out, he didn't know which.

One dog lay dead.

Another wounded.

He crouched and brushed a careful hand down the border collie's wounded flank, his hands shaking with anger and sorrow. There was blood. Lots of blood, but the collie's wound didn't look life-threatening. He studied the splatter. The blood seemed to be contained within the kennel area.

Stay calm, he pleaded with himself silently, and moved on. He peered around the corner, down the office hall. *No blood. She's okay. Karly's okay. No blood.*

Spilled dog food scattered across the hall made him pause.

Good girl. You're trying to slow him down. Buy some time.

A few crushed nuggets by the front entrance indicated she'd tried and failed to get the door open. *What did you do next, Karly? What came next? Show me.*

He rounded the corner, taking in the reception desk, then he saw it. Her office door handle shot full of holes.

His breathing stopped.

Forced his feet to move.

One step. Two steps.

He pushed the door open.

The desk was shoved aside. Paper littered the floor. By the back wall, Thad found her cell phone smashed.

No blood. There's no blood. She's alive.

His held breath barreled out of his lungs with the speed of a bullet.

Anger. Revenge. Fear.

I'm going to get you back, Karly. No matter what it takes, I'll bring you home.

His body buzzed with a cocktail of emotions, but he let the anger burn away the fear. He swallowed to engage and concentrate his senses. See what needed to be seen. He backed out of the office slowly and returned to the kennel area and the wounded border collie, grabbing a towel from the shelf as he passed.

"Thad?" a male voice called.

"In here," Thad replied. He applied pressure to the dog's hind leg, and stroked his head.

Karly would want this.

She'd want him to take care of her animals.

He glanced over his shoulder at the sound of footsteps.

"Sheriff. Whoever took Karly is gone. Based on what I saw, she put up one hell of a fight." He pointed. "The shepherd over there is dead. This one will be okay if we can get him to a vet."

"Karly's blood?"

There was blood splatter across the floor,

now on his clothes, his hands. "Don't think so. There's no blood in her office. Karly's still alive. She made it to her office before she was captured." Thad pointed to a pool of blood. "That's her partial footprint there. The evidence leads toward the back door, not toward her office. She did her best to leave us a clue, and I'm sure she walked out of here on her own."

"Good observation. I think you're right. There just might be an opening on my staff for someone like you."

"I know that look." The flicker of the sheriff's eyes made Thad's gut churn. "My captain got it any time he didn't want to tell us something. What is it you're not saying?"

"I need to make a phone call," Joe turned to leave, but Thad stood and grabbed him by the sleeve.

"You know something, and I want to know what it is."

"This isn't just about Karly. This is big. We need to call in backup."

Big? What the hell does that mean?

Thad leaned in. "We need to start looking for Karly—now! You knew there was a threat, and you did nothing to protect her." Explosive anger made his voice low and ominous. "You closed off that ridge for a reason, so I went to have a look. There are tracks on the ridge heading west. I didn't have time before, but I bet if I follow them, I'll find Karly."

Joe's jaw muscles pulsed. "You go anywhere near that ridge, I'll have you arrested."

Thad took a step back. "Then you find her. Bring her back. Close off the highway. Roads. Call in the state troopers. Do whatever you need to do, but get her back." He crouched to attend to the dog to deflect the sheriff's reproach.

"Joey?" Mara called as she walked in through the open door.

"Don't come in here. This is a crime scene."

Mara's hand gripped the doorframe. "Fine. I'll stay here, but I have something to say." She lifted her chin. "For the past two years, you've been mighty secretive. I've never asked you for details. I've never pushed. I won't ask now. However, as your wife and as part of this community, I'd like to remind you that Karly is one of ours." She reached to smooth Buddy's hackles, to ease her service dog's concern. "More than that, she's my friend and business partner. If I find out Karly's been taken because of whatever you've been so secretive about lately, and there was something we could have done to prevent it, then you might not want to come home for a while, because I will say things you don't want to hear."

"Mara—"

"No." She held out her hand. "Call the FBI or DEA or CIA, or whomever you've been having your secret late-night calls with, and get them here, *right now.*"

Joe placed a hand on the back of his neck and squeezed. "Mara, what you're asking is risky. What's going on here is bigger than big. I don't know everyone involved. Shit. I don't even know who to trust. Certainly no one in this town."

"That's not true. There are plenty of people in this town you can trust," Mara said.

Go, Mara. Thad stood to add his presence and support.

"If there are people you don't trust in the department," Mara lifted her defiant chin another inch, "have them come here and process the scene. It'll get them out of the way, and keep them focused. Brianne is safe. Your mom picked her up. Camilla's on her way here. If we hear or sense anything odd, I'll call you. Plus, no one will think twice about me carrying my cell phone around. I'll record everything." Mara waved her phone in the air.

"Call Tony now. I want your brother here as well." Joe gave Thad a once-over. "You up for some surveillance?"

Surveillance? "Always." *But if I see Karly, screw the surveillance.*

"Good. I'll put a call into Chase and Rivers and have them meet at your place."

"Sounds good."

That makes four. Thad had been in the covert operations long enough to know that six was the optimal number, but for Karly, he'd go alone if he had to. "I ran into General Bryant at the Tool Shed, before I came here. Ashley's dad knows tactical operations. He and Bill Mason should be able to help. That makes six."

"What about Grant Newhall, Jenna's husband?" Mara asked.

Joe shook his head. "No. Newhall doesn't have military or first responder training. Everyone else does."

Mara shook her head. "Okay, I get that, but I don't want anything to happen to you. I know you. If Sam's killer slips through because you don't have enough people, you'll never forgive yourself. For the past four days, you've been tense. Something's happening. I can feel it."

"Woman, you're too smart for your own safety."

"Based on your reaction, I'd say you don't

think they have taken Karly far. Am I right?" Mara stepped closer, but it took a couple of tries before she found and placed her hand on her husband's forearm. "You saved me once. You can save Karly."

"Faster than a speeding bullet, right?" Joe planted a kiss on the end of Mara's nose.

What did you get this town into? Thad paced away before he let his adolescent anger return and he took a swing at the guy.

Joe turned to Thad. "Don't do anything stupid, or start searching on your own. I think I know where Karly is being held. I'm waiting for confirmation now. If I'm right, we'll definitely need as much backup as possible."

Thad stood. "If you know where she is, let's go."

"You don't know who we're dealing with, and I do. You go up there now, you'll get shot before you even get close to that place. There are cameras everywhere. Believe me when I say these people are your worst nightmare. If you go charging into that compound, you and everyone inside will be killed, including Karly. There already are several lives in jeopardy. Give me time to make a few phone calls, and get a solid plan together. We'll meet at your cabin. There are people in this town watching, so you need to keep this quiet. Trust no one."

Does that include you?

Joe's eyes darkened, and he assessed Thad. "We'll get Karly home safe. You just need to trust me."

"You just said to trust no one."

Joe's face turned into a block of granite with deep grooves and lines. "I know you want Karly back. So do I."

"Then stop trying to convince me to stay put and call in your backup."

"Thad?"

"I heard you. I'll stick tight, but I'm warning you—if something happens to Karly, that's on you."

CHAPTER NINETEEN

Twenty-one minutes later a car, a couple of trucks, and a patrol cruiser pulled up his drive.

Thad stood on his porch. The what-if monsters plagued his every thought.

What if Joe is wrong?

What if Karly has been moved out of town? Out of the state?

What if she's hurt and needs help?

What if...

Joe was the first out of his car. Gabrielle, the DEA agent he'd seen before, came next. The rest followed. A couple of feet from the cabin, Joe tossed Thad a Kevlar vest and helmet. "Put those on. You might need them, and no arguments. I have more equipment you'll need in my trunk."

"Yes, sir." Thad rolled the lighter than normal vest over to study the label. His startled gaze met Joe's. "What's a small-town sheriff doing with the good stuff? The military can't even get this gear."

"Wait until you see what's in my trunk. I've been stocking up. Where we're going, we'll need every advantage we can get."

Thad assessed the men walking up the gravel path behind Joe. The air practically crackled with energy.

"Thad," Chase nodded curtly.

Thad held out his hand to Chase, then Rivers. As usual, Rivers didn't say anything, just studied his face. Rivers, who always saw a whole lot more than anyone else noticed.

Bill Mason followed, along with Ashley Bryant's father. Bill had mentioned General Bryant preferred to go by the name Dale.

"Gentlemen." Thankfully, Joe's voice

sounded more confident than Thad felt. "I'd like to introduce you to Special Agent Gabrielle Dalton. She's part of a Joint Task Force team that has been assigned to Elkridge."

She's not just here to observe.

"Call me Gabby," she said, studying each individual, assessing the newly formed team. "I've just got word from our inside contact. Karly is safe. There are no plans at this time to relocate. Our contact has bought us some time. So let's take the time to map out a plan."

"You know as well as I do we can't wait." Joe rumbled with frustration. "Get your people in there now. Karly's a civilian. We need to get her out of there."

Gabby turned on Joe. "It's not that simple, and you know it." If the DEA agent had been two inches taller, they might have been nose to nose.

"Then bring us up to speed so we do know what we're dealing with." Chase pushed his statement toward Joe, to get his attention and possibly defuse the tension.

"May I?" Joe removed a rolled map and aerial photographs from his bag and pointed at the kitchen table.

"Help yourself." Thad stepped back. "Whatever you need. Just hurry."

Joe pointed to the back of Lonely Ridge, and the river running alongside. "Years ago, old mining shafts were turned into underground caverns to grow marijuana. By growing their crops deep in the ground, they prevented satellites from detecting the heat signals from the grow lamps."

General Bryant stepped up to the table to survey the map. "What else have you got?"

Joe pointed at an old logging road. "This is where my brother was shot." He moved his finger an inch to the west. "This is the opening to the compound where Karly is being kept. There are three ventilation shafts here, here, and here."

"Compound?" Thad asked, unable to mask his skepticism.

"Best-kept secret in Colorado." Joe pointed. "When Colorado legalized marijuana, there was no need to maintain underground processing. It was too expensive. The growers became legitimate businesses and bought warehouses closer to town. There is still some illegal activity in the forest, but the state is using drones to suss out the growers."

"If the businesses went legit," Chase leaned in to look again at the map, "then why are these caverns, or whatever you call them, still used?"

"Heroin and women." Gabby's intent scrutiny swept the room, pausing at each person.

"Women? What about women?" Thad's heartbeat ramped up.

"The compound was converted into a heroin and meth repacking and distribution facility. Drugs are smuggled in for packaging, and then transported into Canada and other US states." Joe dragged one of the photographs closer. "See this tree-bare spot? It's a landing strip."

"I've seen a couple of small planes lately, but I figured they were hobbyists out for a ride," Thad grumbled.

Rivers pointed to an Indian reservation in the bottom corner of the state. "Federal Regulations don't have jurisdiction on tribal reservations. Anyone can land a plane just about anywhere, and it would be hard to trace. The local tribes need cash, and the drug dealers need safe distribution routes." Rivers drew a line with his finger across the map. "Anyone could fly in and out of here without being noticed."

"But what about the women?" Thad asked again.

"The place needed to be staffed."

He could do without Gabby's superior attitude. "Let me guess." Thad crossed his arms. "Women smuggled in illegally."

"Yes, but these guys are greedy and smart— real smart." Joe pointed to another road leading in from the west. "Drug traffic can be disrupted, so they've diversified. Pregnant prostitutes and sex slaves from California, Oregon, Washington, and Utah are being smuggled in to work the lines until they deliver. Once the babies are delivered, the whole operation shuts down and moves to a new location. It could be six months, a year, or more, until the facility is used again. That's why it's so critical we do this right. If we screw up, there's no telling where they will set up next."

Thad concentrated on the DEA agent. "What am I missing? Why pregnant women?"

"They are less likely to steal or use the drugs. Once the babies are born, the child and fetal material are sold on the black market. The women are then transported back into the sex trade in a different state, with a different handler. According to my intel, a group of women and a large quantity of heroin will be moved in the next couple days."

"But why Karly? She's not pregnant."

Gabby looked at him, her eyes softening a smidge. "No, but based on my intel, when the women are moved, she will be moved with them."

"We need to stop this now." Thad said a couple of decibels below bullhorn level.

Thad was more than ready to take down every one of the bastards involved with selling women and children, but when it came to the bastard who took Karly—he wanted vengeance. Personal vengeance.

Joe put his finger on the entry point of the underground cavern and gave Thad another measuring assessment. "You've had some trouble getting around." Joe pointed at his leg. "I can't have anyone on this team who can't perform."

"I'm good." *And I'll keep telling you I'm good until Karly's back home safe.* No way was he sitting this one out. "You just worry about making sure no one gets out the front. If Rivers can help me locate that underground vent, we can hopefully gather some more information until backup arrives. If shit goes down, I'll get in and out, no problem."

No problem. What the hell am I saying? No problem, my ass.

"If something happens, hold your position." The command in Joe's voice left no room for interpretation.

A cell phone rang and they all checked their phones. Joe put his to an ear. "Yes?" Joe's face went blank. "No. We're not waiting." Joe gave the statement an authoritative punch. "No. You don't understand. I've got one of my people up there. Our plan is to make sure no one gets in or out, but if we are spotted, we're going in, and your two-year operation will be blown. Then I suggest you get word to your inside man. You have less than an hour."

Joe ended the call and looked at the group. "Backup is two, maybe three hours away. We are on our own until then."

A new load of adrenaline shot through Thad. "Rivers, can we get close enough to find out where they're keeping Karly?"

Rivers pointed at Thad's chest. "You sure you won't freeze up when someone points a gun at you?"

Thad gritted his teeth. "We all have a job to do. I'll do mine. You just worry about doing yours."

Joe opened his mouth to say something, but Rivers waved him off and got up in Thad's face. "I know you can do your job. I just wanted to make sure you know it."

Rivers' face cracked in what Thad could only guess was a smile. He wanted to push Rivers aside and race out the door, but he resisted the urge.

"Enough with the niceties," Joe said. "You are all deputized. All that means is you have the authority to make sure no one leaves that compound until backup arrives. Chase and I will make our way to the front of the compound. Thad, Rivers, you two will hump in from here. According to our inside source, this shaft is the closest entrance point to where Karly is being held." Joe turned toward the general. "Did I cover everything?"

"Not quite." Dale moved closer to study the map. "Mason and I will cover the air strip to make sure there is no movement from that direction. That way you have all the exits covered. If something goes wrong, the rendezvous point is here." The general circled with his finger a small ridge just above the compound. "But nothing will go wrong...right, gentlemen?"

"That's right, because we're going to get in position and make sure no one comes out of that compound." Joe nodded. "We'll wait until our backup arrives. No one moves unless I give the signal. Stay out of sight. Understood? I don't want anyone getting shot."

Or killed. Thad understood perfectly. But if he got a whiff of Karly, all bets were off.

Please let this be a nightmare, Karly fought her way out of a drug-induced fog.

Fear licked the back of her throat.

Her vision turned from muted grays to fuzzy colors. She blinked, then blinked again. Her tongue was thick and dry. Her body moaned. Everything hurt. Her hands and feet tingled with tiny pinpricks from lack of circulation. Nothing worked. Every muscle screamed out in pain. She tugged against the metal wrapped around her wrists, only to be rewarded by pain shooting up her arms. She tried freeing her feet. Same result.

A hacking cough broke through her internal panic and expanded her awareness.

Who's there?

A scream welled in her throat, but she gulped back the terror and hid in the silence.

Where am I?

With every breath, she memorized her sterile surroundings. Trays of what looked like instruments of torture. Cots pushed against the wall. Cabinets full of supplies. *Oh, God. Are those chains?*

She fought to remember. Something. Anything.

A man's hot breath. Running. A pinch on the neck. Gloating laughter in her ear. He called her by name. *How did he know my name?* He called her something else...*coño*, maybe?

She wrestled with the metal binding her wrists. The clink of a chain against the cot's frame triggered panic. Nearby voices made her lower her eyelids into a squint. She forced her trembling muscles to still.

A tattooed hand reached from over her shoulder, landed on her breast, and squeezed. A bitter acid taste burned the back of her throat. She dared not move.

"Macedo, what the hell are you doing?" a woman she couldn't see demanded. "You know better than to handle the inventory."

Inventory? What the hell does that mean?

Karly cracked her eyes open enough to see a petite woman in a white lab coat looking at her. "Taking that woman from town was a very stupid move. People will start looking for her, if they haven't already."

Her kidnapper stepped closer to the woman, his nose inches from her face. "Watch your mouth, bitch. I run this place."

She shoved him, rocking him backward, and held her ground when he rebounded. "If you run this place, why are you still taking orders, huh? Big guy? Tell me that."

The man reached toward her face, but a swift hand slice deflected the move. "Don't touch me. I'll remind you again. I have poisons. Something that will make your dick shrivel until it's black and oozing with puss. You will beg me to cut off your goods. You think you know pain. You don't. I can get to you any time, any place." She emphasized *can* to the point even Karly cringed. "Plus, I have important friends, unlike you, so don't try it."

The man's skin flushed white. "One of these days, Doc, you'll push too hard, and find yourself on a bus to hell."

"And this place isn't? I don't see any

sandy beaches or fruity drinks with little umbrellas, do you?"

A woman's groan deflected Karly's attention, but she didn't move.

The doc pulled the stethoscope from around her neck. "I have a patient to check on. Why don't you go see how the women are doing with the heroin shipment, okay? Leave me to do my job."

When the man leaned in to take a sniff, the doctor pushed back. Macedo responded with a demonic, horror-movie laugh.

This nightmare was worse than any thriller movie—and she'd only watched a few. She hated the violence. The edge-of-your-seat fear. Characters who played their parts too well. Macedo could have been an excellent character actor, only he wasn't acting, and she wasn't sitting in a movie theater eating popcorn and sipping on a thirty-two-ounce soda. This was real—too real.

She bit her lip.

Crying out wouldn't help. Neither would

bursting into tears.

The collar around her neck was attached to a chain bolted to the wall. She wasn't going anywhere.

Oh, please, please, please, someone get me out of here.

The doctor spoke in a low murmur, too low for Karly to hear.

Seconds stretched into an eternity before Macedo's looming form passed between Karly and the light when he left the room.

"You shouldn't hold your breath, it's not good for you." The doctor pressed fingers under Karly's chin, checking her pulse. "I'm Doctor Abbott."

Karly jerked her head away, her lungs burning. "Where am I?"

"Didn't you hear? You're in hell." The doctor pressed her fingers to the vein again, counting and looking at her watch. "You must have pissed somebody off."

Karly twisted her wrists, trying to get free. "There must be some mistake."

"There's no mistake. Macedo only follows

orders. If you are here, someone wanted you here."

I've got to get out of here.

If the fear didn't kill the oxygen in her lungs, the despair would.

She twisted her wrists and tugged at the restraints, but the metal straps didn't budge.

"Where am I? What is this place?"

"Listen to me." The woman clasped her jaw and yanked her chin up. "If you want to live, you need to stay calm. Watchful. There are half a dozen men just outside that door, so don't think about trying to escape. You won't make it far. I've sedated you as long as I dare to keep Macedo away. Now get some rest, you'll need your strength." She turned. "And, you," she said to the other woman. "If another contraction comes while I'm gone, use short breaths."

"Please, don't take my baby." The woman's plea ended on a sob.

Take her baby?

Karly tried getting a good look at the person talking but the collar stopped her.

A memory stirred. Mara had said Jenna's sister had been afraid someone would take her baby. *That's why she left town. I wonder if...*

The doctor grabbed Karly's wrist, tugged, and leaned in to whisper. "I'm going to uncuff your hands and feet, but please don't try anything stupid. You'll only get hurt."

No. Don't trust her. Don't trust anyone. She forced her lungs to draw in air.

"I'll be back." Dr. Abbott smoothed hair from Karly's face after releasing her hands and feet. "Stay quiet. Trust me, you don't want anyone coming in here to check on you, especially Macedo."

The woman disappeared through a metal door. The door clicking shut sounded like a cage locking. A whimper broadcast Karly's fear.

The woman was right. She needed to stay calm, strong, brave. *Thad thinks I'm brave.*

Thad. He'd look for her. She just needed to believe. Act brave, even if she didn't feel brave.

She'd have to fight.

CHAPTER TWENTY

Using her numb arms, Karly pushed against the mattress to roll over. Once there, she stared at a petite Asian woman whose belly was visibly rolling and rippling. The woman clutched the mattress edges with sweat streaming down her face, her eyes clenched tight, probably trying to hold off the pain.

Memories of Karly's miscarriage flooded her with dread—the unpredictability of childbirth. Feeling isolated, alone. Praying for a good outcome. Knowing the result was out of her hands. *Please let this baby survive.*

"Hey? Hey? Talk to me." Karly reached out to touch the woman and provide comfort, but the neck restraint held her back. "What's your name?"

"I'm Sung," the other responded through short bursts of air from a hospital bed complete with stirrups, handles and birthing bar. "Sung Wen. Who are you?"

The heart monitor blipped in time with the woman's heartbeat.

Karly traced each tube and electrode with her eyes to a different piece of equipment. "I'm Karly Krane. Where am I?"

"Be careful." The woman pointed at her neck where the leather collar chafed her skin. "They get mad and punish you if you bruise.

Oh, God. Stay calm. You need to stay calm. She tugged at the leather again, just to be sure she couldn't get free.

"It's locked. You won't be able to get it off." Sung lifted her position, probably wanting to get more comfortable, and groaned.

Helplessness rolled in. Karly folded an arm under her head to reduce the strain on her neck. "Maybe if we talk it will take your mind off the pain."

The woman arched upward, muscles clenching as she curled in on herself when another contraction hit.

"Breathe. Short breaths," Karly advised. "That's it."

Unable to reach the woman, she could do nothing but watch while contractions ripped through the woman's small frame.

Karly wanted to ask how long she'd been there, where Dr. Abbott was going to take Sung's baby, how she could escape, but adding stress to an already terrifying situation wouldn't help. "You'll be fine," Karly promised, even though she had no idea if it was true. "We need to figure out a way to get out of this place."

Hysterical laughter filled the room.

"What's so funny?" Karly regarded the laughing woman with confused delirium.

"Honey, where did they transfer you in from?" Sung mumbled past the pain.

"Transfer? I didn't transfer from anywhere. I was taken."

"Taken? You weren't sold?" Sung looked away. "Most of us worked hard to get here." Her voice quivered with pain. "The price of admission is pregnancy." Her voice stayed soft, even, unemotional. "For six to seven months we get a pass. No pimps. No johns. Three hot meals a day, and all we have to do is package product. Dr. Abbot thinks this place is a hellhole. To slaves like us, this is paradise."

Slaves? Paradise? "You got pregnant on purpose?"

"You are a naïve one. No. I didn't get pregnant on purpose, but where I come from, there's no choice. Just like we had no choice when our parents sold us, and we were shipped here. Three-quarters of us died in that container. We didn't choose this life. We just decided to stay alive."

To live. If this type of thing was

happening in Karly's backyard, then apparently she'd been living in a bubble.

"Where do you go from here?"

"The first time I went back to LA, the second time Las Vegas. I don't know where they'll send me next."

"You've been here before?"

"The is the second time I've been to this place. It isn't so bad compared to other locations. My last handler sorta liked me, so I got a few more freedoms. I'm hoping my former owner might buy me back."

"Buy? You mean like in purchase you?"

"You remind me of another girl I met once. She didn't belong here any more than you do."

Karly could taste the fear of the unknown. "What happened to her?"

She rolled her head to the side. "I helped her escape."

Hope surged through her mind. "Would you…"

The door opened and forced her back into a silent cell. Dr. Abbott moved toward them at supersonic pace. "Time to get this baby delivered."

"What will happen to Sung's baby?" Karly couldn't help asking.

The doctor pushed a cart filled with metal things that looked downright scary. The doctor's expression turned dark. "The fewer questions you ask, the better off you'll be. Stay quiet. Stay small. Be invisible if you can. And, whatever you do, don't let Macedo get a rise out of you. He likes to play, and enjoys watching women react."

Two densely tattooed men entered through a sliding door on metal tracks. Karly glanced into the hall, but all she could see was another wall. The men came closer, and her instinct to run made her roll away, but the chain prevented from moving more than a foot.

Helplessness settled on her chest.

"What are you doing?" the doctor asked. "That one needs to stay here."

"Macedo said to move this one to the warehouse," a Hulk-looking guy responded.

"Suit yourself, but if something happens to her, if she goes into spasms because of the drugs, or her heart stops, the blame's not on me." The doctor turned away as if she didn't care, and made Karly question just which side the doctor was on.

The bulky guy, who looked more like a middleweight boxer than a thug, hesitated. He didn't look like he had an ounce of fat on him.

"Move her, Sanchez," his partner demanded. "Macedo can deal if anything happens."

Sanchez yanked on her leather collar and pulled up, forcing her to stand. He unlocked the collar, releasing her from the restraint, then pushed her toward the door. She had no choice but to go.

At the door, she turned just in time to see Dr. Abbott's intent, silent warning. *Stay small.* Sung cried out in pain, and the doctor's attention was diverted. The door slid shut, and any hope of remaining with the doctor faded. A quick glance left and right revealed a long hall with more closed doors. There would be no escape.

Sanchez yanked her forward by the neck. Ten feet away was another door, leading to another room. A few minutes later, she was shoved into a dark, empty room and attached by metal cuffs to the far wall. "Wait, don't leave me here," she begged.

Her captor started to turn when his partner bellowed, "Out. Now."

The sound of doom was the door locking. Darkness closed in. Karly's insides quaked.

The only light came from under the closed door. She slid down the cold wall and curled into a ball. The hand chains weren't long enough for her to get as small as possible. Minutes ticked by like water from a leaking faucet. The fear overwhelmed.

Tears streaked her face.

Desolation clogged her lungs.

She could scarcely breathe, and wondered if she made a sound whether the other women could hear her. She picked up her chain and clunked it against the wall...waited...then tried again.

Nothing. No return noise. No small hello.

Sung's conversation circled back around. The tiny Asian woman wanted to be here. She believed this place was paradise. If this was paradise, Karly wanted a refund. She'd settle for a three-star...anything...as long as the place didn't have armed men stalking the corridors.

Unless the armed man was Thad. Had he stopped by the kennel? Did he know she was missing? Did anyone know? What if he tried to find her?

These guys know what they're doing. Will Thad be shot? Killed?

A high-pitched whimper echoed off the walls.

Her only thought...I'm going to die.

CHAPTER TWENTY-ONE

T had belly-crawled toward the main building and up to the ventilation shaft. Rivers had cut the wires to disable the air exchange fan a couple of days prior. Why, Thad didn't know, but at this point he didn't care. The prep work was a good thing, or Thad would have had to figure out how to get past the two-foot long, thin metal blades.

"Team one in position." Joe's communication came in clear. Thad lowered the volume on his ear buds, and adjusted his helmet's chin strap.

Thad glanced over his shoulder to make

sure Rivers was behind him. His teammate was a yard back. The guy didn't make a sound.

He appreciated the space, because the fierce hatred he was feeling might burn just about anything within range to a crisp. He hoped Karly was still alive, because if she wasn't... *No. Don't go there. Focus on the mission.*

Approaching the vent, Thad listened for movement, then activated his mic. "Team two in position." He settled on his back and extracted a tool kit from his pocket.

Sweat poured into his eyes as he began removing the screws holding the fan. Screws and bolts were the easy part. Getting past the fan, dropping into the room below—unseen, unheard—would be a bit tougher.

The last bolt wouldn't budge. Frustration bunched the muscles under his shoulder blade. Thad shifted to get better leverage. One tight bolt wouldn't keep him from getting to Karly.

The bolt unexpectedly released. Relief

burst through him seconds before two men entered the hallway, one from each end.

Thad pulled back, automatically sending Rivers a two-men present signal. He hoped Rivers understood military code. If he didn't, both of them were in trouble.

"What's up?" the taller man in the hall asked.

"Last one's delivering now. Macedo said to get the women ready for loading. The new one is in the isolation room. I'll get her and meet you in the loading bay. We leave as soon as the baby's delivered."

Leave? Oh, no you don't.

The image of a dead Afghani mother holding a screaming baby flashed across the screen in his mind, distracting him. Bile stirred in his gut. He closed his eyes and forced his muscles to relax.

The tink-tink-tink of a bolt rolling down the shaft, tightened every muscle in his body.

Rivers caught the bolt, his eyes flashing a what's-wrong-with-you? warning.

"Did you hear that?" The tall man looked up at the vent.

Thad's breathing stopped.

The tall man took a step closer.

"Hear what?" The smaller man snorted a laugh. "You're being paranoid. It's just a field mouse." He shook his head as he pushed through the door. "Come on. Macedo gave us orders." But the tall man lingered. He lifted onto his toes to see into the vent. The crackle of a two-way radio echoed in the hallway.

"Sanchez, you there?"

The man turned and placed the radio close to his mouth. "What's up, boss?"

Thad released his breath slowly.

"Get the women and drugs loaded now. We've got company. It looks like the big bosses came to give us a sendoff. Macedo wants everyone in place."

Thad looked back at Rivers, who held a finger to his lips. Thad wanted to bust through the vent and dice Sanchez into tiny little pieces, but he did nothing except rest his forehead on his long-sleeved black shirt to blot away the nervous sweat pouring down his face.

When the men disappeared through the exit, Thad hauled his hands down his face.

Shit, that was close. Thad shifted to double-check the hallway was clear.

Rivers didn't need to say anything, his eyes said it all.

Thad pressed his push-to-talk unit. "Team one. Sounds like more people are coming in through the front. We've got at least two here, with one on the radio," Thad conveyed on a whisper.

"Team two. We've got more than just company." Joe's voice came in clear through his headset. "Four vehicles just drove in through the main gates. It looks like someone is hosting a party."

Thad looked at Rivers, who'd heard the same message. "I bet you're right," Thad responded. "The guy inside said the big bosses are coming in. What's the ETA on our backup?"

"Our play dates are still asking for more time."

"The cake will be gone by the time they arrive," Thad played along.

"Hang tight."

Thad rolled his eyes. He looked at Rivers, who still hadn't moved.

If something were going to happen, it would happen fast—too fast to react to in their current position. His clear and focused military mind calculated, weighed, and measured the options. Karly was being moved. He couldn't wait. He had to do something.

He signed to Rivers he was going in. Rivers grabbed his sleeve and yanked. He locked his fingers around River's wrist to get him to release his arm. *Don't try to stop me, buddy.*

Rivers opened his hand and released Thad's shirt.

Good. We have an understanding.

Thad pulled the vent, rotated the box, and passed it back to Rivers. Then he dragged himself to the edge of the vent and listened for movement, then shifted and dropped into the hall. Seconds later, Rivers dropped in behind him without a sound. Thad leaned back against the wall in a chair position and held out his hand. In one swift move, Rivers put a foot on Thad's thigh and straightened to lift the fan back in place, then lowered back to the tiled floor.

Thad's breath stopped mid-inhale at the sound of footsteps. A quick shuffle, and both he and Rivers backed into a narrow doorway off the main hall.

Rivers tapped his arm and silently diagrammed the layout beyond the hallway door.

Karly, hold on. We're coming.

Thad checked his weapon again. Fully loaded. Footsteps pushed him deeper into the shadow of the doorway.

"Move it, sweet cheeks." Thad recognized Sanchez's voice.

"Please. I'm going as fast as I can."

Karly. A sweeter sound he'd never heard. *She's alive! Thank God.*

Thad peeked around the doorframe edge and through the exit door's window. Karly looked pale and scared. Anger turned the world in front of him red. These a-holes were toast. Rivers took a position beside him, gesturing toward a door behind him with a warning. Thad acknowledged Rivers and headed the opposite direction. With a quick look through the glass window, he took inventory.

A van.

Seven women walking in single file, bound in chains.

Two men, armed.

Where's Karly? She was just here.

He pressed his radio button. "Team one, several women are being loaded into a van," Thad whispered. "There's a loading dock back here, and a tunnel that's not on the drawing you showed us. Do you know where it leads?"

"I wasn't aware of any tunnel. And, you

shouldn't be able to see a loading dock from the air exchange shaft. Give me your position." Joe's frustration came through loud and clear.

Thad glanced at Rivers, then leaned out to take another look. A female in a medical coat and Karly, both supporting another woman, emerged from a door on the far side of the open space.

A short, stubby man came from another direction. "Get her loaded," he ordered.

Karly! Hold on, love.

"Team two. What is your position?" Blasted in his ear.

Thad signaled to Rivers that he'd spotted Karly. He recognized the short guy with tattoos covering his neck and face as Macedo, because of the man's accent. He was the boss, and the man Sanchez spoke to on the radio. Sanchez monitored the doctor's progress as she supported the wobbly woman while she stumbled toward the van.

"Leave her." Macedo waved with a gun.

"No." The doctor continued to move

forward. "I'm not going to leave an asset behind. She'll be fine."

Karly lifted the small woman's arm and placed it over her shoulder, then continued on with the doctor.

Thad dropped his head back against the wall, closed his eyes, and made a plan. Seconds passed, then he signaled to Rivers, before radioing. "Team one, in loading dock. Van ready and loaded with women. Three men. One woman. I'm going in."

"Wait!" Joe hissed.

He couldn't wait. He wouldn't allow that van to take off. Not with Karly in it.

Thad tried the door handle. It moved. He silently pushed the door open. He duck-ran and slid behind some tables stacked against the wall. He didn't dare look back, because there were only two possibilities. Either Rivers was behind him giving him a WTF look, or he wouldn't be behind him at all.

Thad moved to the other side of the tables and inched forward to get a better look.

His heart pounded.

Sweat trickled down, stinging his eyes.

He blinked to focus.

Think. Stay calm. His finger pressed on the cold metal of his gun.

Someone started the van. He mentally mapped the targets.

Three men, one woman.

Seconds later, Karly got out of the van to help load supplies. His opportunity to act had come.

Thad checked for Rivers. He'd moved into position on the other side of the door.

Options turned from gray to black and white—stop that van.

He aimed, calmed his breath, and fired, hitting Sanchez and the little guy. His second bullet missed Macedo, and he fired again.

He eased his finger off the trigger.

Shit.

Macedo had Karly in a chokehold, holding a gun to her head.

Thad's heart raged. *Come on. Give me a shot.*

His life's purpose became laser focused. He'd pledged to die for the country he loved. He was expendable. Today he'd have the privilege of dying for the woman he loved.

Thad gave a signal to Rivers and hoped the guy had good aim. He pushed to his feet and moved out from behind the tables.

"Let her go." He took a step forward, his gun aimed perfectly, then he spread his arms wide. Macedo knocked Karly to the ground.

P-taff. P-taff.

Thad's body jerked. He gathered his strength and fired at Macedo.

Pain burned across his torso.

P-taff.

Air whooshed out of his chest.

He heard a scream as he fell back into blackness—his soul released from his body and started to drift.

KARLY'S SCREAM ricocheted off the walls.

All sound disappeared.

She began to crawl toward Thad.

Gunfire erupted from behind her. She froze. Covered her head. Fought her instinct to run.

Time slowed. She saw images of her parents, brothers, friends, and then Thad.

No. No. No. Oh, Thad.

Her focus narrowed.

Thirty feet away, Thad lay on his back, unmoving.

A sob robbed her of breath. She reached for Thad, but the rest of her body didn't follow.

When more gunfire didn't come, she slowly searched the loading dock. Dr. Abbott grabbed her by the arm and lifted. Justified vengeance reflected in the doctor's eye and shocked Karly into letting go of the doomed images flashing in her mind. "Get in." Dr. Abbott dragged her forward. "We have to get you and the rest of the women to safety."

"I'm not leaving him." Karly turned toward Thad.

A jerk of her arm spun her around. "Listen to me." The doctor's fingers dug into her arms. "You stay here, and you'll end up just like him. We gotta get out of here. Now."

"No. I'm not leaving him." The doctor tightened her grip. When additional men came through a side door, the doctor shoved her into the van. "Move! Now."

P-taff. P-taff. Bullets whizzed past Karly's head. Her mind went blank as her arms and legs scrambled into the back of the metal box.

A pair of hands pulled her farther into the cargo area. Wide eyes of the other women focused on the men lying on the floor in pools of blood. Others looked sympathetic, while a few turned away. The sex trafficking victims sat next to each other on narrow benches on either side of the van, chained to the wall by their necks, their feet shackled to a bolt in the van's floorboard.

As the van raced away from the loading

dock, all she could see were the bottoms of Thad's feet, getting smaller and smaller. She'd been wrong. Her heart hadn't been broken. Not completely.

It was now shattered.

The image of Thad's high school drawing surfaced. Screws and bolts and springs strewn across a table, pieces of a heart no longer functioning—like Humpty Dumpty, never to be put back together again.

She looked, connecting with each one of the women, one after another.

Every one of them had experienced loss.

She sensed it.

She could empathize with how every one of them felt, and they with her.

Forever damaged.

Totally broken.

CHAPTER TWENTY-TWO

K arly didn't allow herself to cry. She couldn't. Not here. Not surrounded by women who'd visited the grand halls of hell and survived.

The van slowed and came to a sliding stop. "Is everyone okay back there?" Dr. Abbott asked through the front sliding window.

Why do you care?

No one answered.

Karly and Sung were the only two not chained. Karly crawled toward Sung, and brushed the hair off her face. The heat from

Sung's skin made her pull back. Concern replaced her fear.

"Sung. You have to hang on."

Karly glanced at the van window, then made her way to the front. "Everyone is okay, but Sung doesn't look good. I think she's got a really high fever, and she keeps going in and out of consciousness."

"Good to know. I need to find a safe place where we can wait this out."

"Wait what out?" Karly asked, not totally sure if she was prepared to know.

Concerned eyes met Karly's through the rearview mirror, but the doctor didn't reply. Karly studied the road ahead. Like a fence, trees lined both sides. Ahead, a rock formation jutted out of the ground, its outline black against the night sky. The monolith looked familiar—very familiar. She leaned closer to the window. "I know a place that's safe."

"It can't be in town."

"No, it's secluded. There's a small cabin about a mile from here."

"Perfect. Give me directions. I need to get to a phone and call this in."

The doctor pasted words together like a CSI character on television. Was the doctor an undercover cop? "Who do you want to call?"

"My boss."

Her boss. Karly studied the eyes reflecting in the mirror. Dull as a rock. She still had no idea which side the doctor landed on—the good or the bad. She'd hold onto the distrust a little while longer.

Thad didn't have a phone, but she wasn't about to blow her only chance of landing in a place she knew like the lines on her palm.

A few minutes later, after taking a right just after that tree, and a left on that dirt road, the van bounced and rocked up a familiar dead-end road and stopped next to Thad's cabin. The wooden structure stood strong against the darkening night. If only she felt as strong.

Oh, Thad. He'd come for her. He tried to save her, and she'd gotten him killed. Guilt swarmed into every nook of her soul, and wept for a precious life cut short. The pain seared her heart and throat and eyes. She wanted the agony to cut her open. Surgically remove her remorse. Allow the pain to shrivel her insides into small, crumbling pieces until she disappeared.

But she couldn't.

These women needed help. She wouldn't just leave them. They all reminded her of a precious pup that had been abused and abandoned and needed to find a forever home. She wove through the knees of the women and searched for a weapon, anything to help free them. She tugged and pulled an inch-thick chain loose from the wall and wrapped it around her hand, then crouched in a ready position, waiting for the back doors to open. She'd punch, claw, and scratch her way to freedom if she had to.

"Karly?" Dr. Abbott sounded firm and in control. "I'm going to open the doors slowly. I need your help getting these women inside the cabin. They should be looked at. Are you willing to help me with that?"

Damn. She maintained her calm.

"Karly? I know you are there."

Karly glanced back at the women, and then again at the door. "How do I know I can trust you?"

"You don't." There was no movement on the other side of the door. Sung groaned and rolled her head back and forth, pain flickering in her eyes.

A thrum-thrum-thrum pounding in Karly's ears blocked out sound. A hand landed on her shoulder. She flinched, and nearly screamed. Karly turned. A frail woman withdrew her shaky hand.

Someone had called the woman Julia, but she didn't look like a Julia. Thin as a stick, with sunken eyes, and long, oily hair. Add a hot shower, plus twenty pounds, and some makeup, she'd look like a Julia, but not today. The hostage stared at Karly, then her gaze moved toward the door. The silent message was clear. For some reason, Julia trusted the doctor.

She released a resigned breath. "Do I have your word you will not harm these women?"

"You have my word."

Karly pushed back to sit on the bench beside the frail woman.

The little voices in Karly's head mocked her efforts to be superhuman. Her head dropped back against the van's interior wall. "Then I'll help. You have *my* word."

There was a click of a mechanism engaging, then the back doors swung open. Seeing the raised gun, Karly froze. Her rage escalated. She'd been a fool. Then Dr. Abbott opened both hands, palms out, gun pointed at the sky.

The heat of Karly's anger turned down to a low boil.

"It will be okay." The doctor studied each woman in turn. "You're safe."

Karly gasped when the doctor placed the gun in a holster hidden by her oversized white coat.

"I'll get all of you to safety, but have patience." The authority in Dr. Abbott's voice sent a wave of calm through the huddled women. "We need to get Sung inside first. I don't want her hemorrhaging." The doctor looked at Karly. "Can you find something to cut through those chains?"

"Why don't I just drive everyone into town? They'll be safe there."

"Because they won't be safe."

The doctor's adamant statement stalled her plans for driving off in the van. "Why not?"

"That town is more corroded than a car in a junk yard. There is no one there you can trust. Not in this town. Staying here is our best chance of getting out of this alive. We are a liability now. If they find us, we are all dead."

Karly moved in to help lift Sung. "Please tell me this nightmare is over."

"We're almost there. I hope it will be wrapped up soon."

Karly jumped out of the van, then

stopped when a hand clamped to her forearm. She looked at the fingers gripping her and turned back to the doctor. "You asked me to trust you. You'll have to trust I won't run."

"Then let's get these women inside and fed."

The doctor released her, yet she didn't move away. "Dr. Abbott isn't your real name, is it?"

Sung groaned, just as her eyes fluttered and she regained consciousness. The doctor shifted her patient to get a better grip. Once she got Sung standing, she turned to Karly. "For now, just call me Sandra. Let's get everyone inside. I don't know how long we can stay here, and I want everyone unchained and able to move if we need to relocate."

Question after question zipped through Karly's mind. She wanted answers, but instead nodded and went in search of something to cut through the chains.

Bolt cutters would have made life easy, but

she had to settle for a mallet and tire iron. Forty minutes later, she washed her hands in the kitchen sink while observing the women, whose names and brief history she now knew, sat or lay crowded in Thad's small living space. The nine women were safe inside. All were exhausted, scared, and doing whatever worked to maintain control over their shattered lives.

"Ladies. There's food here," she announced while peeking around the corner into the living room.

Three women stood. The others held back. She picked up a plate containing soup, crackers, and cheese, and managed to give them a fake smile, the kind that says everything's fine when it isn't, then headed toward the bedroom.

"You're looking better." Karly set the plate on top of the dresser and turned back in time to see Sung's attempt to smile. The doctor pulled the blood pressure cuff of the woman's arm.

"There's a fire going," Karly continued,

"and I've handed out all the blankets and clothes I could find."

"There's no phone here." The doctor's frustration ebbed into the room. "I need a phone, anything to call for help. Do you know if there's a radio, anything like that?" Sandra helped Sung by propping pillows and an old blanket behind her.

"Many of these old cabins don't have phones. There's a cell tower. We just need to find a working cell phone." Karly sat on the edge of the bed and handed Sung the soup bowl and spoon. "About four miles from here is the Newhalls' place. I could run for help."

"Newhall." A flash of anger flared and ripped across Sandra's face. She shook her head. "You wouldn't be safe. I can't risk you going. We need to stay here. Together."

"Buck Newhall is a lawyer in town."

"Still, you'd be surprised how far the corruption has spread. We still aren't sure of all the players."

"I could go to the Bryant' or Clairemonts'."

"No. It's not safe." Her emphasis on the word safe became more pronounced. "My boss will be looking for me. If we don't hear from someone within an hour, I'll go for help. I don't want any of you risking your lives."

"It's dark out, and I know these hills, because I've lived here all my life. I could be gone and back in an hour."

"Please, let's just wait an hour. Then we'll reassess."

As soon as the women are fed I'm going, whether you like it or not.

Sung pushed to a seated position. "Is my baby safe? You promised me my baby would be safe."

"Your baby is in good hands. I was able to get him transported out before we were forced to move."

"He? It was a boy?"

Sandra smoothed back Sung's hair. "You had a healthy baby boy." She leaned in closer.

"You need to stay strong for him. I have a feeling you two will be reunited soon."

Sung eased back onto her pillow, the tension around her eyes and mouth easing. After several seconds of silence, she rolled her head toward Karly. "What kind of soup is this?"

"Tomato. It's all I could find that I could warm up."

Thad wasn't much of a cook after all.

The past tense drove a knife into her gut. He was gone, and it was all her fault. Grief welled, and she tried to push the sharp, aching guilt into a dark corner for now. She had to survive—for him.

Karly took Sung's hand.

"You did good for a newbie," Sung squeezed her fingers. "You're still a bit green."

Oh, God. She couldn't hear kindness, or she'd just lose it.

"Don't move. Hands up. Hands where I can see them. Now." The command boomed through the room.

Karly's heart raced. *That voice. Oh, God.*

Sandra raised her hands slowly. "You're hurt."

Karly turned. "Thad?" Her eyes opened wider.

You're alive.

The words stuck in her throat. Excitement. Relief. Gratitude. A tumble of emotions piled one on top of the other.

"Karly, walk slowly to me." Thad aimed his gun at the doctor.

His beautiful amber eyes flicked to her for a second, then back to the doctor. "Karly, move, now. Move away from the bed."

Her mouth dried. "Thad, wait." She stood with her hands out and took a step.

Pop-pdd-pdd-pdd. Thad screamed. His body stiffened. His face flushed red.

"No!" Karly screamed.

He flopped to the floor. His body convulsed.

Her heart skidded to a stop. "Thad?" She dove forward and landed on her knees beside his body. He didn't move.

Please. Please. Please. Oh, God, please let him be all right.

She turned toward Julia. "Where did you find that taser?"

"In the cabinet by the front door." Julia hovered near the door, looking ready to collapse. "He had a gun," she said by way of explanation.

Karly looked up to see sorrow in Julia's eyes. "I know. But he's one of the good guys." Karly motioned toward Julia's hand. "Just put the taser down, and don't let Cassandra hit anyone with that fire poker."

Cassandra stood behind Julia, poised like a baseball player standing at home plate, ready to whack anyone within striking distance.

The doctor picked up Thad's weapon, but it wasn't necessary. He didn't move. Sandra removed the electrodes sticking out of Thad's legs.

"Thad?" Karly rolled him over. "Thad?"

His eyes flickered open. "Karly?"

She shifted toward the doctor. "Can you help him?"

"Do you know this man?"

"He came to rescue me. Macedo shot him."

Sandra leaned and dropped Thad's gun on the nightstand, then knelt beside Karly. "First things first." She unplugged the headset from the mic to remove the handset from Thad's vest and clicked. "Hello? Over? Hello? This is Dr. Abbott."

Sandra pulled the Velcro on Thad's vest and gently lifted.

"How did you get access to this channel?"

Karly recognized the voice and wiggled her fingers for Sandra to turn over the handset. "Sheriff Joe, this is Karly. We're at Thad's cabin. Dr. Abbott is in need of some medical supplies. She says it's not safe to leave here. Is that true?"

"It's true. Stay put. Karly, it's damn good to hear your voice. Is Thad with you?"

"Yes, but he needs medical attention."

"Okay. Hold for a second. Let me get

people headed your way." Joe shouted for someone. Another few minutes passed in silence.

Sandra continued unbuttoning and unbuckling so she could assess the extent of Thad's injuries.

"This is Special Agent Bantner." A voice finally responded. "To whom am I speaking?"

Sandra took control of the handheld.

"It sure is a nice day for a picnic," Sandra said with a lilt. "The sun is shining, and the trout are running in the river."

What the hell?

"What shall I bring?" Came the reply. "Fried chicken or sandwiches?"

"Neither. I like salads." Sandra's excitement was like watching a puppy waiting for chow. "It's good to hear your voice, sir. I've got nine females here, and one male. Two need medical attention. If you can arrange transportation, I'd be obliged."

"Where are you?"

Sandra looked at Karly, who said, "We're

at Thad Lopez's cabin on Lonely Ridge, just past the elk pasture on the right."

"That's not helpful." A snort echoed through the radio. "The sheriff says he knows where you are. We'll find you. Sit tight."

Thad's eyes flickered open again. This time he groaned and tried to move.

Thank you, God.

She had never been a religious person, but maybe today was a good day to start.

He reached out, and she grabbed his hand. "I'm here, Thad. It's okay." When his muscles engaged to rise, she pushed and Sandra also leaned closer to push his shoulders back to the floor.

"Stay," Karly told him, and wondered if "sit," or "down," or any other command would get through to her wonderful blockhead.

Karly unbuckled his helmet while the doctor stabilized his neck with a rolled-up towel.

Sandra lifted the vest's chest plate to

look.

"Is there any blood?" Karly choked out, not wanting to know.

"Nope. The bullet didn't go through. He's going to be stiff and bruised, but he should survive." She used the penlight from her coat pocket and went about her examination.

Fear, joy, and worry jostled for Karly's attention. The past few hours had destroyed the world as she once knew it. Nothing would ever be the same. The only bright spot —Thad was alive.

"Will he be okay?" she asked, hoping for the best and prepared for the worst.

"He'll be fine. Bruised and sore, but no bullet holes or breaks."

He lifted a hand toward her face. "Karly?"

She reached for his hand and placed it against her heart. "I'm here."

"I came for you." He blinked a couple more times and tried to move his head. "I don't ever want to live without you. Not again. Will you marry me?"

Her heart hopped and skipped then took a nosedive. *He couldn't mean marriage.*

Thad blinked, then blinked again. "Karly?" He slurred her name.

"No, don't move. Just lie here. I'm safe. You're safe. Rescuers are on the way."

"Thad." Sandra angled in so he could see her. "Help is on its way. I need you to relax, okay?"

Thad didn't respond further, or ask any more questions.

Good thing, or Karly might need some oxygen.

Thad couldn't be serious. *Marriage? He's caught up in the moment. That's all.*

Besides, she couldn't marry him. Now more than ever, she understood that.

Lights from a vehicle making its way up the drive made some women slink away from the windows, and look for a place to hide. Others sat immobile. Passive. As if their fate had already been set.

Karly rested her hand on Thad's chest, grateful to feel its gentle rise and fall.

Everything will be okay. It's going to be okay, she repeated over and over again.

"Nobody taser or hit anyone who comes through that door unless I tell you to," Sandra said, moving toward the living room. "Understood? My boss is one of the good guys. I expect there's a medical helicopter and paramedics on the way. Help should be here shortly."

A man in an FBI jacket with a bulletproof vest, thirty pounds of equipment around his waist, and the confidence to move mountains walked in. He scanned the room.

He wasn't dressed for a picnic, but Karly was glad to see him regardless.

"Ladies, I'm FBI Special Agent Bantner. A team is on their way to escort you to area hospitals and see to your needs. We will need to take your statements. Rest assured, we will do everything within our power to keep you safe."

"What about my baby?" Sung asked, barely able to stand, clutching the doorframe, doing her best to remain vertical.

Sandra rushed across the room and put an arm around Sung's waist to prop her up.

The midsize man walked farther into the room. "Sandra, would you like to tell them?"

For the first time since Karly met the doctor, a sliver of emotion escaped and peeked out of her eyes. "I told you before your baby is safe, and I meant it." Her eyes glistened with excitement. "In fact, every one of your children is safe."

Julia stiffened. "Macedo told me he sold my baby. That I would never see her again."

Sandra allowed Sung to hold on to the doorframe and moved across the wooden planks to crouch in front of the frail woman. Julia crossed her arms over her stomach, rocking back and forth in a self-soothing motion.

"Julia, look at me." Sandra waited until the desperate face lifted and Julia returned her look. "That's what we wanted Macedo to believe." Sandra placed a hand on Julia's knee. "I handed your baby over to an undercover special agent for marked, traceable cash. This money has helped the FBI track additional illegal activity. The babies they sold were all taken to a hospital, cared for, and have been waiting to be reunited with you. Or, if you choose, you can permanently surrender your rights, and we will make sure your children are placed in safe homes."

Julia lifted a shaking hand to her face. "I can't be a good mother. Not like this."

Sandra looked to Bantner, who provided a nod. Sandra brushed away Julia's tears with her thumb. "I understand. We'll provide you with counseling and other assistance to get you back on your feet for those of you who want it." She met the eyes of each woman in turn. "There isn't any fine print. The offer's legit."

The sounds of chopper blades ended the conversation and jump-started a flurry of activity. Paramedics rushed into the house. Sung was loaded and rolled toward the Flight for Life helicopter. A minute after that, several ambulances came howling up the lane. The survivors, too overwhelmed, or physically incapable of standing, began getting the help they needed. Thad was the last to be loaded.

"I'll go with this one." Sandra made the statement in such a way that no one was going to argue.

"Is there room for me?" Karly asked.

Sandra put an arm around her shoulder. "We'll make room." She winked.

Thad had given into the pain medication for now, but she had things to say.

Things she'd left unsaid.

Things he needed to hear.

CHAPTER TWENTY-THREE

Karly hesitated at the hospital room door.

Thad lay in the sterile bed, with tubes and a heart monitor attached. His gown lay open, and Karly could see the purple bruising from the bullet impact spread across his chest. The silly, honorable man was lucky to be alive.

Chase sat slumped in a chair next to Thad, then stirred. "You're back."

"Hi," she whispered her greeting. "Thanks for sitting with Thad while I visited with Sung. I got to hold her baby."

"Sounds like she'll be okay." Chase

hitched himself up into a more vertical position.

"She's tough." Karly wandered farther into the room "She's had to be. As long as they don't take her baby away from her, she should be fine."

"I've seen a lot of stuff, but man, I had to lock it down when I saw the conditions those women worked in. Is it just me, or is the world getting more violent?"

"It might be that we're just more aware because there are cameras everywhere recording everything we do. Before we lived in a bubble, ignorant of the greater world around us."

"Yeah, maybe you're right."

"I can't imagine what it was like for them. What happened to me was nothing in comparison, and I was terrified." *I almost got sucked into that world.* Shivers ran up Karly's arms. "At least all of them will now be free. Sung is being relocated to a safe house." She drew in a thankful breath.

Although there are things I wish she hadn't told me. Things I'll never forget.

Obligation pressed in. Thad was right. Once the knowing was out there, there was no going back to being naive.

"I'm glad I got to spend some time with her, and meet Haun Thad, her baby boy, before she left. He's got this full head of thick black hair and tiny nose. He's so adorable."

Chase's jaw dropped. "She named her baby after Thad? You've got to be kidding me. That guy?" He winked as he started to chuckle.

"Yep."

"Please don't tell him." Chase looked at Thad. "His head is already too big."

"I heard that," came a grumble from the hospital bed.

"You're awake." A tremor of nerves created a fragile border around her words, brought on by another wave of concern. "How are you feeling?"

"I've been worse," he croaked through

dry, cracked lips. He reached for her. "Come here, you." He lifted an arm, reaching for her.

She sat on the edge of the bed. To connect. She cupped his hand in hers, thankful for the warmth of the blood still pulsing through his veins. "Sung wants me to thank you."

He shook off her praise and looked away.

"No. Don't blow this off. You came for me, and you helped save not only me, but the rest of the women. You forced them to move us before they were ready."

"It's what soldiers do. It's no big deal."

Chase smirked. "Doesn't mean that taking one on the pads doesn't hurt. Dude, look at your chest. It's one massive bruise." Chase pushed to his feet, turning to give Karly a small grin. "Guess he thinks he's Superman and can stop speeding bullets."

Thad's eyes narrowed, and his middle finger extended. Chase shook his head, chuckling. "Glad to know you're on the mend, buddy. Maybe I should go." Chase took a step backward toward the door.

"No. No, stay." Karly twisted around. "He was just kidding. I want to know what happened after Thad decided to miraculously come back from the dead and run after a van full of women."

"It was total chaos. The general was right."

"The general. You mean your father-in-law? He's involved?"

"After you went missing, Joe pulled everyone from town he could find that he trusted, and who had first-responder training. We didn't have time to wait for the JTF team. As soon as the first weapon was fired, he was telling us to watch out for fireworks. Sure enough, the traffickers were trying to blow up the evidence, but they hadn't planned on someone deactivating the fuses."

"I bet that was the doctor's doing. She's been undercover this whole time. Can you believe it? A woman was the inside man. Sort of ironic."

"I'm not surprised. I've met my share of

female Marines. I wouldn't mess with them. Definitely ball-busters."

The look on Chase's face made her laugh, although it faded when the attending doctor walked in the room.

"Mr. Lopez," The physician dropped the medical chart in the plastic holder on the door. "You have severe bruising and a couple of cracked ribs. I've just looked at your X-rays, and I'd like to keep you overnight for observation. If all goes well, you can leave in the morning."

"Nope. Not a chance."

The doctor's body stiffened, his expression stern. "May I ask why?"

Yeah, why? Karly turned and waited for Thad to respond.

"I've had my fill of hospitals. A little bruising is nothing. I can heal at home."

The emergency room nurse came to a stop beside the doctor, and propped her hands on her hips. If stares could disintegrate someone to ashes, Thad would be burned toast. "I told you he wouldn't like your suggestion."

"It wasn't a suggestion." The doctor adjusted the stethoscope around his neck, his expression indicating he was choosing his words carefully. "Special Agent Bantner would like you to remain here until he has a chance to talk to you."

The nurse, who'd been fussing with him since he was rolled into the ER, gave him a narrow-eyed assessment. The six-foot Amazon's demands had been hard to put off, but Thad managed, until now.

"Fine. I'll stay, only because my cabin doesn't hold heat, and only until Bantner gets here."

"How about something for the pain?" The doctor reached under the blanket for his foot. "Do you feel that?"

"Yep. Everything is working fine, and I don't want anything that'll knock me out. Just something to dull the pain."

You're as stubborn as a terrier. Karly walked over to rest her hand on Thad's shoulder. "Thad. Please listen to the doctors. They're here to help. I'll go to the cabin and get you a change of clothes. I can be there and back in an hour."

"I'd make that two, maybe three." Chase chipped in. "You still need to give your statement, and that will take some time."

"Fine. Three hours."

"Finally, someone with some common sense." The nurse's mouth bent into a weird shape. Karly assumed it must be a smile because she couldn't imagine what else it might be. "As your reward, I'll make sure they put a sleeper chair in the room when he's moved."

"Thank you. That's kind of you."

The nurse patted her on the shoulder before leaving the room.

"I've got to check on a few things and give Ashley a call," Chase said. "Thad, get back on your feet soon, 'cause I'm not in the habit of hiring some lazy-ass who wants to lounge around in bed all day." Chase reached out to shake Thad's hand. "Take care, man. You took some risks, but they paid off. But don't you dare try being a hero on my crew, or you'll be fired."

Thad released the former Marine's hand. "Don't worry. I'll put a tracker on Karly. She won't get out of town without me knowing about it."

Chase looked at Karly, then looked back at Thad. "Please tell me you're not that dumb."

The room erupted in laughter until Thad cringed and grabbed his chest to ease the coughing.

Karly turned. "Chase, thank you again for your help. I...ah..." *Blast those tears.*

"It's okay, Karly. You're welcome. See there, buddy?" Chase tapped Thad's leg. "That's how you respond to a lady."

"Would you just get out of here? I want some alone time with my woman." Thad let the finger fly again.

My woman? Where did that come from?

There was that push-pull again. Yes, she loved him. No, she couldn't be with him. A black thundercloud of gloom settled over her heart.

Thad pulled on her hand to bring her closer. "Hey. Are you okay? What are you thinking?"

She tried clearing the despondency but the storm of sadness only intensified. "I'm all right." She shifted on the bed. "Just fine."

"Karly?"

"I'm fine, really."

"What happened—"

"I already told you in the ambulance on the way here, they didn't hurt me."

"Physically, yes, but mentally? If Macedo wasn't already dead, I'd hunt him down. The bastard had no right to touch you."

"Stop worrying about me."

"It's my job." He lifted her hand to his lips. "I know you're brave and strong. Come here, I need to touch you. Make sure this isn't a dream."

She leaned in for a quick peck on the cheek, but he apparently needed more. His hand slid around her neck and pulled her against him. His lips were a bit colder than usual, but still soft, sweet, full of promises she couldn't accept.

"I almost believed I'd never see you again," he whispered against her mouth. "That scared me."

Me too. She straightened.

Thad reached for his plastic water jug. "When I came back to Elkridge, I figured the most adventure I would have was dealing with an occasional snowstorm or fire, maybe looking for a lost kid. I had no idea I'd be deputized to help break up a drug and sex trafficking ring."

"And to think all that was going on, and no one had any idea what was happening." She glanced out the window toward the west. Instead of seeing the mountains, she saw her image reflecting off the hospital room window.

Black smudges of mascara underlined her eyes...or were the dark patches from lack of sleep? She slumped while a little voice whispered, *you need to get some sleep,* but she pressed the ignore button on her internal warning system.

She slid the rubber tie out of her hair to retwist and retie the long strands. "I certainly never thought I'd be attacked, drugged, and chained to a wall."

Reliving the memory caused a shiver to roll up her spine. The rancid smell of a man's breath. The frantically barking dogs.

Brutus. Hedge.

"That reminds me, I should call Mara and check on Hedge. See how he's doing after his surgery."

So many people had been hurt. The need to take a shower and wash all the ugliness away became overwhelming. Karly pushed a hand through her hair, now regretting she hadn't taken the nurse up on her offer of a shower.

A hand touched her arm, and she jumped. "You're safe. It's just me."

Thad pulled on her arm, but she tugged back.

"No. I appreciate your concern, but

please don't baby me. I'm not about to let Macedo or anyone impact my life. I can't...I won't let it happen." She crossed her arms. "How do you military guys manage? Doing what you do? Seeing what you do?" *Deal with the humiliation? People's questions? The memories.*

Thad's finger with the oxygen monitor tapped-tapped-tapped on the bed coverings. "It helps that we've experienced some of the same things together. It helps to talk to someone."

"But how do you start talking? I mean... how do you find the words?"

"I suggest you start with the FBI debriefing, and then take it from there."

"Yeah, I still need to give my statement. I'm not looking forward to that."

Thad squeezed her hand before slowly releasing his grip. "You never answered my question."

"What question?"

"I asked you to marry me."

She stood and backed away from the bed.

"You were serious?" *I thought you were delirious.* "Let's not talk about it right now." *Maybe in a hundred years.*

"I don't want to be without you another second of my life. I want to get married, Karly. Have lots of kids. Help you with your business."

Kids. There it was again. The reason she couldn't be with him, in black and white.

She held her hands out in front of her to create a barrier. "You've been back, what, a month? You coming home, the kidnapping, my business…it's a lot to handle."

"Are you telling me don't want to get married?"

Yes, I am. "You're just freaked out because of what happened."

"No, I'm not. I really want to marry you. Today, tomorrow, before the end of the month."

She paced away, and then back. "Thad, please, I can't go there. Once everything calms down, you'll be relieved that I turned down the offer."

"Is that you're final answer?"

"I'm sorry. It has to be." She brushed past the nurse on her way out the door.

"Whoa there, mister. Where do you think you're going?" she heard the nurse say.

She hit the escape bar on the stairwell door at full speed, yearning to race back to her kennel and start cleaning every surface in the place.

Clean her life.

Find a way to move forward.

Breathe again.

Halfway down the six flights of stairs, she remembered she needed to give her statement.

The air in her lungs collapsed. She grabbed the railing and collapsed on the last step.

Oh, Thad. I'm so, so sorry.

This is all my fault.

CHAPTER TWENTY-FOUR

An FBI agent held the door of the huge khaki tent open and waited for Karly to step inside.

Apprehension squeezed the walls of her lungs, making the simple process of breathing difficult. She inhaled a long, slow breath and walked into the beehive of activity. Lights hung from the metal tent frame, and a propane heater dispensed warmth in the center. The hum of a generator could still be heard over the many voices. Small workstations sat in rows like school desks, filling the room. In the back, another door led to a second tent.

"Karly?" a familiar voice called from the second doorway of the double-wide tent.

Relief eased out in the form of a sigh.

Sandra beckoned to her. The older male agent waved her on, and she made her way to the back.

A genuine warmth for the woman made her quicken her step. "I'm not sure what to call you. Sandra? Agent? Doctor? Wonder Woman?"

"Oh, God. Don't start that, I'd never hear the end of it. My name is Sandra, and I am a doctor, except my last name is Johnston, not Abbott.

"You are a doctor, then."

"Yes, and I work for the FBI. I just wasn't a field operative until I took this assignment. I lobbied hard to get this job. It was personal." The doctor's eyes lost focus for a second, misted, then cleared. "My sister was abducted about three years ago. She disappeared in Philadelphia, and I was able to track her to Dallas."

Karly gasped. "You went undercover to find her."

"Well, no, not exactly. In my free time, I started reading, searching the web, putting pieces together. A friend sent me the internal memo correspondence. The task force was looking for someone with a medical background to go undercover. That's when I pulled in a few IOUs. I went through a six-month intensive training, and then the integration process started. That took another six months."

"Did you find your sister?"

"I did, just not in time." The doctor's eyes blinked and flickered like a neon sign about to go out. A tentative smile slid into place, but it wasn't real. "Come. There's food in the back. Let's get you something to eat."

Karly forced her exhausted body forward and bolstered her resolve for what came next. But when Julia looked her way, Karly remembered why she was doing this, and her spirits lifted. Julia was sitting with an agent who was furiously typing information into a computer. She waved her thin arm, and her eyes brightened.

Karly rushed over to give Julia a quick hug. "I've been hoping to see you before you leave."

"They tell me I'll be transported out sometime tonight to a rehab facility. I'll be there at least a couple of months, then I'll be placed in a group home for awhile. I'm gonna clean up so I can get my babies back."

"What wonderful news." Karly looked at Sandra, who was waiting patiently. "Would you email me? My email address is KarlyKrane@gmail.com, Karly and Krane are both spelled with a K."

"KK. I'll remember. Don't worry. Somehow, I'll get you a message."

"I'd better get back. I need to give my statement." She leaned in for one last hug, holding on for a second longer than was appropriate, but she didn't care. Let the social standards board bust her. She'd been through hell, and didn't care about those little things anymore.

She took a step back. "Take care of yourself, Julia. Live a good life."

Julia released her hand and Karly slowly walked back to Sandra. "Where's the rest of the group?"

"Everyone is safe. Some are being treated for dehydration. Others have opted to get some rest at nearby hotels. Some wanted to meet with the family counselors we flew in for support. Everyone here wants to help the survivors adjust before they are reintroduced to their kids." Sandra slid a foldup chair next to Karly. "As soon as one of the agents becomes available, we'll get your statement recorded. I'm sure you want to go home."

"Will this take long?"

"Not as long as the others. Some of these ladies were sold by their parents, transported to the US with false documents, and have been on the streets for months, even years. That type of history takes time to record."

"While Thad was getting X-rayed, I went to check on Sung. She looks much better." Her smile took a dip. "It's sad, though. The whole time we were talking, she wouldn't let go of her baby's bassinet. I think she was still afraid someone would take her son."

"I'm glad you got to talk to her."

"I saw the US Marshals arrive. She's going into protective custody, isn't she?"

Sandra shrugged, and her brows furrowed. "Sung and her sister have been slaves for a long time. She knows too much."

Slave. What an awful word. "I hope she finds somewhere safe to live, with a good job, so she can raise her little boy."

"That's what we hope."

"Over the years, I've listened to sex trafficking reports on the news. Until this happened, I didn't pay too much attention. Macedo told me he would make me disappear. He was going to sell me. That's what he meant—wasn't it?"

Sandra put a hand on top of hers. "Look, I know you're scared, but it's okay. I've been working for the past two years to help bust this massive cartel for selling babies and fetal matter. I started in Philly, then moved to Dallas, then Los Angeles, then the trail led me here. Over two hundred arrests will take place in the next twenty-four hours. Anyone who might come after you is either dead or in custody."

"But I'm not pregnant." *And I can't get pregnant.* "Why did they decide to take me?"

"They wanted free river access to the compound. With you out of the way, they could move up and down the river without your dogs barking and drawing attention to their activities. Plus, it was assumed you could be moved out of the area easily. You were marked for transport to Vegas with the rest of the women."

A shrill voice echoed through the trailer. "Take your hands off me."

Karly leaned back and stared down the long narrow space. A shockwave rocked her system. The sheriff was leading Vivian Newhall, Jenna's mother-in-law to a chair, and then locked her handcuffs to a table. The sheriff escorted in Richard Clairemont, the town's wealthiest real estate agent, and repeated the process.

"Excuse me for a moment." Sandra exited through the doorway. As voices escalated, Karly moved to the black mesh window in the canvas to watch. Sandra had disappeared.

Clairemont's face was red and blotched. "I'll have your job for this." The dire warning had no effect on anyone in the vicinity. "Give me a phone. I'll call the mayor."

"I can loan you a phone," Joe said in a slow, even voice, demonstrating he didn't take kindly to the elitist's demands, "but I don't think you'll be getting a hold of the mayor."

"He'll answer *my* call."

"Not from a jail cell, he won't."

"How dare you!" Clairemont's spittle landed on the sheriff's shirt front.

The scene reminded her of a television show, only this time she knew all the characters personally.

"I've read you your rights," Joe reminded, "but I have to ask, why heroin and sex trafficking?"

Clairemont gave the sheriff an indignant look. "I don't know what you're talking about."

Sheriff Joe opened a file containing several pictures. "Look familiar?" Joe dropped a picture on the table beside the belligerent man. "Your business trip to California last month to set up a transfer of drugs and women? How about this one? You were meeting with a land developer, but you weren't going to develop the land—were you? You just wanted to have clear access to the river to transport your goods more easily."

"I'm being framed. You don't have one piece of evidence that ties me to anything. I insist that you release Mrs. Newhall and me this instant."

Sandra moved into the scene and stood next to Joe. "Good evening, Dick. Mrs. Newhall. Nice to see you both again."

Both of the prestigious community members' faces instantly paled, and their eyes widened. "I don't think we've been properly introduced. I'm special agent Sandra Johnston, member of a special joint task force." She moved next to Joe. "Sheriff Gaccione, I don't think you have been properly introduced to the man in front of you, either." The sheriff watched Sandra curiously as she leaned back against a desk and folded her arms. "Meet Dick Clairemont, the man who murdered your brother."

"That's preposterous!" Clairemont tried to stand, but the table beside him lifted. Papers and a computer slid to the end. Joe shoved the arrogant SOB back into the chair.

The sheriff's expression transformed from astonishment, to a flash of rage, to a simmering bitterness, before the professional mask voided all emotions. He turned to the doctor. "Are you sure about this?"

"Yep, he bragged about it. He even took

Sam's personal videocam recording. He's such a narcissist, he couldn't bring himself to destroy the computer chip. When I found it, I made a copy and had the conversation transcribed. It's sitting in an evidence locker back at headquarters."

Clairemont became quiet as a mouse trying to sneak past a cat. However, the sheriff had the look of someone who was longing to pounce, extend his deadly claws, and strike the fatal blow.

"Nothing to say, Vivian?" Sandra prompted.

"I insist on talking to my lawyer." The socialite's chin rose with indifference, though Karly caught something sinister in her eyes.

"Smart choice, since we will be adding the kidnapping of Karly Krane to the list of charges."

Vivian sat up straighter. "Kidnapping? Now you're reaching, doctor. Why would I do something like that?"

"That's what I wanted to ask you. After

your daughter escaped from your little operation, why did you break your rule? You didn't like the scrutiny. You were the one who gave the order—no more townspeople were to be taken. Why Karly? Why now?"

Her eyes narrowed, and her voice became venomous. "Daughters should always obey their mothers."

"What?" Karly pushed through the door. "What does my mother have to do with this?"

Vivian's mouth flattened.

Sandra looked at her. "Don't blame your mother, Karly. She's just as much a victim as you were. Like I said before, Dick wanted your land. I just wanted to hear Vivian admit it."

Karly took a step closer and focused on Vivian. *All the job applications. The pressure to interview. My mother is so gullible.* "So, when manipulating my mother with lunches and shopping trips didn't work, you decided to put me out of business by releasing the animals."

Joe's chuckle was humorless. "I bet she didn't count on the whole town pitching in to help."

"I know she didn't," Sandra added. "She was furious and ordered Dick to get Karly out of the way. And of course Dick agreed, since he was eager to snatch up the property for pennies, or tie the property up in court. Either way, Karly's business would be closed, and he'd get the river access he needed."

"Stupid people." Vivian's barely audible mumble expanded in the small space.

"No, Vivian." Karly moved toward the woman, and leaned down to look Vivian directly in the eye. "The townspeople of Elkridge are supportive and kind. Only you don't know it, because you've never wanted to be a part of the town. You always wanted to be above everyone else."

Joe shifted, his eyes watchful. "Looks like she'll get her wish."

Karly turned to Joe. He shrugged and pointed. "She won't be part of this town for a very long time."

Delight danced across Sandra's face. "I hope you like the color orange. I hear orange is the new black. Although somehow, Vivian, I think you'll find the color doesn't suit your complexion. But where you're going, complaints like that will fall on deaf ears."

"How does Mr. Newhall fit into all this?" Karly wrapped her arms around her waist, trying not to fall apart.

"Buck? He doesn't." Sandra looked at Vivian, who seemed to be shrinking more with each passing second. "Vivian wasn't satisfied with owning one of the largest estates in the area. She wanted more, and her husband couldn't provide the lifestyle she craved, so she went to find her pot of gold. Her cut from the sales of drugs and babies provided a way for her to fill her offshore bank accounts. The extra money increased her social status. Once the statements are analyzed, I'm pretty sure tax fraud will be added to the list of charges. She even used poor Dick to implement her master plan."

"That's a lie." Though Dick's belligerent

stare and bulging neck muscles suggested Sandra was telling the truth.

"And all this time," Karly's voice wobbled with shock, "we didn't know what was going on in our own backyard. No wonder so many people in this town have gotten hooked on heroin. Talk about easy to get."

Joe hands gripped his utility belt, and his stance shifted subtly, menacingly. "Finding drugs won't be easy anymore. After the arrests we're making tonight, finding a rehab center will be easier than finding drugs."

Karly looked at Joe. "Did you really arrest the judge and the mayor?"

"Plus half the city council, Cuhna and Beaulieu, a county clerk, and eight people from a drug hideout. Oh, and a drug kingpin, a Shane Boulis, out of Chicago. The general tipped us off about him. That makes twenty-one in all," Joe confirmed.

"Cuhna and Beaulieu, your two deputies?"

"Yep. I knew they were dirty the first time I met them, but there was nothing I could do about it until we got this problem solved."

"The town will be in shock." Karly rubbed her head. Just thinking about the complexity of the scheme gave her a thumping headache. The desolation on the women's faces would haunt her the rest of her life. How could she trust anyone again? So many people she considered upstanding citizens were honey badgers, ready and willing to rip the throat out of their victims for money. Greed. "Will we have to testify?"

"I'm not sure yet," Sandra's soothing hand touched her arm. "Regardless, none of you will be alone. We will be here to support you."

"Maybe I can work with some of the not-for-profits. There are several supplying service dogs to victims of sexual abuse. There is something to be said for unconditional love."

"Pffft. Why bother?" Vivian piped up. "They'll be on the streets again in a matter of weeks."

That's not true!

Putting Vivian in a mini skirt and heels and propping her on a busy corner on the wrong side of the tracks in a crowded city to teach the bitch a lesson sounded awesome. Then again, if she could have gotten away with walking over there and punching the woman in the mouth, she would have.

The woman was a piece of trash. "Do you mind if I give my statement now? I want to check on my animals." *And snuggle with a kitten or get a few thousand puppy kisses.*

"You should know," Joe held out his hand. "Several volunteers stepped up to help. Mara wants you to know everything is being taken care of."

"Oh. Okay." Dang those tears. She promised herself she wouldn't cry. "I'm worried about Thad. Would you look in on him? I was supposed to bring him a change of clothes."

"I'll make sure he's looked after." The commitment in Joe's voice reassured her. "However, he's lucky I don't arrest him for obstructing justice, but we'll discuss that at another time."

Her chest squeezed out a nervous sigh when she saw Joe's face lighten a little when he uncuffed Dick Clairemont to take him over to the processing table.

Finding out the man who'd shot your brother was also the guy you played poker with once a month had to be tough to take.

Life was sure one helluva twisted road, full of curves and steep cliffs.

She hoped her life stayed on level ground for a while, and that Thad could find a way to move on. He deserved happiness.

Then again, what was she going to say to her mom? Or the townspeople?

And she'd thought her life was complicated before.

CHAPTER TWENTY-FIVE

Karly tied the malamute's lead on the railing, next to the bowl of water sitting outside Dreamy Delights bakery. She hadn't slept at all. The knowledge Sung shared had haunted her dreams, and Thad kept coming to her rescue. She didn't want to think about Thad, or her captivity, but that's all she could think about, that and the town.

A virtual tornado had ripped through the town council, courthouse, and local justice system. Only bits and pieces were left, though everywhere she looked, people were moving on with their lives like nothing had happened. Only her life was stuck. She wasn't moving forward, and was trying really, really hard to avoid thinking about the past.

She pulled open the bakery door. Once inside, she took a deep breath, breathing in the sugary fragrance of heaven.

There were good reasons Jenna named her business Dreamy Delights, the scrumptious smells being just one. Never before had Karly fully appreciated the simple freedom of being able to walk into a store the way she did today. The rich oranges and greens and lively artwork added to the ambiance. The picture of the three sows' behinds while the animals ate out of a trough was her favorite. The extra-large oil painting splashed bold colors across the blank wall, and was most likely the reason Jenna selected the piece.

"Hey, lady." Jenna's smile expanded. "I'm glad you stopped in. Come here. I want a hug."

Karly shifted the backpack on her shoulder and reached for her friend.

"How are you? How's Thad?"

The crick in Karly's neck twisted. "I hear he's good. Busy. Healing. I haven't seen him since he got out of the hospital."

Jenna titled her head back. "Really? I thought you two were an item."

"You know how this town likes to gossip."

"What can I help you with?"

"You wouldn't happen to know a couple of dozen people who want to adopt animals, would you?"

"Sorry. I don't. Not at the moment, but I could put up some fliers." Jenna's eyes softened. "Maybe Thad can help. He's gotta know a few people."

"That's the last thing I need." Her breath hitched, and she stopped mid-thought. *I can't believe I just said that out loud.*

"Men can do that. They just jump into the mix without being invited, then one day you turn around and find they are a mighty tasty ingredient."

"Thad is a wonderful man. Don't get me wrong."

"But…"

"I made plans for my life, and they don't include him."

Jenna's bangs lifted with a puff of her breath. "I had plans once, but I was wrong. It's none of my business, and I shouldn't ask, but why not give Thad a chance?"

Why not? That's the question she'd been asking herself for days, weeks. It always came down to what she couldn't give him. She loved him. He wanted kids. She couldn't have them. She loved him too much to deny him the happiness that went with building a life together. "It's complicated."

Jenna's eyes opened wider, and bold laughter rang out through the store. "Those are the exact words I said to Maggie and Gwen when they were pressuring me about Grant." She sobered. "Little did I know, I'd have to eat my reluctance. It tasted a bit bitter. But I can tell Thad is not why you stopped by." She grabbed a tray off the back counter. "I was going to stop by to see you today, but since you're here, you have to try my newest invention."

Jenna never changed.

But Karly had. She'd changed a lot.

Karly picked up the small square cookie on the plate Jenna thrust her way. Chocolate, vanilla, and caramel melded to create an ooh-la-la sensation. "These are awesome."

"You like?"

"When can I get more?"

"I'll box you up the rest of the samples. What do you think of Krane's Konfections, you know a play on Karly Krane and the KK family?"

"You made a cookie for me? I have my own cookie?" Karly raced around the counter to give Jenna a bigger hug.

A blush rolled up Jenna's cheek. "You've always been special. Now, you're just super-duper special. I took your favorite tastes and mixed them together. I figure the town's hero should have a cookie named after her."

A rush of heat exploded from her chest

and burned across her cheeks. "I'm no hero." Not even close.

"Helping a doctor save the lives of eight women? Okay, whatever you say, but I still think you deserve to have a cookie named after you. You've done so much for this town."

"I need another hug." Karly held out her arms, and Jenna obliged. "Thank you." She reveled in the warmth of her friend's hug and let a long sigh escape. She leaned back. "Does this mean I get free cookies from now on?"

"That's the deal. It's your cookie. Whenever Krane's Konfections are in the case, you get a free one, with a purchase."

"Well, smart business lady, I think I just might have to stop in more often."

"I'd like that. Whether or not you buy something." Jenna's unspoken words of friendship were like spring perennials, popping up and blooming just when things looked bleak. She'd received the same friendly support from people at the café and gas station and grocery store.

She'd almost disappeared. Just like Caitlyn, Jenna's younger sister, only worse. At least Caitlyn had escaped and had time to love her son before she died.

"Seems we've both come a long way in the past year."

"It's mind-boggling to think that a year ago I was pretending to be happy on my own. Now I have a wonderful man and business partner, and a happy kid. Nothing could be better."

A small niggle of indecision crawled up Karly's spine. *Maybe I shouldn't say anything.*

"What?" Jenna scrutinized her face, and reached for her arm. "Did something happen to you?

"No, not me." Guilt for stopping by made her start counting the number of cupcakes remaining in the case. "Has the sheriff come by to see you?"

Jenna's fingers tightened on her forearm before releasing. "No. Why? Did my criminal mother-in-law say something about Kyle?"

She should go, let the sheriff handle it, but the heaviness in her gut spoke of responsibility.

Thinking about the woman who'd almost sentenced her to a living hell bubbled up to the anger she'd been trying to keep a lid on.

"No. Vivian hasn't said a word, but there's no doubt she'll go to jail for a good long time. You and your nephew are safe. There's no cause for alarm." The potential effect of her careless words made her nauseated, but she forced herself to continue. Jenna had a right to know. She recognized a deep-seated feeling of rightness, and needed to find a way to make things right.

Did that mean Thad had a right to know as well? She ignored the thought.

"I have some more news for you." Karly slid a chair out from under the nearest table. "Do you mind if we sit?"

Jenna picked up the end of her apron and wiped off her hands. "From the look on your face, this is serious. We might need some coffee and treats."

"Carbs are always good." Karly placed her backpack on the floor and forced a smile, but the outer expression was the opposite of her inner turmoil.

Jenna busied herself behind the counter and returned a few minutes later with a tray. The bitter coffee mixed perfectly with the chocolate yumminess.

"Okay, tell me. What's the news?" Jenna asked while settling on one of her olive green leather-covered chairs.

"Vivian will be charged with several counts of sex trafficking and selling babies on the black market, plus a handful of other charges."

Jenna's leg started bouncing, and she pushed a hand down her thigh. "Grant told me after he got a call from his mother." She tucked a strand of hair behind her ear. "There are thirty-two counts against her, and I believe you're right. She'll be put away for a long time, especially since Grant refused to represent her, and told her to hire someone else. My father-in-law is not speaking to her, and has refused to pay for a seasoned attorney." Jenna passed Karly the creamer. "There's a rumor going around town that Vivian was the reason you were kidnapped."

"It's only partially true. Vivian was manipulating my mom, pressuring her to get me to take another job. When that didn't work, Mr. Clairemont sent one of his men to get me out of the way. But, that's not what I came to talk to you about. I want to talk about your sister."

"Caitlyn? My sister?" She sat up straighter, her hand going to her throat. "Oh, God. Don't tell me."

Karly took a deep breath. *You can do this. She deserves the truth.*

"It's not bad news. Well, at least not for Caitlyn." Karly captured Jenna's hand in hers and squeezed, letting her churning thoughts settle into resolve. "I met a woman while I was being held. Her name is Sung."

Jenna's brows furled. "Caitlyn's been gone

for over five years. How does Sung know my sister?" She hesitated, then her eyes widened. "Please tell me Sung hasn't been a prisoner all this time."

"Well..." Karly's lips folded inward, and she nodded her head in a slow, meaningful way.

"Noooo. How awful." Jenna placed her hand over her mouth.

Saliva pooled in Karly's mouth, and she swallowed hard. "She was sold by her parents and transported here. What's even worse is, she thought being chained and forced to package drugs was paradise. It got her off the streets, but still." Karly pressed her fingers into her temple to relieve the ache that started to poke the back of her eyes. "That's not what I wanted to come to tell you. The important part is Sung knew Caitlyn. In fact, Sung helped your sister escape."

"I knew it. I knew Caitlyn was taken that night." The startled inhalation of breath and the promise in her friend's eyes gave her courage. "Ashley and I agreed she was too methodical to run away without a plan."

Tears filled Jenna's eyes. She fought honorably, biting her lip to hold back the flood, shifting in her chair, looking away, doing anything and everything to hold on.

Karly placed a hand on her thigh and waited. Karly could empathize with the feeling of drowning. Not being able to catch a breath. She'd been barely holding on for years.

"Your instincts were right." Karly tried to infuse her words with a bit of cheer. "During Sung's first pregnancy, she met Caitlyn."

"Was my sister okay? I mean, was she healthy? Had she been abused?"

"Sung didn't say, only that she hoarded food and coached your sister about how to beg for spare change and hide until she could collect enough for bus fare to leave town. She even taught her how to change her appearance."

Jenna's gaze sharpened as her chin

quivered. "I take it Sung didn't leave with her all those years ago, if she was still a captive."

"She couldn't." A deep sorrow made Karly's voice thin. "She was days away from delivering her first child. She told me to pass along how sorry she is about Caitlyn's passing. I told her about you and Kyle. She's grateful Caitlyn got to keep her baby."

Jenna swiped at her nose and leaking eyes. "Where is Sung now?"

Karly reached in her backpack for a tissue. "I don't know. She's in protective custody, but what I can say is she's now in a much safer place. Somewhere she can build a good life."

"Wow." Jenna blew her nose. "That's just...wow."

Uncertainty pressed down and made it hard for Karly to take a complete breath. "Was I right to tell you? Does the knowing help?"

Jenna's shaky hand began to lift her mug to her lips, but she set her cup back on the table. "Yes. I needed to know. If not for me, for Grant." Her voice strengthened and assumed an edge. "He's always blamed himself for his sister's disappearance. They had a fight the day she disappeared, and he thinks her disappearance is his fault." Jenna touched Karly's hand. "Thank you for telling me." She pulled a napkin out of her apron pocket and bunched it in her hand. "What about you? Will you tell someone your story?"

Anxiety rattled her core. Could she describe the kidnapping? Being chained to a wall? The not knowing if she was going to die? Should she? Her experience didn't compare to what Sung endured. Her stomach churned just thinking about what Sung and the other women had lived through.

"I've given my statement to the FBI, and I might have to testify in court, but I hope it doesn't come down to that." A memory stirred, and she studied Jenna while she took another deep breath for courage.

"One more thing." Karly hesitated to

continue, but the need to know on Jenna's face left her no options. "Sung told me Vivian knew Caitlyn was pregnant with Jason's child. She was going to adopt her grandchild through one of her agencies after it was born, to make it look legitimate. Vivian liked the idea that her son and Caitlyn had a child together." Karly felt sick. "Sung said Vivian wanted to keep everything in the family."

"That fruity-frosted-fudgey bitch!" Jenna stood and started pacing, her jaw muscles pulsing. "Good thing she's in jail, or I might be tempted to do something stupid." Jenna walked around in circles a few more times, until she settled enough to sit.

"Thank you." She reached for Karly's hand. "Thank you for telling me. Wait until I tell Grant. You think I'm mad. Wait until he hears this." Jenna picked up her fork like she wanted to jab it into the sweet bars, or something more practical, like Vivian, but she put the piece of silverware back on the table, and let out a long, slow breath. "Is there anything I can do to repay Sung for her help?"

"I don't think so." Karly wished she could do the same. "Sung will have a new name and new life soon."

The slight smile on Jenna's face was about how she felt inside—small, and aware of how many things were not in her control.

"Which leads me to the second reason I stopped by."

"There's more?"

Karly found a way to reflect back Jenna's smiling courage. "Yep. I need to place an order for three dozen cupcakes, and a pan of those Krane Konfections. They're amazing. I'm throwing a thank-you party for my volunteers tomorrow, and I would like to invite you and Grant to come, since I know you both helped get my animals back to the shelter safely, and feed them while I was gone. I want to help this community heal. I would like it if you'd stop by and help me celebrate."

"Will Thad be there?"

"I invited him, but I'm not sure he'll show. I'm expecting about thirty people, so I'm thinking we can make it a party."

"Heck, yeah." Jenna moved to the counter to grab the order pad. "Sounds like an excellent idea." Jenna patted the rest of her tears away. "I had this idea for a joint community fundraiser for the shelter as well."

"Helper Shelter? My place?" Karly shoved the sweet bar in her mouth and let the gooey richness pump some sweetness into her soul. "Oh, this is so tasty." She rolled her eyes, letting the ecstasy fill her pores. "I'd love to hear any ideas. Did I tell you I'm thinking of consolidating, and just focusing on service dog training and boarding? There's an adoption center over in Eagle where I can take most of the remaining animals. Besides, I'm not sure how long Brad Clairemont is going to want to stay in town. He's the only vet, and I would have to have one on record if I stayed with animal adoption."

"No you didn't tell me. You're right. I

don't think Brad will stick around long. I think that's smart to think about that now. Running an adoption place and boarding dogs seems like a lot of work."

"It has been." Karly picked up the box of her treat samples just when the bakery door opened and Peggy Sue rushed in. "Did you hear Vivian Newhall and Richard Clairemont were having an affair?"

Karly looked at Jenna, and they both started laughing.

The town gossip spread rumors faster than mayonnaise on bread, but one thing was for sure, Buck Newhall's office assistant was as loyal as a cocker spaniel. She'd worked with Buck for years, and she wasn't about to let Vivian's antics tarnish her employer's reputation.

"See you later, Jenna." Karly settled her backpack on her shoulder and lifted her hand to wave goodbye.

Thrilled to be escaping that conversation, Karly opened the door just as Jenna said, "Hi, Peggy Sue. Did you stop in just for gossip, or for more of your grandson's favorites? How is he today?"

Karly let the door ease shut.

Another chapter closed.

Now if only she could find some closure for herself.

She needed to find a way to tell Thad the truth.

CHAPTER TWENTY-SIX

Reaching for the rescue's lead, Karly turned and smashed into a passerby. She scrambled to keep the bakery box from toppling, and both bodies from hitting the pavement.

Hearing the muffled gasp, Karly loosened her grip.

"Mara, it's me, Karly."

She empathized with the fear on her friend's face. Being on the teetering edge. Being off balance. Not seeing what's coming. The inability to scream for help. The helplessness.

"I'm sorry." Mara's muscles relaxed beneath Karly's hands. "I should have been paying more attention. I've had a lot on my mind, and I didn't hear you coming."

"We're all a little jumpy these days. It's going to take a while for me not to flinch at every little sound."

Mara reached for Buddy, and Gus, Joey's search and rescue dog, to make sure they were okay. "It will take longer than you think. When Mark attacked me, every time someone entered the flower shop, I wanted to scream. For weeks, I couldn't stop shaking. That's one of the reasons I turned Blooms over to my brother and sister-in-law. I couldn't stand to hear the worry in Tony's and Gina's voices. My brother can be overprotective."

"Well, Mark Walters and Jason Newhall are both dead. I hope Brad Clairemont figures out his life, or he'll wind up like his best friends."

Karly reached for the malamute's leash to

assure the rescue dog that everything was okay. "Where are you headed?"

"To the shelter. I want to help you set up for tomorrow's celebration. I can blow up balloons or something."

"Great. Let's walk over together." Karly shoved the baked goods in her backpack, then looped her arm through Mara's. "How are the Gacciones holding up?"

"Joe has his hands full. The family's relieved Sam's killer has finally been caught, but his Dad's not thrilled about waiting for a trial. It could take years before this is settled. His dad prefers the old west style of justice."

"Oh, boy. There are lots of trees and ropes around here. I don't envy Joe. He has a mess to clean up, that's for sure."

Mara stopped at the corner to wait for the light to change. When Buddy stood and leaned forward, she took a step onto the asphalt. Gus and Karly and the rescue trailed a half-step behind.

"How's Thad?" Mara kept her steady pace.

Thoughts of Thad made the sun disappear under a cloud, and the cold sadness caused a small shiver. A magpie flew from one of the building tops on Main Street to get a better view of the humans passing by.

"I guess he's recovering. I haven't seen him."

"Why haven't you seen him? He's been looking for you."

A shudder of nerves made her steps falter. The malamute looked to her for a new command, but she didn't have one. She reached for the dog's furry ears. "I…he asked me to marry him."

"That's great!"

The silence wafted in the breeze as Karly struggled to catch her breath, her palms sweaty.

"Or not." Mara's brows crunched in confusion. "You're not happy about Thad asking?"

"It's not that."

"Is it because—"

"I can't have children. There, I said it." Karly took a gulp of courage. "I had a miscarriage in high school. Now you know."

Mara pulled on her arm as soon as she made it to the sidewalk. "Stop a minute and listen to me."

A surge of tears threatened, but Karly gritted her teeth and swallowed them back.

Mara's hand slid down to squeeze Karly's before releasing her fingers. "I'm blind. That sucks. It does. For the longest time, I believed no one would ever love me. I was damaged goods. Then Joey came home and proved me wrong."

Karly took Mara's arm and a step toward her home—the shelter. "He's such a good man."

"So is Thad. Give him a chance, Karly. Have you told him about the miscarriage?"

"No. I've tried to tell him a dozen times, but something always happens, and it's not something I can text about."

"He deserves to know what's going on."

"At first I didn't think he had a right to

know, but after awhile, I knew I had to tell him. Every time I tried, something happened, or he started talking about having kids and I chickened out." Karly kicked at a rock near her shoe. "He's always held my heart. He'll never forgive me for not telling him. Besides, my parents never liked him, particularly my mom, and his mom and sister don't like me. Can you imagine what would happen at the wedding?" Karly snorted a laugh, but happiness didn't come along for the ride.

"Who cares?"

A jump of surprise made Karly's breath hitch. "What do you mean who cares? *I* care."

"Why? You've always been the one to try to please your family. You haven't gotten much in return. In fact, when you were taken, not one of your brothers showed up to help, your dad didn't fly in, and your mom locked herself in the house. I ask you again, why do you care?"

"Because they're my family."

"No. Family are the people who volunteer

to help at the shelter. Real friends. The people who care about you. The people who help you." Mara reached for her hand. "Between you and Kym, I couldn't ask for better sister friends."

"Oh, poop-on-a-stick." Karly rubbed her nose with the back of her hand. "You're trying to make me cry."

"I'm trying to help you see and believe that people love you. Including Thad."

"He's the one who dumped me, remember?"

"A thousand years ago. Every day since he's been home, he's tried to make up for it. That guy's been bit by the love tick, and it's sucking the blood right out of him. You need to give him a break."

Karly laughed. "That's gross."

"Made you smile, though, didn't it?"

Mara took a step toward the shelter. Buddy stopped at the next corner and looked for traffic before crossing the street. "What do you say? Why don't you take the day off and let the volunteers set up for tomorrow?"

"I don't know."

"You and Thad both deserve to find happiness. You could go up to his cabin and spend hours having raunchy sex."

"Mara!"

"What? Just because I'm blind doesn't mean I don't have a good imagination, and my hearing is great as well. All that kissy-groaning stuff going on in your office the other day left me hot and horny to the point I had to call Joe and tell him I had an emergency at home."

Karly quickly covered her mouth before Mara heard her giggle. "You didn't."

"I did." Mara took a right into the shelter's parking lot. "There are advantages to being married to a first responder. They tend to get places rather quickly."

Mara, you didn't just go there.

Thad had certainly been a mind-blowing surprise. Even now her nipples tingled at the memory.

Karly looked at her friend. "Do you think

the sheriff's department has a procedure code for a booty call?"

The blush on Mara's face was priceless. Karly pulled her backpack off her shoulder and opened Helper Shelter's front door. The sound of happy dogs and voices echoed off the walls.

She dropped her backpack on the reception counter while memories of Thad's long, lean body pressing her against the wall of her office ignited the pilot light in her belly. She could almost feel the burn of his hand circling, driving her into oblivion.

Just as she was about to go and splash cold water on her face, a familiar voice doused her entire system with a winter's blast of cold air.

Mara tilted her head, turning toward the kennel area. "Is that your mom?"

"Yep." Karly fought to keep the anger at bay. She'd never before held on to the negative, but this time, getting rid of the resentment had been challenging—and the reason she'd been avoiding her mom whenever possible. Hiding didn't seem like an option anymore.

"I guess I should go see what she wants." Karly took a step toward the employee entrance. "I'll be back in a minute."

She walked through the kennel area and followed the nasally voice into the back washroom.

"Mother? What are you doing here?" And, what are you doing dressed in jeans?

"I came to help, hun. You need volunteers. I'm volunteering." She tried to look casual, but it didn't work.

Karly studied the woman as her eyes flicked here, there, and everywhere to avoid meeting her direct scrutiny. With minimum makeup, a T-shirt, and a pair of worn jeans, her mother looked fresh, not made up. Not her usual plastic. Over the years, she'd come to understand her mother. What wound her up. What made her tick. What could crush her to pieces. The resentful anger she'd held on to for the past week began to slip.

"That's kind of you," Karly finally managed.

Her mother cupped Karly's face and gently rubbed a thumb under each eye. "You don't look as tired today. That's good. That's very good." She slid a box across the counter. "I made up flyers to advertise your business, and I talked to my women's bridge club. Several of them are going on vacation soon, and need someone to watch their animals. A lady over in the cat room said they need people to socialize the animals." Her mother's face puckered. "I think that means just petting the things, right? I can pet animals. I can do that. And…"

"Mother?" Karly said, gently pulling her mother into her arms. "It's okay. I'm okay."

Her mother's shoulders began to shake. "I just wanted a better life for you. I love you. I want you to know that before it's too late. I want you to be happy. I'm proud of what you're doing here. Honest, I am."

"Mom?"

"From now on, I'm going to stop trying

to change things. I'm going to be more supportive. Will you ever forgive me?"

The tremors going through her mother released a load of unbearable sadness. Karly tightened her arms around her mom's shoulders, and she held on until the resentment and bitter anger faded.

"You don't need to ask for my forgiveness," she whispered past the lump in her throat, while her mother stiffened. She leaned back to look into her mother's eyes. "I love you, Mom." Her mother seemed to have shrunk overnight.

"Oh, honey. You make this momma proud, but I made my mascara run. I had better check it before someone sees me."

Her mother took two steps and turned back. "Oh, I forgot to tell you. There was only one-ply bathroom tissue in your restroom. I replaced it with a better brand."

Her mom's steps picked up the pace as Karly shook her head.

"Well, that didn't go too badly," Mara said

from the doorway, her mouth dancing with humor.

"No...no, it didn't. For the first time in my life, my mother told me she was proud of me. That's something."

"Yes. That's something. I'm going to go check on her, make sure she doesn't drop a cat when she gets fur on her shirt."

"Good idea."

Karly let the moment sink in. The chatter of people. The yip of happy dogs. The smell of lavender and vanilla.

Maybe, if she could learn to forgive her mother...maybe, just maybe, she could learn to forgive herself.

CHAPTER TWENTY-SEVEN

Three days later, Thad walked into More Than Meatballs with mixed emotions. He'd scarcely seen Karly since getting out of the hospital. At the community celebration, in line at the coffee shop, but that was about it.

The pleasantries exchange felt more like a wasp sting. The initial pain was bad enough, but now the poison was spreading, the pain growing more intense.

Joe had invited everyone to a commemoration for Sam Gaccione at the family's restaurant. He could tell Joe missed his brother. Poster boards were set up with Sam's image, and there was a shadow box with his brother's shield and other memorabilia. The former sheriff would have been proud of the work Joe did to find his killer.

Thad expected several of the townsfolk and people from the joint task force to show, but hadn't expected the place to be so full.

He hoped to see Karly. She hadn't returned his phone calls, and she'd been a little distant and played busy when he stopped by the shelter. He'd give her space, but not enough to allow the love to wither and turn to dust.

Thad spotted Chase and raised his hand in greeting, then he winced in pain.

"From the look on your face, you must be off your pain meds."

Yep. #DrugFree.

Chase's knowing smile made Thad snort a laugh, but he regretted it a second later when his ribs protested. "I don't want to get addicted to prescriptions."

Chase pulled a beer from the nearest bucket of ice. "I don't blame you. If you're not taking anything for the pain, a beer won't kill you."

Thad accepted the symbol of friendship. "So what's up with the feds?"

"My guess is Joe's ma wants to thank everyone who was involved." Chase turned toward the rather round older woman standing in the corner in a pristine white apron, looking more like a traffic cop directing servers than a business owner. "If I were a betting man, I'd say she also wants more answers."

"You mean as to why arrests weren't made sooner?"

"Something like that. My respect for Joe climbed a few pegs in the past couple of days. If I'm reading the signals correctly, he knew about the undercover operation, and had to bide his time to flush out the players."

Chase paused, the beer bottle halfway to his lips. "It would suck not knowing who to trust."

There was that trust thing again. Karly didn't fully trust him. Didn't anybody trust anybody in this town? "I wonder if everyone involved has been arrested."

"I sure hope so, for this town's sake. Dale said they arrested the guy who's been blackmailing Gwen. I guess someone figured out he was transporting drugs and women to Chicago."

"Karly mentioned a Gwen. She's the general's girlfriend, right?"

"Right. I keep forgetting everyone in this town hasn't always been here since the prehistoric age. Gwen owns the thrift store over on Main. Several months ago, her ex-fiancé showed up and tried to blackmail her for half of her trust fund. Guess when Gwen wouldn't turn the money over, the jerk entered into the transport business." Chase took a sip of his beer. "This town is going to need a lot of healing."

"Healing? Who's hurt now?" Ashley asked, sliding an arm around her husband.

Chase tucked his wife under his arm and

gave her a kiss on the forehead. A tendril of jealousy wrapped tight around Thad's heart.

Chase tucked Ashley in closer. "This town, I suppose. It's got to be a shock, having most of Elkridge's council, elected officials, and several deputies arrested. How's Caitlyn's diaper rash?"

"I just called Dad. He already put her down for the night." Ashley touched Thad's arm. "How are you?"

"I'm fine, but this corruption mess will take years to unravel. Those narcissists sure hurt a lot of people, Karly being one of them." Thad looked away so his friends wouldn't witness his struggle with wanting to exact revenge. "Speaking of Karly, have you seen her?" He held back his hope with a firm hand.

Nobody knew she'd refused his proposal, and he'd like to keep it that way. Maybe she'd change her mind.

"I think she's in the kitchen with Mara." Ashley pointed to the stainless steel swinging door.

Chase gave him a friendly smack on the arm. "What are you waiting for? Go find your woman."

Thad winced, making Chase pause and start to apologize.

"Just kidding." Thad winked before taking off for the kitchen.

My woman. If only Karly really were his. He wished Chase had hit him harder. He didn't mind that kind of pain. Physical wounds kept his mind occupied. The mental anguish of not being able to connect with Karly messed with his head. The need to see her, to make sure she was okay, drove him toward the back of the restaurant.

He pushed open the kitchen door to scan the efficiently run kitchen. The line chefs worked their stations while wait staff restocked the salad line. In the rear of the kitchen, Mara and Karly were huddled in the hall, out of the path of scurrying bodies.

Studying the way Karly positioned herself facing away from everyone, drawing her arms inward, keeping her voice soft and her head down, he guessed she wanted to be invisible. The same crushing feeling he had in the months after the IED exploded. Those on the ground assured him nothing could have been done, but he still should have found the bomb before it killed his best buddies. Parents, siblings, and friends lost someone they cared about, and wanted someone, anyone to blame.

The muscles in his neck ached just thinking about the visions Karly must be re-creating in her head.

He weaved around a couple of staff members, making his way to the back toward the exit.

"Hey, Mara. Karly. I just got here. Have you eaten yet?"

The way Karly's skin turned a perfect shade of ogre green, he supposed she wasn't the least bit hungry.

"The food smells delicious, but I think I'll pass." Karly made a weak attempt at a smile.

Mara's hand landed on Karly's forearm. "You need to eat something. You wouldn't allow me to order us lunch today, either. When's the last time you ate?"

She seemed to scan the bulletin board behind Mara's shoulder, studying the schedules and menus and pictures of kids. "I'm fine. I wish everyone would stop worrying about me."

"We'll stop worrying when you're eating and sleeping." Mara moved in closer. "I can tell you're exhausted."

Thad put his arm around Mara's shoulders. "Tell you what. I'll make sure Karly gets a salad or something. How's that sound?"

Mara straightened her walking stick. "That sounds great. The only problem is, I know you're just trying to get rid of me." Mara patted Thad's arm. "See if you can talk some sense into her. I haven't been successful so far."

"I'll come with you." The desperate tone added to Karly's statement didn't sit quite right and made Thad burn. Why couldn't she get that he wasn't someone she needed to avoid?

"I'm good." Mara waved her off. "Besides, I believe you and Thad have some things to talk about."

Thad caught the odd expression on Mara's face. *What's that all about?*

Mara's stick tap-tap-tapped across the kitchen tile until she found her way out the door. Thad took a step closer to Karly, but she held out a hand that was still a bit shaky.

"If you're about to ask how I am, please don't. I might brain the next person who asks me that question with a frying pan."

"Would it help if I told you I can empathize? Crowded rooms, people looking at me, giving advice. There's nothing you can do to stop it. Trust me, I've tried."

"Do the nightmares ever go away?"

"Not really."

"Oh, great." Karly almost strangled her words. "Maybe sleep is overrated anyway."

That's my Karly. There's my stubborn girl.

Pride quickly deflated into self-pity. She wasn't his. She didn't want to be his.

Joe popped his head around the corner. "Hey, you two. I'm about to make an announcement. Grab some beer, food, dessert, or whatever you want, and join us in the back room." He disappeared without waiting for a response.

Karly eyed the emergency exit.

Thad leaned closer to her ear. "I wouldn't try it." He pointed at the blinking light. "The doors are armed."

"I shouldn't have come tonight. I just thought..."

"The only people in that room are people who care about you. There's no need to worry. Let's go in together." He nudged her shoulder and took a step toward the door. "I'll stand behind you if it will make you feel safer."

"Who will stand behind you?" A little spark of humor flickered before vanishing.

The smell of her cherry vanilla lip gloss made him want to kiss her until the spark came back. "We'd better go before Joe sends Mara back in here to get us."

"We'd better."

He followed her through the kitchen door and into the back room. Her steps faltered, but she managed to keep going.

"Ah, good. We're all here." Joe addressed the crowd while Agent Bantner took up a position behind the sheriff. "Thank you for coming tonight." His tone was precise, measured. "As many of you know," he continued, his voice getting a bit louder, "my brother Sam was murdered on the logging road just outside of town a few days before Valentine's. It will be two years in February. A few town residents wanted us to believe it was an accident—a poacher. However, evidence proved otherwise.

"Some of you may wonder why my brother's killer wasn't brought to justice before now. You have the right to ask. If Sam was standing here today, he would have agreed that waiting, watching, and patience was the prudent path to take. Because of your patience, eighty-seven arrests have been made across the country. The DEA has seized $50 million in heroin, and well over a thousand women and children, victims of sex trafficking, have been recovered." Joe coughed to clear his throat. "Agencies across the country are seizing the bank accounts and assets of those involved."

Wow. The beer's barley gurgled in Thad's stomach. *Joe said the trouble was big.* Anger darkened every face in the room.

"Yes, but if Karly hadn't been taken, you wouldn't have made your arrests," Mamma Gaccione accused in her normal hand-flying Italian way. "Agent Bantner, you put our lives in danger."

Way to go, Mrs. G.

Bantner, wearing blue slacks and a powder blue shirt, stepped forward. "From an outside perspective, it may seem that way. However, there were agents monitoring the situation around the clock. If at any time we felt your safety was in jeopardy, we would have acted accordingly."

"That's a bunch of bull hooey," Joe's dad tossed back.

"Dad, Mom, if it weren't for the FBI, DEA, and joint task force," Joe said, "we most likely would never have figured out who killed Sam. The agencies were not required to inform us, nor were they required to put me in a position where I could ensure this town's safety."

"Phft." Joe's mom threw up her hand. "If it weren't for Thad and Rivers, those crooks would've gotten away. We protect our own. We always have."

"Which leads me to my next point, Ma." Joe leaned an elbow on top of his holster.

There's more? Thad's shoulders knotted and bunched.

"In a few days, the special task force agents will be gone. We will still be here. There are still schools to run, traffic tickets to process, and a new city council that needs to be formed. Stella King has stepped up to fill in until a new mayor and board members can be elected. I will do my best to see to the safety of the residents, but we can't do this alone."

"What do you recommend?" Harold, the general store owner, asked.

"This town is full of former military," Thad spoke up. "Maybe we need to form a watch."

"That's exactly what I was thinking. We're in this together," Joe confirmed. "We each need to play our part. When someone steps up for one of the vacant positions, vote—either for or against, it doesn't matter—just vote. Until the elections, pitch in where you can."

Never pass a fault echoed through Thad's thoughts.

"What do we say to those reporters?" Jack Burke asked.

"Invite them into your pub, Jack. Let them get a real feel for what this town has to offer. We've been given a black eye, but it won't be that way for long. Most people have short memories. Besides, we have bigger things to worry about."

Mara, Joe's wife, stiffened. "Like what?"

"Like planning the Christmas Bazaar. Elkridge holds one every year, and this year will be no different."

"I'll plan a dog wash or something else to help bring the community together," Karly offered. "Maybe, Mara and I can get Jenna, and Gwen to help."

Ashley lifted the beer in her hand. "Here's to looking forward." Chase wrapped his arm around his wife.

Karly unfolded her arms. Her body shifted and eased as those in the room with glasses or bottles raised them in a toast.

"Okay, that's enough chatter." Joe lifted his beer bottle a bit higher. "Please enjoy my ma's cooking, and the company of our neighbors and friends."

One pair of hands clapped together, then another, then another, until everyone joined in.

Thad leaned in and whispered into Karly's ear, "Rivers Black is here. I'd like to talk to him. Will you be okay?"

She turned. "You're going to get hit over the head with a skillet. I asked you not to baby me. Go. Go talk to Rivers. We can talk later."

Thad accepted the verbal slap. He understood how she felt, but her sharpness still stung. "I'll be back in a minute."

He passed several tables full of people, grabbed an extra beer from the ice bucket, and made his way to a secluded corner of the room. He took a short sip of his own beer and extended his offering to Rivers.

"Don't drink." Rivers waved off the glass bottle hovering at chest level. Thad left the extra beverage on the table.

"I tried getting ahold of you, but no one knows your number," Thad said.

"Don't have a phone."

"No alcohol or phone." *Typical.* "Tell me something." Thad dropped his voice to almost a whisper. "You fired your gun. I heard it go off. I shot Sanchez in the leg, and wounded the two other guys. The good doctor finished Macedo off. What were you shooting at? I have to think you're not so bad a shot that you missed whatever you were aiming at."

Rivers' eyes didn't blink. His chiseled face didn't move except his mouth. His mouth stretched and elongated. Holy cow. *Was that a smile?*

"I aimed for the doors."

"I'm getting shot at, and you're aiming at door handles."

"Not the handles. The locks."

The silence stretched. Thad could stand there all night and not get an answer unless he asked the right question. "Okay. I'll bite. Why the doors?"

"There were eight men in the compound. Three in the loading bay, and I knew you could take out three, but eight? Broken locks would prevent the others from getting in."

"Wouldn't it also prevent us from getting out?"

"At the time, you weren't too worried about getting out."

A good ol' teary-eyed, knee-slapping kind

of laugh bubbled up from nowhere. He threw his head back and gave into the temporary relief, and extended his hand. "Rivers. Thanks for your help."

"You're welcome." His friend squeezed his hand. "You still seeing your father's ghost?"

Surprise coiled in his stomach. Thad shifted and pulled at the label of his beer. "He's always around, in my head, my dreams. I can't get rid of him."

Rivers' eyes grew dark and severe. "Let your father come. Embrace the memories. Then blow them away. He doesn't matter anymore." Rivers put his hand to his mouth and blew, then thrust his hand into the air, his fingers splayed. "You will be wiser, stronger for it."

Rivers patted Thad on the shoulder and then left the party without a sound.

Contentment sauntered into the room and massaged his shoulders. For the first time in forever he didn't feel worthless. Thad turned to see Karly standing by the dessert table.

He shouldn't hover. She'd get claustrophobic and push him away, but he craved her company. She attracted him like a dog to a fresh slice of ham. He couldn't resist. Didn't want to resist. She'd given him a purpose, and he'd protect her—no matter what.

She turned just as he approached. "Lopez! You almost got tiramisu all over your shirt."

"I wouldn't mind, if you promise to lick it off." He started to smile until her eyes darkened, and her plate started to shake in her hand.

"Thad—"

"Don't worry. I won't ask you to marry me again. Twice is enough."

Her eyes held a wanting—no, more sadness. Both irritated him, because he couldn't figure out what she wanted. One minute, she's telling him don't go there, the next she's sending hold-me signals. What the hell was he supposed to do? He needed a map, and she hadn't even bothered to give him a compass.

"Karly, I know you don't want people to care, but we do. What you went through…"

"I can't do this. Not here. Not tonight."

She slid her dessert plate onto the nearest table and made a direct line for the door, picking up momentum as she went. By the time she got to the door, she was practically running.

"Is everything okay?" Joe asked.

Hell, no. Thad studied his beer, now lukewarm. "Are you sure nothing happened to Karly while she was gone?"

"She said nothing happened. Why?"

"Just curious." Thad set his bottle on the table. "Nice speech, by the way." He glanced toward the door. "But I think I'd better call it a night."

"I was wondering if you were going to go after her or just stand here like an idiot."

"Excuse me?" Thad had the urge to punch something. Joe was standing in front of him, and in the wrong place at exactly the wrong time.

Thad moved back a bit. "What's that smile about?"

He hadn't spent a lot of time with Joe, but that fat grin indicated he was up to something. "My deputies need to be able to think on their feet. If you hadn't, I would have trashed the idea of asking you to come in next week to talk about a job."

"Seriously? I'd love to help rebuild this town—help you put it back together the way it was." He summed up the man. Husband. Soon-to-be father. Protector of this town. He could work for someone with solid integrity, and wouldn't have to do construction work after all.

"Your dad had a reputation for working out his problems with his fists."

"Yeah. So?"

"Rivers doesn't think you're like that. What do you say?"

He wouldn't be reckless anymore, or put himself in front of a bullet just to prove a point.

He had a purpose.

Protect this town.

Protect Karly.

"I think Rivers is right. I'm not my dad. Never have been. My father was wrong about me."

Joe shifted and leaned in. "How so?"

"He said I was worthless. Couldn't do a thing right. Would never amount to much." He looked at the door, then around the room. "Protecting and saving lives isn't nothing. It's worth a lot."

"You got that right." Joe's approval beamed across his face. "Now, get out of here. Go find Karly."

"Yes, sir."

Thad took off at a trot, hitting the front door with enough force to clear the door and make it to the curb in time to see Karly's taillights disappear around the corner.

He shoved his hands in his pockets and tilted his head toward the night sky.

Over the years, he'd had many challenging assignments to protect people who didn't always want to be protected.

Some days were hard, but none were going to be as difficult as this one. Karly didn't want his protection. Heck, she didn't want *him*...well, other than as a friend. His determination kicked in. He'd be there for her, because he'd given her his heart, and he didn't want it back.

Ever.

He'd adjust. Become the man he wanted to be. For himself. For her.

And continue practicing patience.

CHAPTER TWENTY-EIGHT

T had waited three days to let her settle back into her routine before visiting.

The Army taught him when to push forward, when to fall back. He just needed to bide his time. He'd let her run. Eventually, she'd get tired, or he'd capture her heart with love and kindness. Getting her to love him back, well…that might take more time.

"I have awesome news." Thad walked into Karly's office. "Joe's offered me a job."

Karly looked up from her computer. "That's great," she said, although the enthusiasm didn't follow.

"Are you sure you're okay with me taking a deputy job, versus working for Chase?"

"Ummm...Sorry? I'm still trying to switch gears here." She tossed her pen on the desk. "Deputy. That's great news, and it shouldn't matter what I think. It's what is important to you." She pushed her hair off her shoulder and stretched as if she'd been sitting for hours. "When do you start?"

"There's some paperwork and a few tests. Part of the requirement for me to work for the force is getting my leg back in shape and EMDR therapy."

"What type of therapy? I've never heard of the EM...what did you call it?"

"EMDR, or Eye Movement Desensitization and Reprocessing. It's some new psychotherapy that will be useful for helping me get my dad's voice out of my head. Both Joe and I feel talking to someone will help."

"That sounds great."

Ah, that smile. If he could see her

beauteous expression every minute of every day, he'd be a happy man.

"Joe will be hiring some new deputies, and wants me to train them in hand-to-hand combat and tactical maneuvering. He's already hired a female he wants me to test. She's moving up from Denver."

"That's great. I'm pleased for you."

Thad sat on the edge of her desk. The floral scent from her shampoo wafted by, and he wanted to lean in closer to savor her essence. "You seem distracted today. What's up? Something seems off."

"Something's off, all right. My bank account. My business. It's all off."

Thad studied the computer screen and saw a bunch of red. "Is that your financial statement for the year?"

"Yep. Even with not accepting any more rescues, adding volunteers, and cutting back on expenses, I still don't have enough to pay the back bills plus fund operations. I just can't seem to figure out a way to make this place work. Even with the donated food and supplies, I can't do it."

Can't? She'd been using that word a lot lately. She never used to.

The tears welling in her eyes shredded his determination to keep his distance. He pulled her into his arms. "It'll be okay, Karly. We'll figure something out. I've already been working on a plan to create some Facebook ads and get you more traffic to your site."

"You have?" Her eyes expanded with her surprise.

"Yep. I just need to look into a few more things before I share."

Her whole body deflated. "I wanted to prove to my parents I could do this, run a business. They never supported my dream, well, not until recently."

"If the Army taught me one thing, it's that a team of people can accomplish more than just one person."

"It's too little, too late. I've already put in calls to other shelters. They're willing to take some of the animals. I also called my brother this morning. That manager job in Denver's still open. I still have time to get my resume in, not that I know how to write one."

Wow. "An office job?" He wanted to grab her by the shoulders and shake until her common sense returned. "That's what you want to do?"

"What choice do I have? With everything that has happened over the last few weeks, I'm tired of the way people look at me like I'm some rescue that they have to adopt." Karly shuffled papers on her desk. "Plus, my mother is being weird. She cleaned my apartment yesterday."

"That doesn't sound unusual."

"She didn't rearrange the furniture this time or reorganize my closet. Everything was where it was supposed to be when I got home."

"That is weird." Thad handed Karly a stray paperclip that had fallen to the floor. "Who replaced your mother with an alien?" Thad walked around to the other side of Karly's desk. "Just kidding."

"No, you're not." She shoved the papers into one of the filing cabinets. "It's just I jump at every little sound. I have these nightmares. I can't even go running and exercise the dogs, because I'm terrified someone will jump out and grab me. I know it's silly. I need to get over the fear, because I love to run, and the large dogs need to release some energy."

I can appreciate how you feel. "We can run together."

"That still doesn't solve the problem of funding."

"How much do you need?"

"If I maintain my boarding and adoption income average, I'm still short five thousand dollars."

Thad let out an elongated whistle. "That's a chunk of change."

"My point. Even if I train more service dogs, it won't be enough. I need money now. Plus, training dogs takes away from my time running the business. I'm exhausted and running low on chow."

"This kennel has been your dream." Thad pushed. "If you give up now, you might regret it."

"If I can't properly feed or take care of these animals, I'll regret it even more. These guys have already been through enough."

"Promise me you'll give me a week."

"Thad—"

"No. Promise me. Just one week. Let me see if I can come up with something."

"You need to concentrate on your new job."

"Let me worry about my job. We need to come up with ideas for how to keep this place running."

"Have you ever thought it might be better, for both of us, if I leave town? I've seen the way you look at me, and you always seem to want more. I've already told you I can't give you more."

A slow breath eased out his chest. Patience. He needed to have patience. "Let's just take one step at a time. Let's focus on your business, and we can discuss our future some other time."

The muscles in her face worked like gears on a bike, rotating around and around and around trying to get all the muscles working together, but then the ticking motion stopped, and she shrugged. "Okay. You've talked me into it. One week. I'll give it one more week, then I have to start getting these animals placed, or find foster families."

"I'll take the week, and raise you exercising daily."

"What are we, playing poker now?"

There was the pushback he loved. "It's called physical therapy. In your case, it's physical therapy for the mind. You need to keep doing what you love to do. What you went through was horrific, and nobody should have to go through that kind of thing. You need to give yourself a break, Karly. You need to give yourself time to heal."

She put her feet up on her desk, leaned back and crossed her arms. "Are you healed?"

"I'm getting there, but it's taken me much

longer than I ever thought it would. How about it? We can each take three dogs. You can always do the paperwork later tonight."

"Thad Lopez, did anyone ever tell you you're persistent?"

He chuckled. "I've been called a lot of things, but persistent hasn't ever been one of them." Thad stood. "Why don't I get the kennels loaded and the supplies packed while you finish up here?" The skepticism on her face he wanted to erase. "C'mon, it'll be fun."

Her sad eyes lifted to him. "Thank you. You've been a great friend these past several weeks. I'm glad you came home."

Friend. He was starting to hate that word. "Yeah. Me too."

CHAPTER TWENTY-NINE

"Neon, my man, I need a favor." Thad paced across the floorboards of his kitchen.

"Monk. Good to hear from you, buddy. What can I do for you?" There was no hesitation, no what-now tone in his friend's voice. *Support for life. That's military for you.*

"I need to tap into your social media network. I need to raise money, and fast. It's for a good cause."

"Don't tell me that old cabin's got leaks."

"No, man, nothing like that. There's this animal shelter that trains service dogs. Some of the guys coming back need help. I want to raise funds to train the dogs."

"Hey, Kenny? Thad's on the line. Doesn't your sister own a kennel?"

#Busted.

"Neon?" He waited for the shuffling to die down. "Neon. Yo, man. Just forget it."

"Not happening. You need a love fund. That's what you need, and Kenny and I will get you one."

Love fund? He was never going to live this one down. Sometimes there was a downside to having buddies who knew too much. "Maybe this wasn't such a good idea."

"No. It's a great idea. We gotcha covered. Tell me what you're thinking."

Turbulent insecurity tumbled through his chest. *You can do this.* He hated asking for help, but he wanted this for Karly. He rolled his neck to steady his uneasiness. "I want to set up a page on CrowdFund.com, see if I can't get a few people to chip in. I need to raise five grand."

"Dude, I know you're doing this to help

Kenny's sister, but you'll also be helping vets. If we're going to do this, do it right. Set the goal high."

"You know how to do this stuff. What do you suggest?"

"Let's double it, and see where we land."

"Double?" *Wow.* "That's a hefty goal." Thad watched a herd of elk move through his pasture and stop to graze. Every member of the herd depended on the others to alert them to danger, and to keep the group healthy. Just like his friends. "Okay, ten grand. Ask Kenny to help."

At that moment, the clouds shifted and the sun unveiled her brilliant colors.

Maybe this would work.

The heavy burden he'd been carrying slid off his shoulders.

"I ain't gonna ask. He'll help. I won't be able to stop him." Neon puffed out in disgust. "If this is for you, and his sister, he'll fill the love bucket to overflowin'."

It's more than about me. "If I don't get this

money, Karly will give up her dreams. I can't let that happen."

"It's about time you unbolted that door. I've been wondering when you were going to admit to loving that woman." *I already asked her to marry me—twice.*

Love. What a funny thing it could be. He leaned against the counter. "Karly stole my heart when I was in grade school, and she's never given it back."

"Then let me talk to some buddies and see what we can do. Once you get the account set up, send me the link. There's this guy at the hospital in San Antonio. He makes videos of vets returning from the zone. I'll see if he's willing to put together a few clips."

His excitement transformed into real possibilities. "That would be great."

"Hey, Kenny wants to talk to you. Hang on a second." The moments ticked by and Thad waited.

"Monk?"

"Hey, Kenny. What's up? You doing better?"

"Yeah, the sergeant is sending me on a new course next month. All's good. How about you? Are you staying out of trouble?"

The last few weeks slashed through his mind, but he couldn't tell Kenny about the kidnapping. It wasn't his story to tell, and Karly insisted her brother shouldn't be told, especially while he was preparing to leave. Kenny needed to keep his head in the game. Karly's words, not his, because war wasn't a game.

"No trouble here." Thad switched the phone to the other ear. "You wouldn't happen to know if something happened to Karly after I left Elkridge, would you? I get the feeling it's something bad."

"Karly's always been a locked box. Not even a crowbar will open her up unless she wants to tell you what's going on."

"Would someone else know?"

"Our cousin in New York, maybe, but when it comes to Karly, she wouldn't say a word. She's loyal. Always has been."

"I'd sure like to know what she's afraid of.

It's like she's resigned to spending her life alone."

"Wish I could help you out there, man, but Karly's always kept to herself. I'm the closest to her, and I still don't think anyone knows my sister."

Good to know. "Thanks. If you think of anything, shoot me an email."

"Good talking to you. Catch you next time."

Thad ended the call and crossed his legs. The last phone conversation he had with Karly all those years ago replayed in bits and fragments. He'd been jealous. She'd been angry. Both of them said a whole lot of things, yet nothing worth anything.

He needed to get her to open up.

Talk to him.

This time, he'd listen to not only what she said...but what she didn't say. This time, his future was riding on her answer.

CHAPTER THIRTY

"**R**eady to get to work?" Joe walked around his desk to shake Thad's hand.

"Absolutely. I can't wait to get started. I'm looking forward to working with everyone." Thad handed Joe a folder. "Here's my clearance. Doc says I'm good to go."

"Glad to hear it." Joe gestured toward a fabric office chair, then hit the ignore button on his cell phone. "It's Mara. I'll call her back when we're done. Take a seat."

Thad sank into the fabric-covered chair and did his best to keep the nerves from wreaking havoc.

"I'm putting you on rotation." Joe dropped the file on his desk without opening it. "As you know we're shorthanded, and need everyone trained for anything. Stella King will give you orientation. Follow her rules, and you'll get along with her fine. She'll get you set up with a locker and gear. Ernie will walk you through the crime-scene training."

Thad's thumbs pounded on the chair arms in time with the excitement beating in his chest. "Sounds good."

"I'd like you to spend the rest of the day going over the open case files." Joe snickered, a reaction to Thad's grimace. "It will be tedious and painful, but I want you to familiarize yourself with what you can expect, what scenarios might come up."

The sheriff looked at his phone again. "Would you excuse me a minute? Mara's called me twice in the last couple of minutes. It must be important, or she wouldn't have called again."

A little lump of envy got stuck in his

throat. He'd like to get a phone call, to be needed. Karly never called, or texted, or dropped by just to chat.

Joe reached for a post-it and pen. "Slow down, Mara. Give me the timeline again."

Thad wasn't an expert on body language, but he knew when something wasn't right.

"Would you switch to video so I can have a look around?" Joe gave him the come-here finger. Thad moved to the edge of his chair and leaned in to see the real-time video.

Karly's office came into view. Gone were the piles of paper and files stacked everywhere. Everything had been put into boxes. *Had she already given up? She promised a week?*

"I came to do the feeding," Mara's unnerved voice wobbled. "The bowls were missing, so I went searching for them. I discovered someone had already fed the animals." The video jostled up and down as Mara walked past the reception desk, into the employee entrance, down the row of dogs.

"Mara, this is Thad. Can you show us the kennel area one more time?" He watched the image on the screen shift.

"Oh good. You're there." The camera swung around. The wire gates with dogs inside came into view.

"Can you turn slowly in a circle?" Thad studied the picture. "All the dogs are accounted for. She doesn't have any with her, which is odd."

The picture flipped, and a distraught Mara came into view. "I'm telling you, something is wrong. She's not answering her phone. I called her mom. She's not at her apartment. Her truck is missing. I've called everyone I can think of, even you, Thad, but you didn't answer your phone."

"It's my first day on the job. I didn't think my new boss would appreciate me taking personal calls."

Joe shook his head and looked at his wife. "Maybe she's out for a run."

"While Tony was out delivering flowers, I had him check all of Karly's usual running spots. Karly's predictable. She likes routine. I wouldn't have called you if I didn't think something was wrong."

"Okay." Joey's voice conveyed a calm Thad wished he felt. "I'll alert the guys. Thad, can you think of anywhere Karly might have gone?"

"There are a couple of places I might look. If orientation can wait, I'll go now."

"Go." Joe nodded. "Keep your cell phone on in case I need to get ahold of you."

Thad was out the door and down the hall in three seconds flat. His mind raced. *Would she go there? Maybe.*

She was predictable. Mara had nailed Karly's personality perfectly.

He backed out of the parking lot. His heart was pounding.

Please, let her be safe.

Almost twenty minutes later, Thad relayed, "I found her."

"Good. That's really good." He felt Joe's relief by his response. "I'll let Mara know."

"Give me a few minutes, and I'll call you

back after I make sure everything is okay." Thad shoved his phone in his back pocket and made his way down the steep hill to the wooden bridge. The vibration of his footsteps on the old wooden planks made her turn.

"Go away, Thad." The sound of rushing water below camouflaged her words, but he got her meaning. She didn't want him to go away now, she wanted him gone for good.

"You keep telling me to go away, but I'm still here, Karly. I'm here to listen."

"You never listen."

Yes, I do. Thad pushed his hands into his khaki pockets. "I promise I'll listen to whatever you have to say. Just let me stay. Tell me what's going on."

"I can't do this anymore." Karly covered her mouth with her hands, her body caving, a raging river of tears flowing.

"Do what? Karly. What is that you can't do anymore?"

She brushed her nose with the back of her hand. "I can't pretend everything's okay.

That I'm okay. I can't lie anymore." She leaned forward, and his heartbeat throbbed in his temples. The rushing water bubbled and cascaded over the giant boulders below. He leaned against the back railing to see if she would turn away from the edge. She didn't. He needed to keep her talking. "You don't need to pretend with me."

"You left me." She pulled her hair into a bunch and twisted it around and around, trying to make a knot. When the hair wouldn't stay, she dropped her hands to her lap with a whimper, her chin quivering. "I loved you. Why didn't you love me enough?"

"I loved you with everything I had." He rubbed at the scars on his hand. "I believed if I let you go, you'd have a better chance at finding happiness."

She looked back at the water. "Well, you were wrong."

"I *was* wrong, Karly." He hoped she heard his plea. "I'm so terribly sorry I hurt you."

"You need to go."

He took a step, but she scooted away.

"Okay, Karly." He held out his hand, and moved to the edge to sit a body's length away from her. "We'll just sit and enjoy the sunshine, listen to the birds sing, let the water roll by. We'll stay here as long as you like. Just you and me."

The minute hand on his watch churned one tick at a time, like a fifty-pound weight had been attached.

Keep quiet. Listen. She just needs you to listen. He rolled his head on his neck and let sound in. After more minutes than he had the courage to count, she lifted an arm and pointed at a stand of aspen trees.

"He's over there." Her words were barely above a whisper.

"Who? Karly. Who's over there?"

"Charlie."

Thad flipped through memory after memory, trying to think of every animal Karly ever had. Kenny had never mentioned a Charlie.

"He never had a chance." Tears poured down her face, and she began to hug herself and rock back and forth. "It would have been his birthday today."

Shock at the pure agony on her face squeezed the air out of his lungs. He couldn't breathe. He wanted to ask questions, but he clamped his teeth together.

Listen. She needs you to listen. You promised to listen.

She put her palms to her eyes and pressed. "I loved Charlie." Her eyes grew distant and glazed before turning to him. "You need to know that. I loved him. I truly loved him. I would have given him everything."

"Karly, who's Charlie?"

She swallowed hard, and her eyes pleaded with him to understand. "He was our son."

"Our son? We had a son?" *Oh, God, Karly no. Please, no.* A knife stabbed his heart, and twisted, then twisted again, pushing deeper.

Her face crumpled. "I found out after you left."

Oh, man. He pushed to his feet to resettle closer to her. He could no longer feel the sun. A bone-deep chill swept over him until he looked at her and the warmth returned. He pulled her into his arms.

"Karly. Please don't pull away. Let me hold you."

Seconds passed before she dropped her head to his shoulder.

"I'm so sorry I wasn't here. Why didn't you tell me?"

"Why? You need to know why? You didn't love me—didn't want me anymore." She curled tighter into herself, to become small.

"Besides I didn't know I was pregnant for the longest time. Weeks went by. I was so upset because you left that I didn't realize I hadn't gotten my period. Then I started to get sick in the morning. I was scared. Really scared someone would find out."

Her body tightened next to him, and he massaged her arm. She ran her fingers under her lower eyelashes. "I was going to find a way to tell you, then you finally called. I was so happy just to hear your voice, then you told me you didn't want to be with me anymore."

"Karly, if I could only take the things I said back. Change things."

She folded in on herself, every curve and angle laden with despair. "You wouldn't tell me why," she wailed. "I kept asking, but you never would tell me. I just wanted to know why." She shrugged her shoulders. "That's when I got mad and told you never ever to speak to me again."

He pulled her closer. "Karly, I'm sorry. I wish I had known."

She pushed away from his arms and stood. A flash of fury sparked from her eyes. "If you had known, what would you have done? Quit the Army? Come home? You didn't have that choice."

"I would have sent for you. Asked you to come live with me. I would have supported you when I deployed."

"Why? Because of the baby?"

"No, because I loved you. I still love you."

She braced against the railing, her anger

deflated. "It wouldn't have mattered. You didn't love me enough to trust in us."

"I can be pretty stupid, but we were both kids. We made mistakes. *I* made mistakes, but I learned from them. I'm not the same guy I was back then."

"Yes, you are, Thad Lopez. You can be brainless sometimes, but you're still giving and kind. Look at what you did for Lily. You trained Custer." Thad moved a little closer to her.

"Will you tell me what happened?"

She sucked in a deep breath and let it out with a rush. "No one knew I was pregnant except my cousin. She was in town for my graduation, and she talked my parents into letting us go to Denver to shop. I wanted to spend my birthday money on baby stuff without my parents finding out."

She wrapped her arms around her waist and paced a few more steps in silence. "I had it all planned out. I was twenty weeks pregnant. Over the summer, I was going to move into a home I found for single mothers. I saw online they had free parenting classes. I was going to raise Charlie. Get a j-job."

A torrent of tears tumbled down her face, and she closed her eyes. "It was awful," she said in a voice so soft he almost couldn't hear her. "The blood. There was lots of blood." She looked up, her eyes meeting his. "The sales clerk called 911, and I was rushed to the nearest hospital. There was nothing to be done. Charlie couldn't be saved."

"You named our baby after my grandfather, didn't you?"

"He was the only person who ever supported you. I was going to tell you. I was, but I didn't know how, and then after a while I figured out you didn't need to know, until I was telling Jenna about her sister. Then I realized I had to tell you."

He locked his knees to remain standing. The acid in his stomach surged into his throat. "You thought I didn't love you, or our child." *Oh, God. How could I have been so stupid?* "I had a right to know."

"I sent you a letter, but I'm not sure you got it."

"I didn't get any letters from you. We move around so much, it must have gotten lost."

He'd barely survived the past ten years. Years driven by reckless anger. He'd volunteered for anything and everything dangerous, because his dad didn't think he would ever be a man. He'd wanted to prove his father wrong. Prove he wasn't worthless.

Dear God...what have I done?

The anger flowed out of his soul and dissolved. "Karly, I'm so—"

"Don't." She waved him off. "Whatever you were going to say, don't. It doesn't matter anymore. I forgave you a long time ago."

"But how am I supposed to forgive myself?"

"I'm having trouble forgiving myself. Maybe we both need to learn to forgive."

He reached for her hand, but she pulled

away. "Karly. Why won't you let me hold you? You didn't do anything wrong."

"I lost our baby."

He cracked his knuckles one at a time, determination welling. "It's not too late for us. We can start over. Get married. Have a house full of kids."

Her puffy eyes turned to him. "No. I can't. I can never get married."

The bomb blast in Afghanistan had ripped his body apart, but nothing compared to this. "Sure we can."

"No, we can't. It wouldn't be fair, Thad. I can't have kids. I'll never be able to have your children, and you've always wanted a family. We talked about having kids all the time growing up. You wanted a boy and a girl, remember?"

"I've seen miracles happen every day. Maybe the doctors can do something now."

Something tromped across her face, strong and swift. He wished he could read minds. He put his hand on top of hers.

"Would you mind telling me what you're thinking?"

"Maybe I don't deserve to be a mother." She slipped her hand out from under his.

He pulled her into his arms so fast she didn't have time to take a breath. "Don't say that. You're already a great mom. Look at all the animals you take care of. They love you. You take care of them."

He brushed a hand up and down her warm skin. "Karly, I know you don't want to hear this right now, but there's no one else for me but you. I love you. I always have. If you don't want me, then I'll try to understand, but there will be no one else—ever."

"You'd make a great dad. You should find someone, have kids, be happy."

I've already found someone. "But if I'm not married to you, how can I be happy?" Thad reached for her hand again. "Please let me share *this* burden with you. I don't want you to have to carry it alone." He tucked a strand of hair behind her ear. "What do you say?"

"I'm tired. I can't keep pushing you away, even if I think it's for your own good. If you can accept that we'll never have our own children, then...maybe," she nodded slowly, distractedly, "maybe...it would work."

"Maybe what will work?"

"Us. If you're willing to help me have that garage sale we talked about and get rid of some of the baggage, we might have a chance."

"I'll do just about anything to win back your heart." Thad lifted her chin to kiss her cheek, her lips, her nose. "Please, just don't shut me out."

"Are you sure?"

"I've never been more sure of anything, Karly."

"I love you, Thad Lopez. Are you sure your willing to take me—even if all my parts aren't working quite right?"

"In my eyes, you're perfect. And yes, I'm willing. Wait. Did you just admit that we're meant to be together?"

Her eyes narrowed, into a scrunched

scowl. "Lopez? Do you have wax in those ears?" She shook her head, and a puff of happiness sweetened the air around him. "I just said I love you, totally and completely. What more do you want?"

He spun her toward the car park. "Where are we going?"

He spun around and kissed her soundly, making her squeak in surprise. "First, we'll pick some wildflowers and visit our son's grave, and then we'll drive to the clerk's office to get married. Just like we planned."

"I didn't agree to getting married. Besides, the clerk's office was your idea when we were sixteen."

"Yeah, well. It still works."

"I think we should wait."

Every one of his muscles tightened, rebelling against the idea. "Oh, here we go again. You said that the last time."

"Yes, but this time it doesn't matter. This time we both know there is no one else we want to spend our lives with. This time we know we've got the rest of our lives."

A joy infinitely wide and deep filled the valleys of his soul. He'd wait an eternity for this woman. "You're right. As always." He lifted her hand to his lips and gently kissed the back of her wrist. "What was I thinking?"

"You were thinking that you love me." Karly pressed her lips to Thad's. He groaned, and wrapped his arms around her, and proceeded to kiss her silly.

"You taste good. Tell me you love me again."

She closed her eyes and rested her head on his chest. "I love you, Thad."

"What did you say? I didn't hear that."

A slow joy hopscotched across her face. "I said I love you."

"You can do better than that. Say it louder."

She threw her arms and head back and shouted, "I love Thaaaddd Looopezzz."

"There...that wasn't so hard. Now, tell me. What are we going to do about your mother?"

She pushed back her shoulders and lifted

her chin. "I'm not going to worry about what my mother thinks. Not anymore. The only thing I'm going to think about is our future."

He wasn't about to spoil the moment by reminding Karly there was a difference between a fantasy and reality. He'd take whatever came next, as long as it included Karly.

CHAPTER THIRTY-ONE

"Where are we going?" Karly ran along the path behind Thad.

"There's a new running trail I found, just up ahead around the bend, right past this grove of trees."

Karly transferred the leashes to her other hand to pull out a water bottle. "Okay, lead on."

Thad raced up the hill, the larger dogs leading the way. He pointed to the off-road trail and took a left. The trail narrowed, and the dogs crowded close together.

"Thad? You sure this is a good idea?"

"Trust me."

That she did. Trust had taken a while to build, but over the weeks and months, Thad had shown her in every way possible that he wasn't going anywhere. He and his military buddies raised more than twelve thousand dollars to train service dogs, and the social media presence made donations roll in. In every way, Thad showed her the possibilities.

He rushed ahead on the rocky trail, and she raced to keep up until she saw a picture clipped to a branch of a nearby tree. She almost raced past, but the familiar image grabbed her attention.

"Whoa, guys." She tugged on the dogs' leads and retraced her steps.

The picture was of her and Thad on their most recent hike. She'd taken the selfie at sunset. Ahead on the trail, another picture caught her eye, then another. She followed the path of pictures around the bend. White and red rose petals scattered along the ground led her to another stand of trees. Tingles zoomed up her spine as the dogs grew restless. Joyous and tentative emotions rocked up and down like a seesaw. The tinkling of wind chimes focused her attention, and she hurried toward the sound.

A chain of gum wrappers, the zigzag rope like she made in high school strung from tree to tree, made her laugh. In a clearing, Thad stood alone. Waiting. The dogs were tied to a nearby log.

Tears of joy sprang to her eyes. "Did you do all this?"

Thad took her dogs and tied them to a separate tree branch.

"Remember this picture from junior high? Or that one from high school?"

"Did you save all this stuff?" She reached toward the nearest memory. "Look, there's the poem you wrote me."

"I did. I just couldn't bear to let it go, just like I couldn't let you go. I've loved you since grade school, but I didn't quite know how to tell you, and figured showing you works better. Every picture or poem or drawing says I love you in so many different ways."

Love bubbled up and out and cascaded through every cell. "It took you until ninth grade to admit you left flowers in my backpack and books."

"It takes me a while to get it right." He took her hand. "Karly, you must know by now, I've never, ever stopped loving you."

"You rescued me. You came, and risked your life to save me."

"No. You saved me. When I came home, I didn't know what I would find. I was half a man, and you made me whole again."

"You've always thought of yourself as broken." She reached for his face and cupped his cheek. "You've never been broken. Not to me."

He took her hand and kissed her palm. "I've been told by some that I don't express my feelings very well, so I wrote down what I want to say." He lifted a piece of notebook paper from his pocket. "Ready?"

A smile trickled across his face and

ignited in his eyes. Love. He loved her.

She reached for his hand. "Always."

"Karly, thank you for being a listener, even when I didn't have anything to say. You've always given me a soft place to land, a place to call home.

"I love that you never give up when you know you're right.

"I'll never give up on you, Karly. I commit..." He kissed her softly then adjusted the paper in his hand. "...I commit to spending the rest of my life keeping you safe. I commit to creating a home, a place where we can both find peace. I commit to helping you fulfill your dreams, and if they change, I commit to walking beside you all the way. I commit to loving you the rest of my life."

"Karly?" He dropped down onto his knee. "I know I've asked you before, but I don't want to wait, and they say the third time's a charm. You're the only one I want to be with, Karly. Let's spend the rest of our lives together. Marry me."

"Oh, Thad. Yes. A thousand times yes, of

course, I'll marry you. It's the right time." She choked when he slid the most beautiful ring in the world on her finger.

He stood and swung her around in a circle. "The ring's not much, but I promise you I'll get you a better one as soon as we can afford it."

The platinum band with diamonds circling the ring couldn't have been more perfect. "No, you won't. This one's perfect." She spread her fingers to get a better look. "I'll never have to worry about banging this one or getting it dirty, and I'll never have to take it off. I won't take it off." She spotted a picture of her mother.

She closed her eyes. "Are you sure you want to do this?"

"I do. I have two more surprises for you. Are you ready to go see?"

Yes. Yes. Yes. She wanted to jump up and down, and turn back the clocks. Relive their first date, first dance, first kiss...but there were going to be so many more firsts in their lives. "What are you up to?"

"You have to run to the bottom of the hill to find out. Do you trust me?"

She searched his eyes, and the truth was there. "Always."

"Leave the dogs here. They'll be safe. I'll come back to get them. Let's go."

She followed Thad down the steep incline, zigzagging down the trail through tall pines, heading back to the car park. Fifty yards from the trailhead she saw cars, where twenty minutes ago there were none.

Tentativeness made her breath short, but she slowed to take a deep breath. He'd be there for her. Support her. Believe in her. She knew that now. There wasn't anything to be afraid of. Not anymore.

At the crest of the hill, she saw the surprise and raced down the trail. Her family. Kevin, Kurt, her mom, were all waiting. A hundred yards away a soldier got out from the back of a car. "Kenny!"

She glanced at Thad, and raced faster. A foot from her brother, she leaped in the air. Arms caught her and spun her around.

"You're here!"

Kenny set her on her feet. "When Thad called me and told me what he was planning, I was able to talk my commander into letting me come home. For some reason, he likes Thad." Kenny winked and turned to give the love of her life a handshake. "Good to see you, buddy. Well?"

Thad released her brother's hand, and a life-couldn't-be-better lopsided grin stretched across his face. "She said yes."

Mrs. Krane tapped on Thad's shoulder and stepped in front of him. "I never did like you." Karly's breath hitched. "But my daughter has loved you forever. Goes to show she's always had better judgment than I when it comes to the heart. I want to welcome you into our family."

He leaned in to hug her mother. Delight beamed from all the faces except for one petite woman standing back on the perimeter of the crowd. "Sarah?" Karly inquired, not positive of the shy woman's identity.

Thad turned. "Sarah. You came." He stepped out of the circle of people.

Thad's sister made a half-step forward. "Mom had to work, but I wanted to come." She shuffled a bit. "I needed to come."

"I'm glad to see you." Karly stepped in between brother and sister to give Sarah a hug. She could have been hugging a pole, but hung on for a few extra seconds, and then… yes, there it was…the release. Karly pulled back, but still hung on to Sarah's hand.

"I wanted to tell you how sorry I am for the lies I told Thad." Sarah's voice faltered. "I was mad when he left." Her gaze lifted to Karly. "I said things to hurt him. Hurt you. I didn't think there was anything that would ever separate you both."

Karly squeezed Sarah's hand. "Hey. Don't cry. It's not a day for crying. You know, sometimes things happen for a reason. Maybe you did Thad and me a favor."

"A favor?" Thad looked at Karly like she'd lost her sanity.

"Yes, a favor. Sarah gave us time to grow

up and learn what we want out of life." Karly opened her arms again. "Now, give me a proper hug. We're going to be sisters."

Sarah wiped away her smeared mascara. "Now I wish my fiancé and I lived here."

Karly's brow rose. "You can always come back."

"Tempting—but there are no jobs."

"I'm trying to fix that," Joe said from somewhere outside the tight circle. "I'm going to need to rebuild my department, and I'll be looking for a few good people."

Thad placed a warm hand on Karly's lower back. "Are you ready for your last surprise?"

"There's more?"

On cue, Joe and Mara lifted the back of the SUV hatch with two kennels inside.

A fragile surprise began to take shape.

"During our crowd funding event," Thad pulled her toward the car, "I got an email from a guy in Montana. He breeds shepherds, and was wondering if we would like a pair to seed our service dog efforts."

Thad moved her forward, and she saw two sets of puppy eyes staring back at her. "Meet Romeo and Juliet. Our first four-legged family members."

"Oh, Thad. They're precious. But, I thought Shakespeare wasn't a good memory for you."

"People can change their minds."

She turned in his arms. When their lips touched, the people and voices and cars and trees disappeared. What was left was Thad and a profound feeling of contentment.

Finally.

She slowly drew back and opened her eyes.

"Well, Mr. Lopez. It looks like we have a boy and a girl. You're a dad. You got your wish."

"No, Karly. You have always been my wish, my dream, my paradise. It took me a while to figure it out, but the day you become my wife, I'll be the happiest man on the planet."

He leaned in for another kiss.

Thad. It's you who saved my life. You will always have my love.

I'm so glad you could join Karly and Thad on their journey to their happily ever after.

Those of you who have read my books or been part of my newsletter have heard my explanation for why Authors never see their Star Ratings requested by Amazon, so thank you for allowing me to share the information once again.

When Amazon asks a reader to "Rate this book" on their Kindle, Amazon is the only one to see these ratings.

I'm left clueless about how you feel about this book. Your input matters.

Book reviews help me decide what kind

of books I write. Plus, the more people who leave an review, the more likely Amazon is to move a book up in the rankings? Written reviews help other readers find and love a series.

Please continue to rate the book on your Kindle or reader as this helps Amazon, but take an extra moment to pop over to the review section and leave a few words!

Seriously, a few words like, "great story," is enough.

If you have not read my Elkridge Series or the Lonely Ridge Collection, and have no idea why authors keep asking you as a reader to take a few minutes to leave even a couple of word reviews, here's the break down of how reviews work in this crazy business.

Reviews (not ratings) help authors qualify for advertising opportunities. Without triple digit reviews, an author may miss out on these valuable opportunities. And with only a "star rating" the author has little chance of participating in specific promotions, which means authors continue to struggle, and many talented writers give up writing altogether.

Readers aren't the only ones who use reviews to help make purchasing decisions. Producers and directors use your reviews when looking for new projects.

This is why I'm asking for your help.

A few kind words make such a massive difference to me. Your words give me the encouragement I need to continue writing because honestly, I write my books for you, and I'd like to keep delivering the types of stories you want to read.

And, yes, every book in a series needs reviews, not just the first book. Even if a book has been out for awhile, a fresh review can breathe new life into a book.

So, please take a few minutes to leave a short review. Even a couple of words will brighten my day.

Lastly. Thank you for reading this book. I hope to see you again soon. Cheers!

I wish you all the best the day offers, and I hope you enjoy reading the next book in the Elkridge Series.

DEDICATION

To all the honorable men and brave women in the world who give of themselves without asking for anything in return.

AUTHOR NOTES

Dear Readers,

In this story the voices in Thad's head are so negative he can't listen. In his own way, he's a hero—an honorable and giving man—but he doesn't know it, and he certainly doesn't believe it.

All it takes is someone believing in him to create that desperately needed positive change.

I truly believe we are all heroes who can change the world—some of us in small measured ways, others with big sweeping gestures.

We all have the superpower.

It's as simple as granting a smile to a stranger, embracing tolerance, or maybe respecting your neighbors enough to listen.

I've felt small, insignificant, unworthy, at times in my life. Writing has allowed me to change those feelings. I know now I have a voice, just as you have a voice.

Please believe you can be, do, think, anything you want, because you have already made a difference just by opening this book to read.

I implore you, wherever you are, go out and paint the world your own special color.

Wishing you all the best life has to offer.

~Lyz

More Books By
Lyz Kelley

SILVER FOX RESORT
SILVER SPOON
SILVER DOLLAR
SILVER BELLS

SECRETS
BILLIONAIRE'S SECRET
DOCTOR'S SECRET

THE ELKRIDGE SERIES
BLINDED
ABANDONED
ORPHANED
RESCUED
UNMISTAKEN
ATONEMENT
BITTERSWEET

ACKNOWLEDGMENTS

FOR RESCUED

This book was my biggest writing challenge yet. I had to make sure I tied off all the series threads, plus gave Karly and Thad a happily ever after.

My sincere appreciation goes to the Douglas County Sheriff's Department, for providing their technical expertise. To Aimee my plotting partner. To Joyce Lamb for deepening the story elements. To my gracious beta readers, Jenn, Kristen, and Margaret who were brave enough to provide constructive suggestions for improvement. Faith Freewoman and my amazing editor, who sprinkles my manuscript with fairy dust and makes it sparkle. To Carol Agnew, who catches things no one else sees.

And, to you the reader who took this journey with me. If it wasn't for you, this series might have not gotten to the final who-done-it resolution. Thank you for all the support and kindness.

Last but not least, to my husband who understood when I was up at 3 am, or pacing the living room floor talking to myself, or when I slid into the chair for dinner at the last possible second.

You all have my sincere gratitude.

~Lyz

THANK YOU FOR READING:
RESCUED

Award-winning author Lyz Kelley mixes a little bit of heart, healing, humanity, happiness, honor, hope, and honor in all her books that are written especially for you.

She's is a total disaster in the kitchen, a compulsive neat freak, a tea snob, and adores writing about and falling in love with everyday heroes.

Please also consider leaving a review on Amazon Goodreads and/or BookBub. Reviews help readers find new books to read, and authors find their footing.

You can also find Lyz on Facebook and Instagram for news, contests, giveaways, and more exciting stuff!

COPYRIGHT

RESCUED Copyright © 2017 Belvitri
Services, LLC

Email: Lyz@LyzKelley.com
Newsletter Sign Up: www.LyzKelley.com
Facebook: www.facebook.com/LyzKelley
Instagram: https://www.
instagram.com/lyzkelley/

Cover Art by Lyz Kelley

www.ingramcontent.com/pod-product-compliance
Lightning Source LLC
Chambersburg PA
CBHW030537020726
47494CB00005B/1401